ISLANDS OF
DECEPTION

Handwritten inscription: Kathryn, thank you for all of your support & enough. Much appreciated!! Blessings, Chris

A NOVEL

CHRIS G THELEN

**What lies
are below
the surface?**

BROOKSTONE
PUBLISHING GROUP

Islands of Deception

Brookstone Publishing Group
An imprint of Iron Stream Media
100 Missionary Ridge
Birmingham, AL 35242
IronStreamMedia.com

Library of Congress Control Number: 2022923827

Cover design and photography by Brian Preuss

ISBN: 978-1-949856-94-1 (paperback)
ISBN: 978-1-949856-95-8 (ebook)

1 2 3 4 5— 27 26 25 24 23

To my wife, Joanne, who believed
I was a writer before I did.

MICHIGAN

St. James

BEAVER ISLAND

Charlevoix

Traverse City

Lansing

Detroit

Jackson

Ann Arbor

St. James

BEAVER ISLAND

NORTH FOX ISLAND

Charlevoix

Lake Michigan

St. James

Welke
Airport

KINGS HIGHWAY

Beaver
Island
Airport

BEAVER
ISLAND

Lake Geneserath Cabin

Lighthouse and
Coast Guard Station

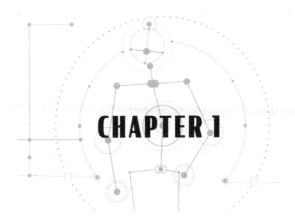

CHAPTER 1

Have some more tuna salad," Cally's mom said as she pushed a ceramic bowl across the kitchen table toward him.

Cally glared at her, then the half-full bowl with curly noodles laced with mayonnaise and flecks of tuna. Another cold noodle salad for dinner; another hot, repressive August day in his parents' house. "No, thanks."

An old metal fan rattled in the kitchen window, filling the quiet as Cally looked up at his parents wordlessly staring at him across the small, metal kitchen table. He didn't want to be here, but he had no choice. The hot, humid air blowing in from the window only made it more uncomfortable.

"You've hardly eaten anything," his dad said.

Cally glanced at his dad's aged face and scowled as he reached for his glass and took a sip. The cool water felt refreshing going down. "I'm good."

They sat for a moment in silence.

His parents seemed to blend in with the faded yellow wallpaper behind them. They looked at him with disappointment. Behind them, a crucifix on the wall looked down on him.

"Why don't you just say it? I'm a hopeless case."

"That's not true, Cally," his mom said.

"You keep reminding me I went to prison for drug dealing."

"But you're out now. We just don't want you to go back to the drug ring," his dad said. "It's your chance to start over—as long as you don't violate your parole."

"We don't want you to slip back into your old life," his mom said. "You've been clean for so long."

Cally felt anger surging.

"When you were in high school, you ran track," his dad said, fork in hand. "Maybe you could pick up running again."

"I was lousy at track. I always placed last. And I barely passed high school."

"That doesn't make you a failure," his mom said.

His dad set his fork down. "Cally, if you—"

"No! I don't want to hear how Jesus transformed your life. Ever since I moved back in, you've tried to tell me what to do! I'm thirty-one. I can run my own life."

"Son—"

"Enough!"

Cally stared at the watermelon pattern on his place mat, trying to avoid his parents' eyes. His sweat-soaked shirt stuck to the chair back, pulling away uncomfortably as he leaned forward. The phone in his jeans pocket vibrated. His chair legs squawked against the floor as he slid away from the table. He pulled out his phone. The name on the screen was Chuck's.

"If that's Chuck, don't answer it," his dad said.

"So what if it is?"

"Don't talk to him. He's caused enough trouble in your life."

"When no one else cared, Chuck was there for me!"

2

"You need to stay away from him," his dad said. "He's the one who pulled you into drug dealing. He's the reason you went to prison."

"He's nothing but trouble," his mom said.

The phone vibrated in his hand. He stood up. "I need to take this call."

"Cally—"

"It's not Chuck!" Cally said as he stormed out of the kitchen and climbed the stairs to his bedroom. The phone kept vibrating in his hand. He sat on his bed and declined the call. Within seconds, the phone vibrated again and Chuck's name reappeared on the screen. Cally declined the call again—and just seconds later it vibrated again. He sighed and accepted the call. "You know we're not supposed to talk."

"Cally! You need to come—now!"

"I'm violating my parole just talking to you."

"Forget that. Cally—they're coming for your family!"

"What! Who?"

"The drug ring."

"Hey, I quit that."

"Doesn't matter. They're coming for your family."

"Why?"

"I have something they want."

"Then give it to them."

"I can't. Just come, Cally. Hurry!"

"What does my family have to do with it?"

"They know I have no family—that you're the only person I care about. They'll start picking off your family if I don't give them what they want."

"Then give it to them! Don't drag me into this."

"I can't. Just come."

"Why?"

"It's the only way to protect your family."

Cally pulled the phone away from his ear. He looked at the framed picture of Chuck and him sitting on the hood of Chuck's Shelby Mustang Cobra—arms around each other wearing big grins.

"Cally! Are you there?"

"I'm here."

"If you care about your family, you'll come."

"What if I don't care?"

"I know you care about Daniel and Sheila," Chuck said.

"They wouldn't dare touch my brother and sister."

"They will."

Cally swore. "Give 'em what they want, Chuck!"

"No."

Cally's body tensed. The mattress springs creaked as he leaned forward on the edge of his bed.

"Hurry—before it's too late! Come to my apartment."

Cally looked at the picture of Chuck and him.

"Cally!"

"Okay, okay! I'll be there as soon as I can."

Cally ended the call and glanced at the time on his phone. He was due to start his work shift in an hour. He dreaded going back into that fast-food place again. The pay was a fraction of what he'd earned when he was helping Chuck with the drug ring. He stood and pocketed his phone.

Cally's mom stood at the bottom of the stairs, wiping her hands on her apron. "Where are you going?"

"To work."

"Where's your uniform?"

Cally walked past her and headed for the door. "I'll be back in a few minutes."

Someone grabbed his shoulder. "Leave me alone!" he snapped. He turned. His dad's haggard face focused on him, trying to stop him. He jerked his shoulder free and left the house.

"Cally . . ."

Their voices faded as he hurried down the sidewalk away from the house, away from them. Feeling nervous, he hurried across the street, looking over his shoulder as he made his way to the back alley. The late afternoon sun felt hot on his back. It was hard to breathe in the thick, humid air.

What did Chuck have, and why was his family in danger? He moved through the back alleys quickly, block after block, until he reached Chuck's apartment building. Slowly, he approached the front of the familiar, three-story building with rotting clapboard siding. It looked worse than he remembered it. Cautiously, he moved along the crumbling sidewalk, looking over his shoulder, stepping over empty liquor bottles, needles, and trash. Hesitantly, he climbed the four crumbling cement steps to the entry door.

He could still turn back, but what would happen if he did? Was Chuck telling the truth about the threat to Cally's family? His finger hovered over the call button for Chuck's apartment. He glanced over his shoulder. An old, candy-apple-red Cadillac slowly cruised by. A man with mirrored, aviator sunglasses peered at him through the open passenger-side window. Cally quickly turned away and pressed the button for Chuck's place. A small, dented-steel speaker above the row of buttons buzzed.

"Cobra," Cally said.

A moment later the door latch buzzed. Cally grabbed the wobbly doorknob and pushed the door open. He took a deep breath, stepped inside, and scanned the vacant hallway in front of him. The door clicked shut behind him. He wiped sweat from his brow and walked past several apartment doors to the stairwell. His body tensed and his breathing quickened as he ascended the creaking stairs. On the second floor, he carefully walked down the empty hallway and stopped at a door with 217 on the front. Muffled conversations rose above the sound of groaning air conditioners from behind the walls. Something moved at the end of the hall. He exhaled a sigh of relief when he realized it was only ragged curtains waving in front of an open window. Cally tapped on the door.

"Who's the boss?" someone asked from the other side of the door.

Cally cracked a smile. "Bruce Springsteen."

Deadbolts clunked open and the door opened a crack. Through the narrow opening, Chuck's face was wide-eyed and filled with fear.

"Cally!" Chuck grabbed Cally's shirt and pulled him in. "Thank God you're here!"

"What happened to you?" Cally asked, studying the gash in the side of Chuck's head.

Chuck slammed the door behind them and re-latched three deadbolts. He pushed Cally toward the couch. "Sit down."

"Why are all the shades pulled?" Cally asked as they both sat. He could barely see Chuck's Bruce Springsteen T-shirt, let alone his terrified face, in the dim glow of a table lamp next to the couch. "And what's with that gash on your head?"

"That's not important." Chuck pulled a handgun out of a drawer in an end table next to the couch and slid it on the coffee table toward Cally. "Take this. It's loaded."

"For what?"

Chuck stared at him wide-eyed, silent.

Cally had never seen Chuck so scared. He always wore a look of confidence. Cally looked at the gun, then Chuck.

"You're going to need it," Chuck said.

Cally waited, then nodded and picked it up. It felt familiar and comfortable in his hand. He quickly slipped it behind his back, perched just inside the waist of his jeans.

"You're the only one I can trust," Chuck said, holding up a small black box, about the size of a deck of cards.

"A computer hard drive?"

Chuck shoved it into Cally's hand. "Guard it with your life."

"What's on this?"

"Enough evidence to shut down the entire crime ring."

"Crime ring?"

"This is bigger than just the drug business we dealt in. It's a massive crime ring involved in all sorts of things. That drive is your bargaining chip, Cally. They won't touch your family as long as you have this."

Cally stared at the backup drive, then looked at Chuck. "What kind of evidence?"

"There's several terabytes of stuff on there—videos, phone calls, text messages, emails, financial transactions. It's all there. That box can put them all away for a long time."

"How'd you get all of that?"

"You know I've always been a geek. The crime ring has me maintain their computer servers. They thought they could trust me more than some outside tech company."

Cally felt himself growing cold. "Chuck—what did you do?"

Chuck ignored the question. "I've been doing a lot of thinking lately—watching how you're working to turn your life around."

"But, Chuck—"

"It's too late, Cally. I decided to do the right thing. Last week I tapped into the crime ring's private network and started collecting as much as I could—and that was a lot, because everything runs through their servers. It's all on that drive."

Now Cally's cold dread was turning to anger. He held up the hard drive. "You didn't need to drag me into this. Why didn't you take this to the police?"

"There are cops working with the crime ring."

"Then take it to the state police."

"I spent yesterday opening up files and checking out what was on that drive. I found out people in state government and the state police are also in on it."

Cally swore. "What am *I* supposed to do with this?"

"Your brother Daniel works for the FBI. He'll know what to do."

"Why didn't you just store this in the cloud and send me a link?" Cally argued. "We could've handled this meeting with an email, and I wouldn't have had to risk violating my parole!"

"Wouldn't have worked." Chuck paused. "Somehow they caught on. They hacked my cloud storage and deleted everything. They know I downloaded a backup copy." Chuck tapped the hard drive in Cally's hand. "They won't stop until they destroy that drive."

"This is the only copy?"

Chuck nodded. "They're onto me, Cally. About an hour ago I was making a drop and my contact told me they knew what I was up to. In fact, he tried to tie me up, but I fought him and escaped. He tried to knife me. I left him bleeding and ran."

"They could be here any minute!"

"That's why you need that gun."

Cally's pulse was getting quicker by the minute. Sweat soaked his hair and face. The humid air in the room felt oppressive. He wanted to leave—leave the drive with Chuck and run.

Chuck stared at Cally. "This is taking too long—you need to take it and go. Now!"

"What about you?"

"It's too late for me."

Someone body-slammed the door.

Cally looked at the door bowing, wood cracking under the force of a second slam.

Chuck swore. "They're here."

Cally gripped the hard drive in his hand as splinters of wood broke loose from the door. He looked at Chuck's panicked face. "Who?"

"The corrupt police."

Another slam against the door almost broke it loose.

"Run *now* or we're both dead," Chuck said, pulling a gun from under the cushion of the couch. "You know the drill. Go!"

Cally slipped the drive into his jeans pocket and sprinted into the kitchen, where he dived into the cupboard under the kitchen sink and slipped through a hole in the wall into the vacant apartment next door. He ran to a window on the far wall. As he stepped onto the fire escape, he heard the door break open in Chuck's apartment, then gunshots. He paused a moment, looking back at the open lower cupboard doors in the kitchen, waiting for Chuck to emerge. He heard muffled shouting, then more gunshots.

Suddenly, Chuck slid through the open cupboard doors and rolled onto the kitchen floor. Cally watched him regain his footing and scramble toward him, panic on his face. "Run, Cally!"

Cally turned away to descend the fire escape, then turned back as more shots rang out and he heard Chuck groan. His friend staggered toward the window—then fell face-first onto the floor. Blood quickly pooled beneath him. Cally could see three large circles of red staining the "Born in the USA" album art on the back of Chuck's shirt.

"Chuck!"

Chuck lifted his head. "Run, Cally! Get that drive to Daniel!" Then his head dropped to the floor.

The door to the vacant apartment burst open. Cally slammed the window shut and fled down the fire escape to the sound of more gunshots. He shielded his head as shards of glass rained down around him just as he reached the bottom of the fire escape. Above, he heard boots on the metal grate. Cally bolted down the alley. He was just pulling out Chuck's gun when he stumbled, fell, lost his grip, and watched as the gun dropped into a clump of weeds. Cally hesitated only a second before jumping to his feet and running as gunfire sounded behind him. He expected the piercing, hot pain of bullets but it never came. His legs kept moving. The sound of his shoes thumping on broken pavement echoed from the fences and garages in the alleys. He squinted in the late-afternoon sunshine and didn't stop until he arrived back at his parents' house.

Sheltering behind a corner of the house, Cally took a moment to catch his breath, his hands on his knees. The fan rattled in the kitchen window facing the alley. His clothes were soaked with sweat. He stood, frantically looking up and down the street. He saw no one—just a half-dozen cars in driveways. He heard kids playing nearby. He wiped his face with the bottom of his T-shirt, took a deep breath, then climbed the steps to the porch and entered.

The screen door creaked and slapped closed behind him. Cally headed straight for the stairs.

"Cally?"

"I'm in a hurry, Mom," Cally said as he climbed the stairs.

"Where have you been?"

Cally stopped halfway up the stairs and looked down at his mom at the bottom of the stairs.

"You need to eat something before you go to work," she said.

"Leave me alone," Cally said, and continued up the stairs to the top.

"Don't talk to your Mom like that," his dad said.

Cally turned and looked down; now both of his parents were at the bottom of the stairs. Their aged faces frowned up at him. He ignored their calls. "I need to get ready for work," he said, as he headed to his room. He stopped a moment at his door, pulled the backup drive from his pocket, and stared at it. He had to get it to Daniel. He would have to take his parents' car.

Cally grabbed a wad of money from his dresser drawer and jammed it into the pocket of his jeans. As he snatched the car keys from on top of his dresser, he heard aggressive pounding at the front door. Someone shouted, "Open up! Police!" He pulled the hard drive from his pocket and frantically looked around his room, trying to decide what to do with the drive. It was likely he was about to be arrested, and if he tried to flee with it now, the police would surely get it and destroy it.

And if they didn't find it on him, the police would search his room. It was a small room, without a lot of hiding places. There was, though, one place where he used to hide his drugs. And there was a secret way he and Daniel used to sneak out of the house when they were teenagers.

He rushed into his closet and pulled out a loose piece of floor molding. He slipped the backup drive into an open space between the studs in the wall and replaced the molding. Then he popped open a panel in the floor to reveal an old chimney with a ladder inside that led to the basement. He climbed inside the chimney, closed the panel above him, and scurried down the ladder. In the basement, he quickly brushed off mortar pieces and cobwebs, then hurried to an old coal chute on the side wall of the basement. He grabbed ladder-like rungs welded inside the chute and climbed out of the basement to the driveway at the side of the house next to the alley. A second later he was inside his parents' car starting the engine. Tires squealed as he backed out of the driveway. He had to make it to Daniel's house.

Cally ran the stop sign at the end of the street and zipped toward the freeway on-ramp. He sped through a yellow light, accelerated down the on-ramp, and merged into traffic. He wove from lane to lane in heavy traffic, trying to recall how to get to Daniel's house. Ahead he recognized the mirrored glass office towers in Southfield as he headed for Farmington Hills. He was getting closer. He pulled out his phone.

"Daniel!"

"Cally?"

"They're coming after our family."

"What! Who?"

"I have something to stop them."

"Where are you?"

"I'm almost to your place."

"You're coming here?"

In his rearview mirror, Cally saw two police cars approaching with flashers lit. Vehicles around him began to pull over to the shoulder.

"Can't talk now, see you soon," Cally said, tossing his phone on the seat next to him.

He didn't want to pull over but thought it best to try to blend in with the other cars. He slowed down and pulled to the shoulder. A freeway sign ahead told him he was one mile from the exit for Daniel's house. His phone rang. Daniel's name came up on the screen. He grabbed his phone and tossed it out the open passenger-side window. A moment later police cars boxed him in and officers surrounded his car with guns pulled.

An officer in front of the car, gun pointed at Cally, shouted, "Out of the car! Hands in the air!"

Another officer, also with gun pointed, yanked open Cally's door. "Hands up where I can see them!"

Cally carefully slid out of the car with his hands raised. Someone grabbed him and shoved him against the car face-first, then cuffed him and started to pat him down. The officer stopped at Cally's jeans pocket, reached inside, and pulled out the wad of cash. Turning slightly, Cally saw the officer pocket the cash. Then the officer turned him roughly around.

A man wearing mirrored aviator sunglasses approached them.

"He's clean, Chief Peters," the officer who'd been searching Cally said.

"Tear the car apart. See if there's a laptop or something in there," Chief Peters said.

Cally studied Chief Peters's face. He looked familiar. Then Cally saw his reflection in the mirrored sunglasses. He looked a mess. His hair was rumpled, his clothes sweat-stained.

"So, I get to bust you again, like I did three years ago at that drug warehouse," Chief Peters said, his face directly in front of Cally's. "We're going to find whatever Chuck gave you."

Cally remained silent.

"What did Chuck give you?"

Cally glared at Chief Peters.

"I'd beat it out of you right now if it wasn't for this audience."

Cally glanced at people passing by in their cars with cell phones pointed at them through open car windows.

"Put him in the squad car," Chief Peters said.

Another officer grabbed Cally's arm and yanked him toward a police car. As they passed his parents' car, he saw officers were tearing it apart. The officer opened the back door of the police car and pushed Cally inside. Cally's head hit the doorframe as he fell onto the back seat. The door slammed behind him. His head pounded with pain, but the air-conditioned car was a relief from the August heat. He looked out the side window and saw Chief Peters with his mirrored sunglasses shouting at another officer as he pointed at Cally's parents' car.

Suddenly the back door opened. "Where did you put it?" Chief Peters said, glaring at Cally through the open door.

Cally remained silent and turned away.

"You have the right to remain silent," the chief said. "But we'll see if you have anything to say when we send you to prison for murdering your friend Chuck."

Shocked, Cally said, "Me? *I* didn't kill him!"

"Tell me where you hid whatever Chuck gave you and maybe we can cut a deal."

Cally said nothing more.

Chief Peters slammed the door.

Cally watched through the side window as the chief turned and shouted at his officers, pointing at Cally's parents' car.

For the moment, the hard drive was safe.

CHAPTER 2

allon McElliot eased his car into a parking space near the Michigan State Capitol and pulled out his phone. "I'm here."

"Meet me on the fourth floor. I'll be in hearing room C."

"Is this about your reelection campaign?"

"Sort of. See you in a few minutes."

Fallon ended the call and slipped the phone into his blazer pocket. Politics, particularly campaigns, nauseated him. He wasn't about to help the governor with her reelection campaign, even if she was a longtime friend.

Cool September air greeted him as he climbed out of his car and looked at the familiar Capitol building in front of him. The bone-colored dome glowed in the morning light. He closed his car door and walked to the main entrance, stopping for a moment to recall the time he climbed the limestone stairway to the ornate entrance for his dad's final press conference as attorney general. Dry leaves skittered across the sidewalk in front of him. Inside the Capitol, he walked down a vacant hallway to the rotunda. The sound of his hard-soled shoes clicking on the black-and-white-checked marble floor echoed from the walls. As he stepped onto the glass floor of the rotunda, he paused a moment to look up at the painted stars at the pinnacle of the dome six stories above him. He shook off the memory of what had occurred here years ago, exited the rotunda, and climbed a stairway that led to the fourth-floor hearing rooms.

"Good morning, Mr. McElliot," a young Capitol Security officer said when he stepped into a lobby area surrounded by committee hearing rooms. "I'll show you to the governor."

Fallon followed the officer to an open door a few steps away. He entered and saw the governor seated at the far end of a large conference table, talking on the phone. The officer closed the door behind him.

She motioned for him to sit in the seat across from her as she talked. "No, Mr. Massey. Not yet. The implementation is in the budget for next fiscal year. We should have final approval by the end of the week."

Fallon sat down. Governor Karen Bauer looked uptight.

"I'll let you know as soon as we release the purchase order." She ended the call and looked at Fallon. "Sorry."

"That's okay, Karen. Who was that?"

"Henry Massey. He's overseeing our transition to their Archipelago software."

"Isn't that the tech billionaire?"

"That's him. He personally made the sales pitch to us."

"Wait a minute. Didn't he make his fortune in social media?"

"Yes, he started the social media company Quick Connect."

"What's he doing selling government operations software? Are you looking to get into cat videos?"

"Very funny, Fallon."

"Seems like he'd have better things to do, like sail his megayacht."

"It's the top-rated government software."

"I don't get why he has such a personal interest in Michigan."

"Always the skeptic, Fallon. Apparently, he loves our state and wants to personally handle the rollout." Karen set her cell phone on the table and leaned back in her chair. "So, how are you, Fallon?"

"You know I'm not a fan of this place."

Karen nodded. "Thanks for coming."

"I wouldn't be here if we hadn't been friends since high school. How's Jack doing as first gentleman?"

"He's doing great."

"How are your girls?"

"Melanie's in her second year of college at the University of Michigan, and Colleen graduates next year from high school."

"Either one interested in politics?"

"They're like you. They don't want anything to do with it. How about your boys?"

"Scott's in his junior year at Wayne State. Trent started this fall at the U of M."

"Any of them taking up your family business of crime fighting?"

"Scott's majoring in criminal justice at Wayne State. Trent is looking at a social justice major . . ." Fallon paused. "You look stressed. What's going on?"

Karen frowned. "Not here, Fallon." She went to a nearby closet, opened the door, and motioned for Fallon.

Fallon joined her inside the closet. She closed the door. Why the sudden secrecy? To his surprise, she slid a panel on the back wall and stepped through the opening. He followed her into a narrow, curved hallway lit by a single bulb. "Are we inside the upper part of the dome?"

"We're between the outside and inside of the Capitol dome," Karen said as she walked to a narrow, metal stairway that hugged the curved wall of the Capitol dome. "This leads to the top of the dome."

Fallon followed Karen up the stairs until they reached a small circular room with a railing at the top of the dome. Fallon peered over the railing at the spot six stories below where he'd stood a few moments before. "I didn't know this was here, and my dad was state attorney general for years."

"This area was closed to the public in the 1950s. I use it sometimes for private meetings. Up here I know no one is listening in."

"What's going on?"

"Corruption in my cabinet."

"Didn't you handpick your cabinet?"

"I did—for the most part."

"Who's the other part?"

"Marjorie Brogan, director of Corrections. I had my doubts about her when I first met her."

"So why did you put her in charge of Corrections?"

"Payback for political favors. The private firm that manages some of our prisons was a major donor to my campaign."

"But, Karen—"

"I know, Fallon. It reeks, but it's the way the game is played. She has a solid résumé in Corrections, but I didn't know her that well."

"What do you think she's doing?"

"We've seen a significant spike in drug use in our correctional facilities since she took over. The same thing happened at the prison she managed in Wisconsin before she came here. That prison was run by the same private firm we contract with to run our prison system, the same one that donated to my campaign."

"What does this have to do with me?"

"Yesterday, Treasury told me they completed an audit of the warehousing system. Corrections is ordering way more supplies than they can possibly consume, but the auditors aren't sure whether it's a software glitch or something is actually amiss. I'm wondering if Brogan and her team are using the warehouse system to distribute drugs outside the prison system."

"Why don't you have the warehouses searched?"

"If we find drugs, that would only get low-level employees arrested. If there is as much corruption as I think there is, we need to apprehend everyone involved in it."

"I can start looking into it tomorrow."

"No. Not in your current position as a state police detective." Karen paused. "Fallon, I want to appoint you as my adviser."

"What?"

"I want you to join my administration."

"You know I hate politics."

"But you won't have to be involved in the politics."

"This place is all about politics. My dad taught me that."

"You'll be focused on state police policy. That will be your cover while you investigate Corrections. Your official title will be Liaison to the State Police. You'll be part of my cabinet and report directly to me."

"I don't know, Karen . . ."

"As part of your cover, you'll research law enforcement policy for me. That'll give you the authority to scrutinize Corrections."

"Give me a few days to think about it."

Karen shook her head. "I need you now, Fallon."

"What's the rush?"

"The new Archipelago software will give us a level of scrutiny we haven't had with our old computer system. As we transition to this new software, we'll have an opportunity to scrutinize the Corrections warehousing system and hopefully uncover anyone else involved in the scheme. I want you onboard before we start bringing the new software online."

"And when are you bringing this new system online?"

"With our new fiscal year next month, starting October first. We'll likely have an initial meeting with Massey in November."

"So I'll get to meet him if I join your administration?"

Karen smiled. "I bet you still don't have a Quick Connect profile."

Fallon laughed. "You know I hate social media."

"There's a billion Quick Connect users around the world. You really should get a profile."

"I don't understand why you're going to use operations management software developed by a social media mogul. Was Massey a major donor to your campaign?"

"Yes, but their product is far superior to anything else on the market. Massey is passionate about making government more efficient. He and some other tech billionaires started the venture capital firm Arpa to create software to run governments. They sell the software at cost."

"You believe their marketing material?"

"We've thoroughly vetted the software. There's nothing like it out there. Nine other states are using it and have raved about the millions of dollars they're saving in operations. Over the next year we'll incorporate all of our departments into one software suite. By this time next year, we'll bring an integration tool online that will give us the ability to operate seamlessly between departments. We'll have total control over state operations like never before."

"Sounds too good to be true."

"Always the cynic."

"You know me."

"That's why I need you, Fallon. You have a knack for seeing things others don't."

"But Karen, I'm a state police detective, not a politician."

"I need you, Fallon."

Fallon leaned on the railing and looked at a group of kids walking on the glass floor six stories below them. He tried not to make eye contact with Karen.

"It's important."

"If I accept, can I bring Chip with me?" Fallon said, turning to look at Karen. "I can trust him with confidential things."

"I know Chip's the best analyst you have. And your friend. You'll have a small budget to bring him onboard with you. This isn't just about stopping corruption, Fallon. Brogan and whoever she's working with are peddling drugs that are killing people. We need to stop them—and by doing that, we'll stop all the violence associated with illegal drugs. Like that case in Detroit last August."

"The one where the guy shot his friend in the back over a bad drug deal?"

"Yes. Horrible."

Fallon smiled. "And here I thought you were going to ask me to work on your reelection campaign."

"I wouldn't think of it. I know how you felt after you worked on my dad's congressional campaign when we were in college."

"I'm only doing this as a favor to you."

Karen smiled. "I also know how much you want to bring corrupt people to justice."

Fallon chuckled. "Maybe I have more of my dad in me than I like to admit. When do I start?"

"Next week. Your office will be in the Romney building across the street from the Capitol. You and Chip will have top-level access to the Archipelago project. You'll be able to work with the implementation team under the guise of collecting data for policy analysis. I'll talk to your lieutenant in the state police about your new appointment this afternoon."

"He's not going to be happy about you stealing me," Fallon said.

She looked at him with sympathy. "I know how much you love being a detective with the state police. I know you'd rather be in the field. I wouldn't have called you if I thought there was another way to go at this. I trust your instincts, Fallon."

"I'll get to the bottom of it."

"Oh." She reached into her pocket and handed Fallon a red, disposable flip phone. "Starting next month, all our state government phones will be routed through the Archipelago server. I don't want anyone listening in on our conversations. I have one just like it. We'll only *talk* on this phone about your investigation. No texting or voice mails."

"My own hot line to the governor," Fallon said as he took the flip phone.

"Use your work phone for everything else."

Fallon nodded, pocketed the red phone, then followed Karen down the narrow, curved stairway inside the dome and back to the conference room.

"Thank you, Fallon," Karen said, gently closing the closet door. She hugged him.

Fallon made his way back down the stairs to the first floor and stopped a moment under the rotunda next to a display case with Civil War flags. Unlike his dad, Fallon had never wanted any part of politics. He recalled the speech his dad had made years before, behind a temporary podium set up years ago in front of this very display case. It was as if it had happened yesterday. The words of his dad's speech—his announcement that he would not seek reelection as State Attorney General so he could work on Bill Clinton's presidential reelection campaign—echoed in Fallon's mind. He sighed and exited the Capitol. His dad was always vying for a spot in Washington.

He descended the limestone steps and returned to his car. He started the engine and pulled out his work phone. "Hey, Chip, I have a new assignment for you."

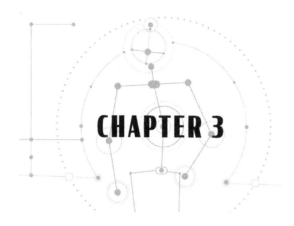

CHAPTER 3

Meetings. Fallon loathed them. When he'd accepted the state police liaison position two months before, he hadn't anticipated so many of them. Now here he was again, walking to another meeting. This time, at least he would finally get to meet Henry Massey—the person he had heard so much about since the State of Michigan signed the contract to implement the Archipelago software.

Fallon stepped into the large conference room nicely appointed with photos of Michigan scenery on the walls and a prominent view, through the large expanse of windows on one wall, of the Capitol building across the street. He recognized most of the governor's cabinet seated around the large, rectangular table. He tried not to make eye contact with Marjorie Brogan as he made his way to an empty chair between the directors of Agriculture and Treasury.

"Hey, Fallon," the Treasury director said.

Fallon acknowledged her with a nod. "That must be Henry Massey," he said as he looked at a man in a finely tailored suit focused on the tablet in his hands as he stood by a screen at the front of the room.

"That's him," she said as Fallon sat down next to her. "We had our first meeting with him last week. He's really taking a personal interest in overseeing this software rollout."

"Or maybe he's just a micromanager," Fallon said as he sized up Massey, watching him busily tap his fingers on his tablet. He looked arrogant, overbearing, and a bit out of shape.

"Let's get started," someone said.

Fallon recognized the voice. He turned to see the governor enter the room and take a seat at the head of the table opposite Massey. "Let's do a quick round of brief introductions, and then you can start your presentation, Mr. Massey."

Each department director gave their name and position. When it was Fallon's turn, he introduced himself and gave his title as state police liaison.

Massey smiled at Fallon. "Crime fighting. Just like your dad."

Fallon looked at Massey.

"Your dad, Nicholas McElliot, was the longtime Michigan attorney general from the late 1960s until 1995," Massey said.

"You did your homework," Fallon said. Why would this guy care about his dad?

"I make it a point to get to know the people I will be working with on implementation projects."

Fallon didn't respond, keeping his expression serious. Why was this man singling him out? Massey hadn't tossed out any trivia about the other cabinet members making introductions.

The Treasury director looked at Fallon, raised an eyebrow, then continued the introductions by giving her name and title.

"Thank you, everyone," Massey said as soon as the last introduction was given. He then launched into his litany of tech talk about the rollout of the Archipelago software.

Fallon studied the logo on the first slide on the screen behind Massey. The word *Archipelago* was cleverly surrounded by an archipelago of island silhouettes that looked vaguely familiar to Fallon—a group of islands he had seen on a map somewhere. "Excuse me, but that group of islands on your logo," he said. "They look familiar."

"Very observant," Massey smiled. "It's the Beaver Island Archipelago. I've always had a fondness for that group of islands and for Michigan." Without missing a beat, he dove back into his presentation. "This suite of software will link the separate islands of each department of Michigan state government under one software—our Archipelago software suite . . ."

Fallon hadn't thought about Beaver Island in years. He shoved the memories to the back of his mind as he glanced across the table at Marjorie Brogan, seated between the directors of the state police and social services. She was all business with a royal blue suit and a stern expression as she watched Massey, then whispered something to the state police director. She stopped when she noticed Fallon looking at her. They exchanged glances; he turned away first and focused on Massey. Her expression had seemed suspicious of him.

"If you're familiar with the word *archipelago*," Massey said, "you know it's a reference to a large group of affiliated islands. Our software ties together a large group of separate units of government into one seamless system. Over the next twelve months we'll bring each department online, and by this time next year, we'll go live with the integration tool that will link all departments together. When that happens, nothing will be hidden. There will be full transparency of all the state's operations."

Fallon caught Karen glancing at him. She nodded. When he turned to look back at Massey, he noticed Marjorie Brogan looking at him. Their eyes met again. He quickly fixed his look on Massey.

"Governor, you will be able to monitor all your state operations in real time with a few clicks," Massey said. He began to demonstrate the inner workings of the software on the large screen behind him.

Fallon couldn't endure Massey's technobabble. He leaned back and shifted his attention to the tablet on his lap where he found Massey's bio equally boring: CEO and founder of Quick Connect, the largest social media platform in the world with more than one billion users;

lead investor in Arpa, the venture capital firm behind the Archipelago start-up company; loving father and husband; philanthropist supporting the poor and needy; the wealthiest man in the world . . . so full of himself.

"Excuse me, Mr. McElliot," Massey said. "Am I boring you?"

Fallon looked up and smiled. "All I'm hearing is a lot of jargon."

"What's your point?" Massey asked.

Fallon leaned forward, letting the silence hang in the room for a moment. He could feel all eyes on him as he kept his focus on Massey. "You're bragging about how we'll have total control of state government with just a few clicks."

"You *were* listening," Massey said.

"That feature would also make it easy for a hacker to take total control of the state's operations."

"Archipelago is bulletproof. I've had a team of friendly hackers attack it daily for the last year. It's impenetrable and far superior to your old software."

"Statements like that are what make it vulnerable," Fallon said.

"I have to agree with Fallon," Marjorie said, nodding at him. She turned to Massey. "As long as our departments aren't linked with an integration tool, it will be more difficult for someone to take control of all our systems."

Fallon was surprised to hear Marjorie agree with him.

"Our firewalls are far superior to anything else on the market," Massey said.

"How can you be so sure? Major computer systems are hacked every day," Fallon said.

"Fallon," the governor said, frowning, "IT thoroughly vetted the software. I also spoke with other states that have implemented Archipelago. The security of the system is sound."

"Thank you, Governor, for that endorsement," Massey said. "Let's continue."

Fallon tried to focus on the presentation as it continued for another hour, but instead he found himself studying the people around the table. They all seemed interested in this new software—all except Brogan, whose body language signaled uneasiness.

"Anything to add, Governor?" Massey asked, apparently wrapping up.

"IT is drafting an implementation plan and schedule," Karen said. "All of you should have a copy in your inbox in a couple weeks. We're planning to go live by fall of next year. Any questions?"

Fallon looked around the room. No one said a word.

"Okay, we're done," Karen said. "If you could stay, Fallon, I'd like a word with you."

Marjorie smirked at Fallon as she stood and left the room.

Fallon remained seated as he watched the rest of the cabinet leave the room. He looked at Massey on the other end of the room, busily tapping on his tablet.

The governor moved to the seat next to Fallon. "You need to ease up a bit."

"You know me, Karen. I'm still a detective at heart. It's my job to question things."

"Yes, always the skeptic," Karen said, then looked up. "Mr. Massey."

Fallon turned to see Massey approaching them.

"I'll send my integration team over next week, after Thanksgiving," Massey said. "Everything looks like it's on schedule to be fully operational by this time next year."

"That's the goal," Karen said.

"I should be going," Massey said.

"Nice to meet you, Mr. Massey," Fallon said. He stood up along with the governor and shook Massey's hand.

"Good questions, Fallon," Massey said. "I like skeptics. They only reinforce the strength of our software."

Massey's comment only reinforced Fallon's opinion about Massey's arrogance.

"Fallon was born a skeptic," Karen said.

"People today are too agreeable. They're scared of conflict," Massey said. "I wish I had more people like Fallon on my team." He looked at Fallon. "You should come work for me."

Fallon was surprised by Massey's offer.

"Keep your friends close and your skeptics closer—that's my motto," Massey said.

"Isn't that supposed to be 'enemies closer'?" Fallon asked.

"'Enemies' sounds so harsh," Massey said. "Not everyone who disagrees with you is an enemy."

"Anyway, Fallon is already working for me," Karen said.

"Well, if the government bureaucracy gets to you, Fallon, give me a call. I'll have a job waiting for you."

"I'm fine where I am," Fallon said, and smiled at Karen.

"Very nice meeting you, Fallon," Massey said. "And always good to see you, Governor."

"I have one more question," Fallon said just before Massey left the room. "Why are you so fond of Michigan and Beaver Island?"

"My grandfather had a farm in the northern lower peninsula of Michigan near Charlevoix. He used to ship grain to Beaver Island."

"No kidding," Fallon said. "My parents had a summer home in Charlevoix."

"I'm aware of that," Massey said.

Fallon frowned. "How did you—"

"I really should be going," Massey said.

"Have a good trip back to Colorado," Karen said.

"Actually, I'm going to Detroit now. I head back to Colorado tomorrow for Thanksgiving," Massey said.

"What's in Detroit?" Karen asked.

"The online retailer Caspian is making plans to test commercial delivery drones in Detroit," Massey said.

"Caspian is the largest online retailer in the world. How are you connected to Caspian?" Fallon asked.

"My venture capital firm Arpa is an investor in the company that's building and testing the delivery drones for Caspian," Massey said.

"You have your fingers in a lot of things," Karen said.

"I like to stay ahead of whatever's next," Massey said. "That's how we remain relevant."

"Well, enjoy your time in Detroit," Karen said.

Fallon watched Massey leave the room. He closed the door and looked at Karen. "There's something about that man I don't like. I feel like he's spying on me."

"You're suspicious of everyone," Karen said.

"He knew my parents had a place in Charlevoix."

"It's no secret. Your dad was well known in this state."

"Did you notice how Brogan fidgeted when Massey detailed the integration tool. She seems scared about the transparency."

"She's dragging her feet on implementing the new system into Corrections. Does Marjorie suspect anything?"

"Not as far as I can tell," Fallon said as he glanced at the screen at the front of the room, then looked at the governor. "Do you think we can trust Massey?"

"You just won't let it go!"

"You're putting everything into *his* basket. I'm not sure it's the right move."

"We scoured Massey's background and the executives associated with Arpa before we signed the contract for Archipelago. Some of the best tech industry leaders are investors in Arpa. They're sincere when they say they want to make government more efficient through software."

"There's a big difference between the digital and the real world," Fallon said. "His background and bio might look good on-screen, but I get a bad vibe from Massey in person."

"I'm used to men like him with huge egos. It's all an act. Just ignore him. We have more important things to talk about. Walk with me."

Fallon followed Karen into the empty hallway. They walked to the elevators and stood a moment as they waited for the elevator doors to open.

"Some of my sources say Brogan is trying to dig up dirt on me," Karen said. "I'm concerned she might try to set me up to take the fall for her drug dealing. If I'm caught in a scandal—even a perceived scandal—it would hurt my reelection chances. That would be her ticket to step in and challenge me for the party nomination to run for governor."

"Where did you hear that?"

"I have my sources. Listen, Fallon—you have to be extra careful not to tip her off about what you and Chip are doing."

"Chip is the best. He's digging into the warehousing system totally undetected. Soon, we'll have a pretty good picture of what's going on."

"You have to catch *her* in the act, not just her flunkies. She has to be totally surprised that we have hard evidence on her. I don't want to give her any opportunity to pin it on me. Don't underestimate her."

The elevator dinged and the door opened. As someone stepped off the elevator, the governor abruptly changed subjects. "Will your boys be at your place for Thanksgiving?"

"They'll be with their mom on Thanksgiving and with me on Saturday. How about you?"

"Everyone will be at our house on Thanksgiving," Karen said as she stepped into the elevator and pressed a button. "You're welcome to join us."

"Thanks, but I'll be fine."

Fallon stood a moment looking at the closed elevator door. Was Massey telling the truth that his grandfather used to ship grain to Beaver Island?

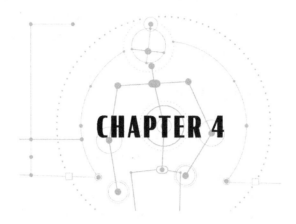

CHAPTER 4

Cally sat on the edge of his bed in his prison cell. He had plenty of time on his hands now. Time to think. It was hard to believe that a year had passed. Why had he responded to Chuck's summons that day? Now he was serving an even longer sentence in prison as a repeat offender. He pressed his forehead into his hands, took a deep breath, and exhaled. The image of Chuck lying on the floor bleeding—dying right in front of him—haunted him.

He stood and walked to the tiny window in his cell and looked at the wooded area beyond the tall fence that circled the prison grounds. Not that it made any difference at this point, but he wondered about the hard drive Chuck had given him. Did it really contain what Chuck said it did? Chuck had said it would be leverage to protect his family. Yet, a year had gone by and Cally had heard nothing about anyone coming after his family. But if Chuck had lied to him, why?

There was only one way to find out if what Chuck had said was true. Somehow, he had to find out what was on the backup drive. But how could he tell anyone where he'd hidden it? All of his conversations with visitors were monitored. Every prison guard, police officer, or government official who spoke with him could be part of the crime ring.

Leaves on the trees outside the prison fence quivered in the breeze. He tried to recall the phrase recited by the man leading yesterday's Bible study. Cally hadn't really been paying attention—he went to the Bible studies only to get out of his cell. That line, though, had stuck with him. Something about the truth setting him free. Did that apply to whatever was on the backup drive? If it held the truth, could it set him free?

Cally sat down on his bed and rubbed his forehead. Actually, the truth had betrayed him. He was locked up for a murder he didn't commit. He was being punished for protecting the truth. He lay down and stared at the ceiling. At least his family hadn't abandoned him. His mom visited him every Wednesday night—she'd be here soon.

He sat up and put his feet on the cement floor. He ran his fingers through his thinning hair and looked around his cramped cell. Not much to look at—a toilet, a sink, and a small desk, surrounded by white cinder-block walls. He walked to the metal cell door and peered through the small window. Across the hall, Louis was looking at him through the window in his own cell door. Louis cracked a smile and gave him a *V* with his fingers—the peace symbol. Cally smiled and returned the gesture. Louis nodded and walked away from the door. Cally liked that he and Louis had an understanding about each other. They enjoyed playing basketball together during their recreation time. Louis believed Cally's claims of innocence. Cally trusted Louis, yet he was hesitant to tell even him about the backup drive.

Cally returned to his bed. A few minutes later there was a tapping noise on his cell door. The door opened and the regular night shift guard, Pete, stepped inside. It was a relief to see him. Pete had a way of calming him.

"Your mom's here," Pete said.

Cally walked with Pete to the brightly lit visitor's area. He passed several other inmates seated with visitors and sat down at the usual pair of chairs facing each other across a table in the far corner of the room, next to a large expanse of windows. He looked through the window at the golden sunlight in the prison yard.

"Cally!" his mother's voice said.

"Mom," Cally said, standing to hug her. Her feeble arms wrapped around him; her face pressed against his chest. Cally released her frail body and helped her sit in the chair opposite him. Her face looked stressed. "What's wrong?" he asked, sitting again.

"Oh, Cally . . ." Cally's mom said, her voice cracking. She began to sob.

Cally pushed the box of tissues on the table closer to her.

She took several tissues, wiped the tears from her face, and blew her nose.

"Your dad," she managed to say between sobs. "I think he . . . he had a stroke this morning."

"What? A stroke! Is he okay?"

"He's in the hospital."

"Shouldn't you be with him?"

"Daniel and Sheila are with him. They told me to visit you like usual, to tell you in person about the stroke."

"I'm sorry, Mom," Cally said. But inside he really wasn't. He wouldn't have to listen anymore to his dad preaching at him.

"Thanks, Cally," she said as she wiped tears from her face.

"What happened?"

"I think it was the protesters."

"What protesters? What do you mean?"

"I don't know what's going on," she said, her head sagging as she sobbed. "There are protesters outside the house. They showed up a few days ago. They stand in front of the house and shout awful things."

"Like what?"

"'Racist!'"

"Why would they say that?"

"Something your dad did."

"What did Dad do?"

"He's not a racist! He reads his Bible every day. He gave up drinking. He believes everyone is created in the image of God."

"If there are protesters there, there must be a reason." His stomach suddenly tightened. Maybe someone *was* coming after his family. "What did Daniel and Sheila say about it?"

"Your dad called Daniel when they first showed up, thinking the FBI could do something. Daniel had Sheila get something called a PPO?"

"A Personal Protection Order—did that help?"

"Not really."

"Did Daniel or Sheila say why the protesters were at the house?"

"Daniel said someone posted racial slurs using your dad's name and our address. He said it was on something called Quick Connect. He's trying to get it cleared up."

"Dad is clueless when it comes to computers and cell phones. He has no idea how to use Quick Connect."

"But, Cally, Daniel showed me. His name and picture are on there! *Someone* put them there. It's turned into this big deal. Reporters showed up yesterday."

"Reporters! Did you talk to them?"

"Oh, heavens no," his mom sniffled as she grabbed another tissue. "I called the police, but they couldn't stop them. They could only enforce the PPO and keep them off our lawn."

"So, what happened to Dad this morning?"

"The protesters . . ." His mom paused to wipe tears. "Your dad was getting all agitated when he saw them show up again. He had a cup of tea to try to calm down, but then he . . . well, he just collapsed. I called 911 and an ambulance rushed him to the hospital."

"Maybe you should be with him."

"As soon as we're done, I'm heading over there. I'll stay with him tonight."

Cally nodded. His mother's tears seemed unending, and he was concerned for her—but not his dad. He was reluctant to admit it even to himself, but he hoped his dad would die so he wouldn't have to look at him again, wouldn't have to remember all the past alcoholic abuse his dad had put their family through.

"Those protesters were too much for your dad."

"I'm sorry, Mom," Cally said. He wanted to comfort her, but he knew that touching her, even just taking her hand, would abruptly end the visit. They were allowed one brief hug of greeting and one to say goodbye, and that was all.

He didn't learn much more between his mom's sobs about the protestors or his dad's condition. Soon visiting time was over. Cally watched as his mom tried to regain her composure. They stood and looked at each other for a moment. Suddenly his mom looked strangely calm.

"Take care of yourself, Mom," Cally said.

She smiled. "I will. And *you* take care of yourself."

Cally gave her the permitted goodbye hug.

She turned to leave, then stopped and opened her mouth as if about to say something. Instead, she pressed her lips together.

"What were you going to say?" he asked.

"No . . . nothing." She bit her lip. "See you soon, Cally."

"Next week."

She stared at him with a blank expression and nodded.

"You okay, Mom?"

"Yes. Next week." She turned and walked toward the exit.

Cally watched as a guard escorted her out of the visiting area.

"I overheard your mom. Sorry about your dad," Pete said as he escorted Cally from the room.

"Don't be. He was an abusive alcoholic."

"Well, I'm still sorry."

Cally walked through a metal detector, then Pete swept his body with the handheld wand. They continued down the hallway to his cell.

"Pete, have you heard anything about protesters at my parents' house?"

"I saw something on the news about it. I guess your dad put some hate speech on Quick Connect and it upset a lot of people."

"Pete, my dad has never used a computer or cell phone in his life. My brother's looking into it."

"Maybe he can clear it up," Pete said, opening Cally's cell door.

As he stepped inside, Cally noticed Louis peering through the window of his cell door. Cally nodded and Louis nodded back, waving the peace symbol with his hand as Cally's door closed behind him.

Cally sat on the edge of his bed in the dark and looked at the small square of light on the floor from the window of his cell door. Chuck had said they were coming after his family, but why had they waited so long? Why now? He lay down and thought. He had to get the backup drive to Daniel, but how? He weighed his options, but got nowhere. It was too much. He tried to forget everything. He let his mind slip into a carefree moment of riding with Chuck in his Mustang convertible with the top down on a hot summer night—wind in their hair as they sped along Detroit's freeways. His eyelids felt heavy.

* * *

A thumping noise startled Cally. He opened his eyes. Chuck wasn't there, nor was he sitting in a Mustang. He propped himself up in bed and heard his cell door open with a clunk. The light coming through the open door blinded him for a second.

"Get up!" a shadowy figure said.

Cally sat on the edge of his bed. Two guards he didn't recognize were standing by his bed.

"Come on!" one guard said as he grabbed Cally's arm and yanked him to his feet.

Groggy but waking up fast, Cally staggered.

"Move it!" the other guard said as he pulled him out of his cell and into the hallway. The cell door slammed shut behind them as they continued toward the cell block exit.

"Where are we going?" Cally asked.

"Quiet!" one guard barked.

The guards yanked him through a door that led out of the cell block and down a long corridor. Cally squinted at the bright fluorescent lights illuminating the white walls. He wrinkled his nose at the smell of bleach. The hallway looked so sterile and clean. He hadn't been in this part of the prison before. Soon they were in a hallway filled with old pictures of wardens staring at him with stern expressions. At the end of the hallway, they stepped into a reception area surrounded by office doors. They pushed Cally down into a chair next to a door marked WARDEN. One guard sat next to Cally with a tight grip on his arm while the other knocked on the warden's door.

Cally glanced at a clock on the wall. Why was he being brought to the warden in the middle of the night without handcuffs?

"Get him in here!" someone said from the other side of the door.

The guards yanked Cally out of the chair, pushed him into the warden's office, and thrust him into a chair in front of a large, wooden desk. A nameplate on the desk read "Thomas Ferguson, Warden." The man behind the desk sat confidently in his high-backed, leather desk chair, wearing a spotless, stiff white shirt and deep green tie. The man's steely blue eyes bore down on him.

"Well, well," the man said with a grin as he leaned back in his chair. "Mr. Robert Callahan Junior. Or should I call you Cally?"

Cally studied the man. He couldn't place him. Had they met before?

"Leave us alone," the warden ordered the guards, pointing to the open door.

Cally watched the guards leave and close the door behind them. He turned to look at the man.

"You have no idea who I am," the man said with a smile.

Cally looked at the nameplate on the desk. "Thomas Ferguson?"

"So, you can read," Ferguson said. "Do you know why you're here?"

Cally shrugged.

"Remember Chief Peters?" Ferguson said. His chair squeaked as he leaned forward. "The man who arrested you on the freeway about a year ago. The chief and I are buddies."

Cally tried not to react to Chief Peters's name. He tried to look indifferent, but inside he could feel fear beginning to stir.

"I've kept an eye on you since I started here as warden last month. You know where something is that we want."

"I don't know what you're talking about." He felt a tinge of relief that apparently they hadn't found the hard drive.

Ferguson leaned across the large desk toward Cally. The smell of stale tobacco emanated from his breath. "We think Chuck gave you a hard drive with lots of information on it. Where did you hide it?"

"All Chuck gave me was trouble," Cally said.

"We scoured your parents', brother's, and sister's places. We searched their digital footprint online. We've exhausted all options . . ." Ferguson paused and smiled.

The room went silent for a moment as they stared at each other. Cally kept a stoic look, even though he was panicking inside.

Ferguson frowned. "Except for beating it out of you! This prison is run by a private firm. The guards who brought you here are my special guards. They answer only to me."

Cally gripped the armrest tighter while maintaining his stone face.

"Where is it, Cally!" Ferguson lunged across his desk and struck Cally across the face.

Cally was thrown back in his chair by the force of the blow. He put his hand to his cheek.

Ferguson sat back in his chair and straightened his tie. "We've been watching you, listening to every conversation you've had since you were arrested. We're tired of waiting for you to say something. We're coming for your family."

"You leave my family out of this!"

"Too late. We've already started."

"The Quick Connect Posts! You're the one."

"You're catching on," Ferguson smiled. "I was surprised how quick it went viral. It doesn't take much these days to incite a mob. Nobody cares about the truth. They only know what they see online."

"You!" Cally resented Ferguson's smug look.

Ferguson chuckled. "Your dad said a lot of hate-filled things online, and now he's paying for it. The stress is slowly killing your parents. When they're gone, we'll destroy your sister, Sheila, and brother, Daniel. Soon we'll post embarrassing things. They'll be so humiliated—who knows what could happen."

"What do you want?"

"We know Chuck downloaded a bunch of stuff from his cloud account. We suspect he dumped it on a small backup drive that he gave you at his apartment. Tell me where you hid it and save your family."

Even if he told Ferguson where it was, there was no guarantee they wouldn't still come after him and his family. Chuck was right. The backup drive was his only leverage. "If you don't stop coming after my family, everything on that drive will be posted to the internet for the world to see."

"If you had planned on releasing that information, you would've done it a long time ago. Obviously, you're the only one who knows where the drive is hidden. I'm done playing games. Tell me where it is."

"No!"

"Your family is as good as dead. I've already killed your dad."

"What?"

"Well, not directly. Your brother contacted Corrections online to tell us your dad died several hours ago. I guess the protesters were just too much for him."

"As if I care," Cally said.

"But you *do* care about your mom," Ferguson said as he turned in his chair to grab the computer screen next to his desk. He swiveled the screen so Cally could see the display.

Onscreen, Cally saw a video of his mom's visit only hours before.

"This is tearing your mom up," Ferguson said, gesturing toward the video. "She looks so frail. We'll keep pushing until she's gone too."

"You leave my mom out of this!" Cally said, lunging at Ferguson. But Ferguson pushed Cally backward into his seat. Ferguson walked around the desk and leaned over Cally, their faces only inches apart. Cally looked up into his eyes.

"You can't stop us," Ferguson said. Their eyes locked for a moment, then he released his grip on Cally and went back to his chair.

Cally took a deep breath and tried to calm himself. He felt helpless. What could he do from prison?

"Where's the backup drive, Cally?"

"I don't care!" Cally said.

"I'm going to make you care," Ferguson said. "Your brother requested a hardship release for you to attend your dad's funeral. Our department director already approved it."

"I won't attend."

"I'm making you attend."

"You can't do that."

"I want you there to see your mom weep. I want you to see the faces of your brother and sister before we ruin their lives. I want your relatives to see you in your orange jumpsuit. You'll have a front-row seat. Who knows, maybe a mob will show up to protest and take their anger out on your family. Guards!"

The two guards outside the warden's office entered the room.

"Get him out of here!" Ferguson shouted.

The guards took Cally's arms, yanked him out of the chair, and pushed him through the door. He heard Ferguson's voice as they guided him through the reception area.

"I'll be praying for your family," Ferguson said.

The guards escorted Cally back to his cell. As they opened his cell door, he glanced across the hall—Louis was watching. Cally nodded at him as the guard pushed him inside. The door locked behind him. He stood a moment in the dark. At least he had confirmation that there must be something important on the drive to make them go to so much effort to get it. But how could he get the drive into the right hands? Who else in state government was working with Ferguson—someone powerful enough to put Ferguson at this prison to watch him?

Cally lay on his bed, his racing mind pushing away any possibility of sleep. He tried to think of something else that would soothe him. His mind drifted to a thought he often used to calm himself—a moment from his childhood. His family was all there, sitting around a campfire at a campsite on Beaver Island, laughing as they told jokes and riddles to one another. He recalled the scent of cedar trees and the sound of the surf from nearby Lake Michigan. A feeling of contentment washed over him. He could smell the campfire smoke on his clothes as his mom zipped him into a sleeping bag in their large tent.

"Good night," she said in a soft voice.

He looked up into her loving eyes as he drifted off to sleep.

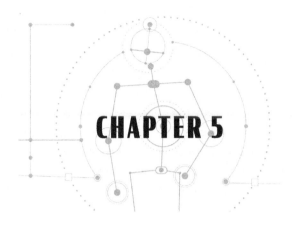

CHAPTER 5

Sitting on his thin mattress a couple of days later, waiting for the guards, Cally asked himself: Would things be different if he had never met Chuck? The question often came to his mind. Sure, Chuck had given him his first hit, but that had been his choice. It wasn't just the drugs he became addicted to, but the easy money from working for the drug ring. He just did what Chuck told him to do. He had no idea the police were involved, or powerful people in state government.

His body tensed. He felt vulnerable. Soon he would be taken to his dad's funeral—or would he? Outside the prison walls they could take him anywhere . . . say to some deserted warehouse, and dispose of him. Except . . . Cally stood and looked out the small window in his cell at the blue sky. Only he knew the location of the hard drive. If he was actually taken to his dad's funeral, he had to find a way to tell Sheila and Daniel about Ferguson's threats and the drive. If Daniel retrieved the drive, he could take it to the FBI and put a stop to this whole mess.

The sound of his cell door opening startled him. He turned to see the warden's special guards step into his cell.

"Time to go, big shot," one guard said.

The other guard yanked Cally's arms behind his back. The metal handcuffs felt cold as they locked around his wrists. A moment later, they pushed him into the hallway and his cell door clanked shut behind him. Cally took a quick glance to his right at Louis's cell door—there he stood, with a big grin, peering through the small window in his door. Cally smiled back. The sight of Louis calmed him. Louis flashed the peace sign.

One of the guards tugged his arm and they walked through a maze of hallways, metal detectors, and heavy steel doors to the main exit. Cally squinted at the bright morning sunlight as they stepped outside. A light summer breeze refreshed him as it crossed his face. The guards thrust Cally into the back seat of an unmarked police car. He fell onto the vinyl bench seat as the car door slammed shut behind him. Inside, the air was hot and stuffy. He struggled and twisted with his hands cuffed behind his back until he was able to sit up.

Through a yellowed, plastic divider between the front and back seats, Cally watched the two guards climb into the car and drive out of the parking lot. Were they really going to his dad's funeral, or did they have other plans for him? He glanced at the rear door panels—no door handles, no window buttons. There was no way to escape, no one to rescue him.

The buzzing sound of tires on pavement filled the car as they accelerated onto the freeway. Cally's shoes vibrated on the floor pan with the revving car engine. The sight of open road felt good. The blur of passing cars and landscape hypnotized him. He closed his eyes, recalling riding in his parents' station wagon as a kid—Sheila and Daniel sitting on either side of him on the back seat; his mom and dad fighting in the front seat, shouting at each other. He missed his brother and sister. Perhaps he would have a chance to see them at the funeral if indeed that was where they were headed.

He opened his eyes and looked at the passing landscape of apartment buildings, factories, stores, and warehouses. Soon they exited the freeway. He recognized his old neighborhood. There was the church he'd attended as a kid, a few blocks ahead. The tall brick building rose above nearby homes with massive stained glass windows and a towering steeple with a spire that pierced the deep blue, cloudless sky. He shifted in his seat so the handcuffs wouldn't dig into his wrists. So many times, as a kid, his mom had hauled him to church so he could kneel in secrecy in a dark booth to confess his sins to a priest hidden behind an opaque screen. He was still doing penance for his sins, he thought, looking at his orange jumpsuit. He chuckled. His family had dressed up each Sunday for church. He wasn't exactly wearing his Sunday best today. Once again, though, he was being dragged to church.

"Looks like a nice turnout!" one guard said with a snicker.

As they approached the front of the church, a large group of protesters stood on the sidewalk a short distance from the church shouting and waving signs that read "NO MORE HATE!" The reality of Ferguson's words hit him. They really were coming after his family.

"Such a nice welcoming party," the other guard said.

Cally studied the angry faces of the protesters as they drove past the church. Their shouts were quickly drowned out by bells ringing in the steeple. Beyond the protesters he recognized family and friends gathered on the front steps of the church. They passed a hearse, and he caught a glimpse of a dark blue casket inside. It was true. His dad was really dead. He felt a sense of relief that he would never have to see him again. He just had to get through this funeral.

They parked on a nearby side street. He felt anxious about getting out.

"Let's get this party started," one guard said, pulling Cally out of the car.

A warm summer breeze greeted Cally as the guards, gripping his arms, guided him toward the church. In the distance he heard the sound of traffic on the freeway. He looked up at the green leaves on the trees, then at the church steeple rising high above them. A white cross stood out against the clear sky. He turned his gaze to the sidewalk in front of the church, where several police officers were pushing back some protesters trying to approach the church entrance. He eyed the pallbearers lined up behind the hearse. They stared back at him.

"We're taking you through the front entrance so everyone can admire your outfit," one guard said as they approached cement steps rising to the main entrance of the church. Cally kept his head down to avoid the condemning eyes of relatives who stood scattered on the steps. They wouldn't understand that *this time* he was innocent, that he'd been framed for Chuck's murder. Why would anyone believe him?

The guards escorted Cally up the steps to two large, oak entry doors. Cally kept his eyes locked forward toward the doors. Just before they reached the entrance, he exchanged a look with an aunt on the top step, then caught the scowling look of a nephew standing next to her. He turned away and heard someone whisper, "That's the son who murdered his friend."

Cally tried to ignore it all as they stepped into the large vestibule of the church illuminated with tall, stained glass windows rising to a vaulted ceiling. An usher in a black suit greeted them and tried to give him a funeral program. He noted his dad's smiling face printed on the front. Cally waved his elbows and nodded toward his back to show that he was cuffed. The man in the black suit apologized.

"We don't need a program," one guard said.

The usher nodded and retracted his arm with the program.

"I'll take it," the other guard said. He stuffed the program in his pocket. "I'll give it to you later."

Surprised, Cally glanced at the guard.

"Are you family of the deceased?" the usher asked.

"I'm his son," Cally said.

"Front pew," the man said as he eyed Cally's orange jumpsuit. "Sorry about your loss."

"Let's go," the other guard said.

Cally recognized more relatives as the guards escorted him across the vestibule of the church toward the sanctuary. To his left, he spotted Daniel and Sheila. He didn't recognize them at first—Daniel with a monochrome outfit consisting of a black suit, shirt, and tie; Sheila with a tasteful black dress and black pumps. They looked surprised to see him. He smiled when they walked toward him. This was his chance to tell them about the backup drive.

"Can I talk a minute with my brother and sister?" Cally asked as he tried to stop.

One guard tugged on him. "Keep moving."

"Give him a minute," the other guard said, funeral program poking out of his shirt pocket.

"Okay, one minute."

"Is it okay to hug him?" Sheila asked.

"Make it quick," the guard said gruffly.

Sheila embraced Cally. When his head was next to hers, he whispered in her ear, "Evidence hidden in my closet."

"So good to see you, Cally," Sheila said as she released her embrace and stared at him.

Daniel's embrace was next. "They're gunning for you," Cally said when he was next to Daniel's ear.

"I know," Daniel said as he released Cally.

Cally stared at Daniel.

Daniel nodded.

"Thanks for requesting the hardship release," Cally said.

"I'm glad they approved it," Daniel said with a smile.

"Where's Mom?"

"With Aunt Catherine, over there," Sheila said, nodding toward the other side of the vestibule.

His mom was crying in the arms of his aunt.

"She's a wreck," Daniel said. "Those protesters really upset her."

"I can't believe they're here," Cally said.

"It makes me angry," Daniel said.

"Mom said Dad had a stroke," Cally said.

Daniel nodded. "Sheila and I were there when he died."

"It was . . . well, he went quick," Sheila said.

Cally nodded and looked at Daniel, then Sheila. They seemed apprehensive, nervously looking around the room. He wanted to tell them more, but Ferguson's guards flanked him.

"Enough family time," one guard said as he grabbed Cally and started to pull him toward the doors to the sanctuary.

"Hey!" Daniel said, reaching for the guard's arm. "Give us another minute."

The guard pushed away Daniel's hand.

Cally felt the tension in the air as the two glared at each other for a moment. He was surprised to see Daniel open his suit jacket just enough to expose his FBI badge clipped to his belt and his gun in a holster strapped to his side.

"We know you're FBI," the guard said with a stern look.

"Watch yourself," Daniel said in a hushed tone, eyes focused on the guard.

"Stop," the other guard whispered. "People are starting to look."

The guard looked at his partner, then Daniel. "Watch your back, Callahan," he said.

Daniel turned to look at Cally. He smiled and patted him on the shoulder. "It'll be okay, Cally. We'll get through this together."

Cally looked at Daniel. What was going on?

"Everything will be all right, Cally," Sheila said.

Cally nodded.

"Come on," the guard snapped as he grabbed Cally's arm and pulled him toward the pews in the sanctuary.

"Wait! Are you taking him to the cemetery after the service?" Sheila asked, stepping in front of them.

"He's going back to the prison after the funeral," the guard said.

"Can't he go to the cemetery?" Daniel asked.

"No. He has permission for the funeral only," the guard said.

"That changes our plans," Daniel said.

"I guess this is it," Cally said.

"Keep your spirits up, Cally," Daniel said. "Think about that promise I made about you and me taking a road trip someday."

"What promise?"

"Don't you remember? When I got my license in high school, I told you I would take you on a road trip someday."

"Well, that won't happen for quite a few years," Cally said as he looked at the guards.

"Even so, focus on that," Daniel said as the guards took Cally into the sanctuary.

Flanked by the guards, Cally looked up at the high, vaulted ceiling as they walked down the long, center aisle toward the front pew. He tried not to think about the disapproving stares of relatives and friends, focusing instead on the gold stars painted on the ceiling. He already knew the total number from when he did the same thing as a kid to relieve his boredom each Sunday. His concentration was broken by someone wailing behind them. He turned to see his mom frantically running down the aisle toward them.

"Cally!" She fell against him and almost knocked him down. He instinctively tried to grab her, then remembered his hands were cuffed.

One guard steadied his mom while the other stopped Cally from falling.

"Oh, Cally!" she said between sobs as she leaned on his shoulder. After several seconds, with the guard steadying her, she stepped back and looked into Cally's eyes.

"Mom," Cally said.

They looked at each other for a second.

"It'll be okay," she said. But she looked uneasy.

"Mom?"

"I'm fine," she said between sniffles.

"Mrs. Callahan," the guard said, "we need to get Cally seated."

"Come with me, Mom," Sheila said, taking her mom's arm as the guard released his grip.

Daniel arrived and stood by Sheila and their mom. "Watch the incense," Daniel said, looking first at Sheila, then at Cally. "Mom's allergies have been acting up."

Cally didn't recall his mom having allergies. Perhaps it was something new caused by her frail health.

"Come on," the guard said as he moved Cally toward the front of the church. "Time to sit down."

The guards escorted Cally to the front pew. They sat him down on the far end of the pew, then sat next to him like bookends on his left and right. Soon Daniel, Sheila, and his mom joined them on the other side of the pew. His mom looked at him and smiled as she wiped her eyes with a tissue. He nodded back at her. She was acting strange. Despite her tears, she seemed like she was not in deep mourning. Could she, like him, be relieved his dad was dead—that she didn't have to put up with him anymore?

A soft organ prelude began, and all heads turned toward the center aisle as his dad's flag-draped coffin rolled toward the front of the church with three pallbearers on each side. When the casket stopped in front of the altar, a priest dressed in a robe walked over to it and uttered a brief blessing. He then walked back to the altar and began the funeral mass.

"We are gathered here today to mourn the loss of our brother, Robert Albert Callahan Senior," the priest said. "We celebrate his life and what he brought to this world and this community. In doing so, we prepare to . . ."

The words of the priest faded as Cally stared at the casket. Celebrate his dad's life? Cally didn't feel like it. All he could think of was the countless times his dad had beat him as a kid during alcoholic rages. Cally looked away from the casket, away from the altar and the priest. His eyes were drawn to a statue of Jesus with outstretched arms, standing tall on a small platform next to the altar. The open arms looked so welcoming.

The priest concluded his opening prayer, then sat on a chair on the altar. Everyone in the church followed his lead and sat down. A woman stepped up to the pulpit and read a passage from the Bible: "These things I have written to you who believe in the name of the Son of God, that you may know that you have eternal life . . ." Cally felt the disapproving stare of the priest as the woman continued reading. He looked back at the statue of Jesus. The woman finished the reading and returned to her seat as the priest stepped up to the pulpit.

The priest spoke about some admirable man of character. Cally knew he must have been talking about his dad, but he didn't recognize the man the priest eulogized. Had the priest said something about his dad being a man of faith? If his dad's faith was about abuse, Cally didn't want it. The words of the priest faded as Cally's thoughts drifted back in time to a camping trip to Beaver Island as a kid—the one time he remembered his family laughing together.

"Robert became devoted to Jesus late in life," the priest said, and Cally looked back. "It transformed his life. With great sadness, we say goodbye today, but it is with joy that we can say one day we shall be reunited with him."

That was the last thing Cally wanted—to be reunited with his dad. He glanced scornfully at the casket, then took another look at the statue of Jesus.

A loud wail filled the cavernous church, echoing off the tall, vaulted ceiling. It was his mom, weeping hysterically. The priest hesitated a moment on the altar, looking at Cally's mom. Daniel nodded at Sheila, who gently escorted their mom out of the pew and toward a side aisle. Daniel followed. Cally wanted to help, but the handcuffs reminded him of his situation. He felt very alone as he watched Daniel and Sheila disappear down the side aisle with their mom. The heads of relatives and family turned as she passed. The priest stood silent for a moment as their mom's wails echoed in the church, then faded.

Tears streamed down Cally's cheeks as he realized that his hope of getting the hard drive to Sheila or Daniel was now leaving the church. He doubted Sheila would find the drive based on what he'd whispered to her. Soon he would return to his cell with no hope of ever getting the truth out. And there was nothing he could do about it. The truth would remain hidden. He turned to face the front of the church and watched the priest walk down from the altar to the casket, followed by an altar boy wearing a robe and carrying a large gold incense burner suspended by a chain. The priest opened the incense burner, lit the incense inside, and closed the lid. Smoke rose from the burner. The priest slowly walked around the casket, swinging the incense burner back and forth on its chain. Aromatic smoke drifted upward, creating a smoky haze above the casket.

Cally was startled to hear a sizzling sound emanate from the incense burner and to see black smoke start to pour out of it. The priest instantly dropped the incense burner. It hit the marble floor and broke open, spewing its contents near the casket. A second later came a loud bang and a flash of light. People screamed in panic. Dense, black smoke began to fill the church.

Cally froze. What was happening? He looked at the astonished faces of the guards. He struggled to breathe as smoke engulfed them. There was another large bang and a flash of light from the altar, followed by two more explosive bangs from somewhere behind them. Cally dropped to the floor and tried to crawl under the pew. Was it an explosion? Was the church about to crumble on top of them? Panicked screams were everywhere. He could hear people running and coughing. His eyes watered from the dense smoke. He tried to press his face to his shoulder to breathe, but it was hard with his hands cuffed behind his back.

"Stay with me!" one guard said between coughs as he crawled next to Cally, still maintaining a tight hold on Cally's arm. Someone grabbed his other arm.

"Let's get out of here!" one guard said between coughs as he tugged Cally to his feet.

"Unlock my cuffs!" Cally said, struggling to stand.

"No!" the guard said, then he swore. In the enveloping, dense haze, Cally could see that the guard was close to panic.

"Forget him," the guard said. He let go of Cally's arm and disappeared. The other guard also released his grip on Cally's arm, then crouched next to him, coughing as he rubbed his eyes.

In the thickening smoke, Cally spotted the illuminated red letters of an exit sign. He coughed. It was getting harder to breathe. He had to get outside. The smoke stung his eyes. He was staggering toward the exit when a shadowy figure appeared in front of him wearing a gas mask, with a rifle hanging from his shoulder. Cally instantly dropped to the floor and tried to wriggle under the pew. Could it be Ferguson or one of his goons, here to finish him off? Someone grabbed his leg and pulled him out. As soon as Cally was free of the pew, someone put a gas mask on his face. Why would one of Ferguson's goons do that?

With his lungs still full of smoke, Cally still coughed, but breathing was easier through the gas mask. He tried to see what was happening through the mask's foggy glass as the man with the rifle guided him from in front of the altar through a side door. The smoke wasn't as thick in the adjoining room. They trotted down a narrow hallway before the man abruptly stopped, bent down, and pulled open a trapdoor in the floor, revealing steps leading to the basement. Cally knew those steps well from when he was an altar boy. So many times, he and the other altar boys had gone into the church basement to smoke after mass. How did this man know about the basement access?

The man whipped out a bolt cutter from under his black jacket and cut the chain linking the cuffs on Cally's wrists, then cut the chain off of each cuff on his wrist. He motioned for Cally to climb down the steps. Heart racing, Cally hesitated, then decided he had little to lose— this might give him another chance to get the hard drive to Daniel. The man followed Cally down the ladder, closing the trapdoor behind them. The man turned on a flashlight and slipped his rifle off his shoulder onto the floor. The air was clear of smoke in the basement.

"Who are you?" Cally asked, not sure if his voice was audible through the gas mask.

The man took off his gas mask and tossed it onto the floor next to the rifle, but his identity was still hidden by a black ski mask. He remained silent as he removed Cally's gas mask and motioned for Cally to follow him.

The beam of light from the man's flashlight broke the darkness as they moved down a long corridor. Without the gas mask, Cally could feel the cool, damp air on his sweaty face. He followed the shadowy figure in front of him, wiping cobwebs from his face as they moved through the basement. Somewhere above them he heard the faint sound of sirens. The corridor looked vaguely familiar. He thought it led to an exit. A moment later, the man threw open a door and they stepped into a courtyard behind the church.

"Hurry," the man said. "Follow me."

Cally ran with the man to a black Shelby GT500 parked in the courtyard, then stopped, unsure what to do.

"Get in!" the man yelled, quickly climbing into the driver's side.

Cally hesitated only a second, realizing that he had little choice but to follow. The engine started and revved with a throaty sound. The sirens grew louder. Cally quickly climbed into the passenger side.

"Buckle up," the man said as the car lurched ahead, tires squealing. Cally's body hit the back of his seat as he buckled himself in.

The car raced out of the courtyard down a service road and onto the street near the church. Cally watched an ambulance and two police cars zip past them with sirens blaring and lights flashing. He turned to look out the back window at the disappearing church. A police car made a quick U-turn.

"They're coming after us!" Cally said.

"Quiet!" the man commanded as he jerked the steering wheel and locked the brakes.

The car swerved sideways, pressing Cally's body against the door. Cally watched as the man took his foot off the brake and simultaneously punched the accelerator, pointing them down another street. He felt his body press into the back of his seat as the car accelerated. The man's eyes were fixed forward.

"Who are you?"

"I said, 'quiet!'"

Cally thought he recognized the voice, even though it was muffled by the ski mask. He turned and focused on the road ahead, tightening his seat belt.

After three more aggressive turns, they lost the police car. Cally continued to grip his armrest as they sped through the streets of

Detroit. He watched the man. His mannerisms seemed familiar. "I think I know you."

"Not now," the man said as they slowed a bit before the man jerked the steering wheel.

Cally's shoulder hit the door panel as they turned into a parking garage and blew through a little wood bar that blocked the entrance. He winced and ducked as fragments of wood flew over the hood and windshield. They raced through the parking garage, squealing around each corner as they sped past each level. Finally, the car skidded to a stop on the top level. Cally sighed and released his grip on the seat.

"Get out!" the man demanded as he unbuckled his seat belt.

Cally released his seat belt and climbed out. He glanced at the clear, blue sky. The midday sun felt warm on his face. He turned and watched as the man standing on the other side of the car ripped the ski mask off his face. "Daniel! What the—"

"No time to explain," Daniel said, pulling a duffel bag out of the back seat and plopping it onto the roof of the car. He opened it and tossed some clothes to Cally. "Put these on."

Cally caught the clothes, watching Daniel as he shed his black jacket. Underneath, he wore a tan T-shirt with the words *Traverse City* embroidered on the front.

"Hurry! Change into those clothes," Daniel said.

Cally quickly shed his orange prison jumpsuit and slipped on the jeans and T-shirt. He looked down at the lettering on his shirt and smiled when he read "Pure Michigan."

"Here's some running shoes," Daniel said as he tossed them over the car. "I think I still know your size."

Cally caught the shoes and put them on. He tossed the prison jumpsuit into the car.

Daniel zipped the duffel and grabbed it from the car roof. "Let's go."

They ran to the exit door and hurried down the stairway to street level. Cally stood behind Daniel as he opened the exit door a crack and peered outside. Through the opening, Cally could see an empty alley with a silver pickup truck parked a few hundred yards away.

"That's our ride out of here," Daniel said, jogging toward the truck.

Sweat dampened Cally's shirt as he followed Daniel to the truck and climbed in.

"Here, put this on," Daniel said, tossing a baseball cap to Cally and starting the engine. "If we're going fishing, we have to look the part."

"Fish Michigan" was embroidered on the front of the cap. Cally put it on.

"It's our cover," Daniel said, putting on sunglasses and his own cap, which sported an embroidered fish. He lowered his window.

They exited the alley onto a street lined with office buildings and proceeded at an inconspicuous speed. Cally lowered his head when he saw two police cars approaching a few blocks ahead of them. He watched as they raced by in the opposite direction with sirens blaring, lights flashing.

"That was close," Cally said.

"We're already a few steps ahead of them," Daniel said as they drove onto the freeway. "If we're lucky, we'll put a few hours between us and them."

Cally glanced behind them. No police cars. He took a breath. "Were Mom and Sheila in on this?"

Daniel nodded. "Sheila took Mom out of the church right before I triggered the smoke bombs and flash-bangs."

"Those weren't bombs?"

"If they were, the whole church would've come down and crushed us all. All I needed was a massive smoke screen and simulated explosions to create chaos."

"Where are Mom and Sheila?"

"Windsor."

"Canada?"

"Yes. We decided it was better to split up."

"Are they safe?"

"Yes. A friend of mine arranged a place for them to hide out. Would you stop looking out the back window?" Daniel asked.

"If they catch us, we'll both go to prison for a long time. You ruined your career with the FBI!"

"Nobody knows I helped you escape. Because I work for the FBI, I'm the last person they'll suspect."

Cally sighed, continuing to look nervously out his window as they headed out of Detroit. "You knew they were coming for us."

"When those fake Quick Connect posts appeared with Dad's name, I went to a tech guy I know to see if he could take them down," Daniel said. "He went a step further and traced the posts and fake profile to a man named Tom Ferguson."

"You know about Ferguson?"

Daniel nodded. "Why is he after you?"

Cally looked out the window for a moment.

"It's okay to talk now, Cally."

"The drug stuff Chuck and I were involved in is part of a big crime ring. Ferguson is part of it. That's why he was made warden of Jackson State Prison a month ago so he could keep an eye on me."

"I knew it!"

"So why didn't the FBI go after him?"

"When those posts first appeared, I tried to convince my boss to do that. But she said it was a personal matter that I needed to take to the courts—that we had more important things to worry about than fake social media posts. I did what I had to do."

"But you broke the law."

"I had to do something before it was too late." Daniel glanced at Cally. "Before you were arrested on the freeway, you called me and told me they were coming after our family—that you had something to stop them—but you never told us what you have or who is after us. Why?"

"Because I knew they would be listening to every conversation I had in prison."

"You could've told Sheila when she was preparing your defense."

"I couldn't risk it. The attorney meeting rooms could've had listening devices."

"No one is listening now. Tell me."

Cally sat silent. Since the moment he stepped into Chuck's apartment a year ago, he hadn't told a soul what happened. He'd been yearning for a chance to tell Daniel about it, to enlist his help in getting the hard drive into the right hands. So why was he reluctant now?

"What do you have, Cally?" Daniel asked. "Why would Ferguson come after us?"

"You know I stayed away from Chuck and the drug ring when I got out of prison."

"But you were with Chuck when he was killed."

"I didn't kill him!"

"I know that, but why were you coming to my place that day?"

"Chuck told me there were people in the Detroit Police Department and state government involved in the crime ring—maybe even the state police. He wanted me to give the evidence he had to you because he knew you worked for the FBI—that you would know what to do."

"What kind of evidence?"

"Chuck gave me a computer hard drive with video, texts, emails, bank records—all kinds of evidence to identify who's involved in the crime ring. Chuck told me it was the only leverage we had against them."

"And they know you have it."

"Chief Peters grilled me when he arrested me. He knew Chuck gave me the drive."

"Chief Peters! I've worked with him on some cases. Who else?"

"Whoever made Ferguson warden must also be involved."

"Someone in the Department of Corrections." Daniel rubbed his chin. "Whatever is on that hard drive must be pretty damning."

"They killed Chuck. They almost killed me!" Cally sighed and closed his eyes. He couldn't shake the image of Chuck dying in front of him. "They'll do anything to keep the evidence on that hard drive from getting out."

"Where is it?"

"Hidden at Mom and Dad's house."

"The police tore the house apart after your arrest. They—"

"It's in a safe place."

Daniel smiled. "You put it where we used to hide our weed when we were in high school."

Cally smiled at Daniel. "Then I used the secret chimney passage to escape to the basement."

"The one we used to sneak out of the house when we were teenagers."

"Mom and Dad never found our weed or that secret passage, and the police never found the hard drive."

"Well, we sure can't go back there now. Everyone will be looking for us."

"Including the Catholic Church!" Cally looked at Daniel. "I can't believe you blew up a church, Daniel."

"They were only smoke bombs and flash-bangs. When I was a kid, I told myself someday I would blow up that church so I wouldn't have to go there anymore."

"You could've killed someone! That smoke was pretty thick."

"It was just a smoke screen to get us out of there."

"They *felt* like bombs!"

"That was the idea. I also used the church audio system to make it sound like a bomb. I wanted the media to think it was retaliation for that hate speech. I used Ferguson's hate posts and protesters against him."

"You put a lot of planning into this." It seemed like a lot for one person to pull off.

"You still look worried, Cally. Trust me. We're not going to get caught. The best way to blend in with the crowd in Michigan on a Saturday afternoon in the summer is to look like you're heading north for a fishing weekend. We'll blend into the tourist crowds. The last place they'll expect us to be is out in the open."

"Are we going to Traverse City?" Cally asked as he looked at Daniel's T-shirt.

"No, to my cabin on Beaver Island. We'll hide out there until things cool down enough for us to go back to Detroit to get the drive."

Cally had never been to Daniel's cabin. He remembered Daniel buying it about ten years ago when he'd left his job with Peninsular, the company he'd worked for for a few years after leaving the Air Force, to join the FBI. Cally thought about it, then said, "You never did tell us what you did for Peninsular."

"You know I can't tell you. I signed a confidentiality agreement. All I can say is that they are a global security company."

Cally nodded and looked out his open window. No surprise there. Ever since Daniel left the Air Force, he never talked about his work. He was always so secretive. He looked out the back window at the traffic behind them.

"No one is following us, Cally."

"How can you be so sure? Can't they track your phone?"

"This is a disposable phone."

"You're making it sound too easy," Cally said. "By now every police officer in the state must be looking for us."

"I know what I'm doing. We made a clean escape."

Cally checked the road in front of them. The warm, fresh air blowing through his window felt good. He looked at Daniel.

"What's eating you, Cally?" Daniel asked.

"You had help with my escape."

Daniel kept his eyes on the road.

"Who helped you?"

"It's complicated, Cally."

CHAPTER 6

T
oilet paper?" Fallon said as he looked at Chip standing next to pallets of large boxes stacked in the State of Michigan warehouse.

"Shhhh," Chip said, pointing toward a door.

Fallon turned to see the shift supervisor approach. "Are you two about done with your audit here?" he asked when he stood in front of them.

"About done," Fallon said.

"You know—I don't think I've ever had someone from the governor's office check out our warehouse operation, especially on a Saturday," the supervisor said.

"How long you been working here?" Chip asked.

"About twenty years."

"You've seen a lot of change," Fallon said.

"Nothing like that Archipelago system we're bringing online," the supervisor said as he pointed to a robot moving a pallet of boxes. "Stuff practically comes in and out of here by itself. And now with those drones—pretty soon we won't even need delivery trucks."

"What do you mean?" Fallon asked.

"I've heard that Caspian will be testing delivery drones in Detroit," the supervisor said. "The way I see it, it's just a matter of time before drones start delivering stuff to our doorstep."

Fallon wanted to keep the man talking. "Yes, Henry Massey mentioned that in a meeting a couple months ago."

"The billionaire Massey who started Quick Connect?" the supervisor asked.

"That's the guy."

"I didn't know he was involved in Caspian."

"His venture capital firm Arpa invested in Caspian's delivery drones."

"These tech guys are going to take over the world," the supervisor said as he shook his head. "It's just a matter of time before this whole place runs itself, and then I'm out of a job."

"Don't worry, you're union," Fallon said.

"Well, that's one bright spot," the supervisor said.

"Does anyone inspect the deliveries when they come off the truck?" Fallon asked.

"That Archipelago system does all the checking. If those zebra stripes on the boxes coming off that truck don't match the orders, we get an alert," the supervisor said.

"Does anyone visually check what's in the boxes?" Chip asked.

"Not until they get to their destination. We barely have enough people to make sure all this automated stuff is working right."

Chip looked at Fallon and nodded.

"I think we're done here. Thanks for your help," Fallon said.

"No problem," the supervisor said. "It's nice the governor takes an interest in how things are working out here, away from the Capitol."

Fallon and Chip walked to Fallon's car. "Looks like another hot August day," Fallon said as he climbed in his car and rolled down his window.

"Sure does," Chip said, settling into the passenger seat and rolling down his own window.

"What's so hush-hush about toilet paper?" Fallon asked. He started the car and drove out of the parking lot.

"I pulled a roll of toilet paper out of one of the boxes," Chip said. "It had small white packets with a white substance rolled up in it. The box was tagged as originating from a Detroit supplier I suspect is a shell company used to pack the drugs for distribution through the state's warehousing system."

"I hope no one saw you open that box."

"I made sure no security cameras caught me," Chip said. "About a half-dozen Corrections facilities receive double the amount of toilet paper they received in past years."

"Maybe it's the food."

Chip chuckled. "I doubt it. When I visited those locations, there was no excess toilet paper in storage. It's the perfect way to make the boxes disappear from the system—as if they've been used."

"That's what I like about you, Chip—you're very thorough."

"If we do a surprise raid and catch whoever is picking up those boxes, we can shut them down."

"We could, but that wouldn't get us Brogan and the rest of the crime ring, only her underlings. Stay on it, Chip. We need hard evidence linking her and whoever else is in on this."

"No sweat. I wish I could say that about your car. Why don't you get a car with air conditioning?"

"You know I love this old Dodge Dart. They don't make 'em like this anymore."

"And I'm glad they don't. This car was built before I was born."

"How old are you?"

"Thirty-five next month."

"You're right."

Fallon felt his phone vibrating in his shirt pocket. He pulled it out.

"This car is about as outdated as that phone," Chip said as he looked at the red flip phone in Fallon's hand.

Fallon opened the phone. "Hey, Karen."

"Fallon! Did you hear about the bombing at a church in Detroit?"

"No."

"It's all over the news. A prison inmate escaped from the church during the chaos. He was there on a hardship release for his father's funeral. Now he's missing."

"Why are you calling me? This sounds like a Corrections issue."

"The guy who escaped is the one who killed his friend about a year ago—the one involved in a drug ring."

"You think it's connected to Brogan?"

"Brogan approved the hardship release so the prisoner could go to the funeral."

"That's not unusual."

"Fallon, I've got no evidence to back it up, but I feel like she's behind the escape. I need eyes on the ground at that church. I don't want anything covered up."

"Chip is with me. We'll head over there right now."

"Fallon, don't you know someone at the FBI?"

"There's a detective there I know quite well. We did several overnight stakeouts together."

"Can you trust him?"

"Yeah. He's solid."

"Would he tell you what they know about the bombing without telling his superiors that you contacted him?"

"For me he would."

"Good. If anyone asks why you're at the bombing site, tell them you're representing the governor's office—that she wants the information directly from her state police liaison. I'll text you the address of the church."

Fallon ended the call and put the phone back in his pocket. He pulled out his work phone.

"What did the governor want?"

Fallon told him as he called his FBI contact. "I hope you didn't have plans for today."

"You know I don't have much of a life outside of work," Chip said. He pulled out his phone. "I'll see what the news has to say about it."

Fallon's call went to voice mail. "Hey, Daniel. This is Fallon McElliot, call me when you get a chance."

"It says here a prisoner escaped during a funeral at the church. Robert Callahan Junior," Chip said.

Fallon was silent as he glanced at Chip, then back at the road.

"What's wrong, Fallon?"

"Callahan is the same last name as my contact at the FBI."

"Pretty common name," Chip said. "It's probably a coincidence."

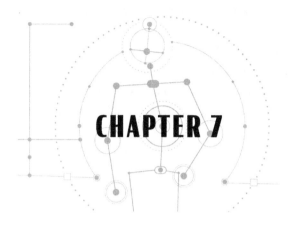

CHAPTER 7

S tanding outside the main entrance, Fallon studied the church. He traced the lines of the ornate steeple up to the cross on top, then lowered his gaze to all the people wearing jackets with different acronyms on the back scurrying in and out of the church.

"DPD, MSP, FBI, ATF—it's a law enforcement alphabet soup," Fallon said as Chip stepped next to him. "What did you learn from the state CSI?"

Chip showed Fallon a toaster-sized metal box sealed in a large plastic bag. "State police found this detonator in the choir loft hidden under a pew. Looks like they used a cell phone to trigger multiple smoke bombs and flash-bangs. There's also this." Chip held up a small black box. "They used this to broadcast explosion sounds through the church audio system."

Fallon examined the detonator. "Is there any way to trace this stuff to the buyer?"

"There's a partial order number stamped on the box. They're working on tracing it."

"This was no bombing," Fallon said, handing the box back to Chip. He looked at the church. "I saw plenty of bombings in Afghanistan. Half the church would be gone if it was a bomb. I'm guessing it was all a diversion to help Callahan escape."

Fallon stooped and picked up a sign with "No More Hate!" printed on it. "What's with these signs?"

"Cops say there was a group of people protesting."

"Why?"

"Callahan's dad posted some hate speech on Quick Connect before he died."

Fallon examined the sign. It was preprinted, not hand-lettered. This felt too staged to him. "Do the police think the protesters set the smoke bombs and flash-bangs?"

"They're not telling me anything."

"If Daniel calls me back, he can tell me what the FBI knows. Did anyone see Callahan leave in a getaway vehicle?"

"My contact at the state police tells me the Detroit Police pursued a car leaving the scene at a high rate of speed. They lost him and then found the car abandoned in a parking garage near downtown Detroit. The car was rented to an Albert Kaline."

"That figures."

"You know him?" Chip asked with a puzzled expression.

"He was one of the best baseball players of all time for the Tigers."

"Must've been before my time," Chip said with a smile.

"Like so many things."

"So," Chip smiled. "Whoever rented the car must be someone very old."

"Or an avid Tigers fan," Fallon said. "I'm guessing he used a phony address."

"Trumbull Street."

"Appropriate. The old Tiger Stadium address."

"State police checked the email used to book the car, but there are no leads there."

"See if you can trace that email to something."

"I doubt I'll find anything, but I'll check."

"He would've had to use a driver's license and credit card to rent the car. Did they check that out?"

"The guy had a Michigan driver's license with Al Kaline's name and the Trumbull Street address in Detroit," Chip said. "The credit card was also in Kaline's name."

"Callahan had some pretty sophisticated help."

"I'll be back at the car on my laptop checking the IP address for that email if you need me," Chip said.

"I'll snoop around a little more." Fallon pulled out the red flip phone and called the governor. "Where are you, Karen?"

"I'm walking to the Capitol. It's safe to talk. What do you know so far?"

"This was no bombing."

"But the media is saying it was a bombing. They're calling it a domestic terrorist attack. The public is getting whipped up about this."

"This was all about freeing Callahan. They used smoke bombs and flash-bangs for a distraction."

"This is trending big time on social media. I talked to Brogan a few minutes ago. She seems very anxious about this prisoner escape. She kept saying, 'I'm going to get him.' It was a bit over the top."

"That surprises me. I was wondering if she might be behind the escape."

"I don't think so. She sounded pretty surprised and upset about the whole thing . . ."

The phone went silent.

"Karen? Are you there? You sound worried."

"I am. Something else has come up. This is strictly confidential, Fallon. Massey called me a few minutes ago and told me they misplaced a delivery drone Caspian is planning to test in the Detroit area. They think it was stolen."

"Why would he call you about that?"

"He said these commercial drones are capable of carrying large payloads. He didn't want to alarm me, but he told me someone could arm it with a bomb and fly it into something. He urged me to have you personally look into it."

"A drone is stolen and his first thought is that someone might use it to deliver a bomb? Does he know something we don't?"

"He said he and the director of Homeland Security have been working on surveillance drones to monitor major transportation hubs. The director asked him if one of his drones could be commandeered and used for a terror strike. He insisted it could not, but it's the first thing he thought of when he found out one of his drones was missing. He wants you to find it before it's used for some nefarious purpose, which would jeopardize his contracts with Caspian and Homeland Security."

"Homeland Security doesn't know about the missing drone?"

"No—but this may be related. They picked up some chatter about a potential terror attack to the Beaver Island ferry. Yesterday they sent one of their detectives to investigate." The governor paused, then said, "Fallon, Massey specifically asked if you could help find the missing drone before Homeland Security finds out. He thinks if they find out, it'll leak and create a lot of panic."

"Why me?"

"He likes your skepticism and your inquisitive mind. He thinks you'll find it and stop it before it's too late—before this gets out. I have to agree with him. Your intuition is usually spot on."

"Doesn't Massey have a way to track that drone?"

"He said they tried, but someone disabled the navigation."

"If the drone is that large, can't the FAA track it on radar?"

"Airport radar is designed to track airliners, not drones. I know Homeland Security is working on a drone radar, but it's not operational. Go. Check it out. If you don't find anything, at least you'll get a few days in Charlevoix."

"I haven't been there in years."

"You could catch the morning ferry from Charlevoix to Beaver Island to get a feel for things."

"I'll leave for Charlevoix as soon as I finish here," Fallon said as he looked at the hearse, then the church. "There's one more thing I want to check out. I'll call you when I'm in Charlevoix tonight."

"Keep me posted."

Fallon ended the call and slipped the phone into his pocket. The area around the church was eerily quiet. The smell of smoke hung in the air. Funeral programs were scattered on the ground. Fallon noted a pair of black high-heel shoes with a broken heel on the sidewalk. His eyes were drawn to the empty hearse parked in front of the church. No one seemed concerned about the body. Where was the family of the deceased?

He climbed the stairs to the main entrance of the church and stepped inside, walking through the vestibule into the sanctuary. Through the faint haze he saw a flag-draped casket parked in the center aisle near the altar. What kind of family would leave the body behind? Didn't they at least have enough respect to retrieve the flag?

He bent down and picked up a funeral program from the floor. The cover had a photo of a white-haired man with the words "In memoriam, Robert Albert Callahan Sr." He folded the program, slipped it inside his coat pocket, and walked toward the altar. The church was empty except for a few police officers combing the pews near the altar. He stepped over an incense burner on the floor and stood a moment next to the casket, then carefully removed the flag. He wondered what branch of the military Mr. Callahan served in as he gently folded the flag and placed it on a pew.

Colored light from the stained glass windows reflected on the coffin's shiny exterior. He ran his hand along the smooth lid. He felt unsettled.

"Hey, officer," Fallon said to the police officer closest to him. "Did you check the casket?"

"Why would we do that?" the officer asked.

Fallon nodded and pulled out his pocketknife. He slipped the blade into the hexagonal keyhole.

"What are you doing?" the officer asked.

Fallon sprang the lock open.

"Hey!" the officer said, moving toward Fallon.

Fallon opened the casket.

The officer stepped up to the casket, and then he and Fallon stood together a few seconds in silence. "It's empty!" the officer said at last.

"Except these sandbags. You might want to report another missing person," Fallon said as he patted the officer on the shoulder.

Fallon walked back down the aisle toward the exit. On his way down the outside steps, his work phone rang. He opened it and saw a number he didn't recognize.

"McElliot," he said as he answered the call.

"Fallon!"

"Who is this?"

"Your old buddy Tom."

"It's been a while."

"I saw you at last year's police academy reunion," Ferguson said.

"What do you want this time?"

"What makes you think I need something?"

"Because it's the only time you ever call me."

"Okay . . . so I need something. Did you know I'm the new warden at Jackson Prison?"

"I heard. What do you need?"

"I don't want to discuss it on the phone. Can you come to my office?"

"In Jackson Prison?" Fallon said as he stepped onto the sidewalk and stood next to the hearse.

"Yes . . . Aren't you in Lansing? I heard you're working for the governor."

"I'm in Detroit at the Catholic church bombing site. I'm sure you heard about it. It's all over the news."

"What are you doing there?"

"Monitoring the situation for the governor."

"I need you here as soon as possible!"

Fallon stood silent as he looked at the empty hearse.

"Remember, Fallon? I had your back—"

"That was a long time ago, Tom."

"Come on, Fallon. We've always covered for each other."

Fallon didn't respond. It made him angry every time Tom implied he owed him for the time he saved his life in Afghanistan.

"Fallon?"

"I'm here."

"You owe me, Fallon."

"Okay, okay. I'll see you in a couple of hours."

Fallon ended the call. He hated doing favors for Ferguson, but maybe he could also get some useful information for the governor about the escape.

"Hey, Chip," Fallon said as he walked to his car.

"What's up?" Chip asked, looking up from his laptop perched on the hood of Fallon's car.

"Can you get a ride back to the office?"

"I'm sure I can," Chip said. He pointed to several blue-uniformed officers standing near a state police car.

"I'm going to chat with the warden at Jackson Prison to see what he knows."

"At least I don't have to ride in this clunker car of yours," Chip said.

Fallon chuckled as he walked to the driver's side door, then turned to look back at him. "Oh, Chip—can you look into Callahan's background? See what you can find out about his arrest and trial."

"Looking for anything in particular?"

"I'm not sure, but see what it says about his ties to the drug ring. I'll catch up with you later." Fallon climbed into his car, then pulled out the flip phone and dialed the governor.

"Learn something new?" she asked.

"No, I just want to let you know that I'm going to talk to the warden of Jackson Prison before I head up to Charlevoix. I want to see what he knows about Callahan."

"Isn't that Tom Ferguson—the same guy who was your partner when you were with the Detroit Police?"

"A long time ago. We also served together in Afghanistan. We're not exactly close anymore."

"Do you think he might have some additional information on the escape?"

"Maybe."

"Let me know if you uncover anything of interest."

Fallon ended the call and climbed into his car. He started the engine and sat still for a moment. The worn vinyl seat, the column shift, the idling V8 engine—the car was like comfort food to him; like eating a meal of meatloaf, green beans, and mashed potatoes. It was a brief moment of solitude. He put the car into gear and headed for Jackson Prison.

* * *

When he arrived at the prison, he drove down an access road to the main entrance. The prison grounds were familiar to him. His dad was always trying to make sure Fallon never strayed and dirtied the McElliot name and his dad's political career. He still resented his dad taking him to the prison when he was a teenager and locking him in a cell to scare him out of getting caught up in criminal behavior. Decades later, the prison grounds didn't look much different.

The guard in the security station checked Fallon's ID and opened the gate for him. Fallon parked his car outside the administration area of the prison. Before he locked it, he grabbed a couple packs of cigarettes from the glove box and slipped them into his coat pocket. At the administration entrance, he once again used his state ID to enter, then made his way to the warden's office. At the end of a long hallway, just outside a reception area surrounded by offices, he was startled to see a portrait of Ferguson hanging next to pictures of former wardens.

"Can I help you?" a man behind a desk asked as Fallon stepped into the reception area.

"Fallon McElliot. Here to see Tom Ferguson."

"Have a seat. He should be done in a few minutes."

Fallon ignored him and stepped up to a door labeled "Warden."

"Hey! Wait." the receptionist said.

"This is urgent," Fallon said as he reached for the doorknob.

"Sit down!" the receptionist instructed sternly.

Fallon turned the knob.

"I'm calling security."

"Do what you need to do," Fallon said as he stepped inside the warden's office. He was startled to see a woman seated directly in front of the warden's desk.

"What the . . ." the woman said.

"Marjorie Brogan!" Fallon exclaimed.

"What are you doing here?" Marjorie asked, standing abruptly.

CHAPTER 8

'm sorry, Warden Ferguson. I called security," the receptionist said, stepping up next to Fallon in the doorway.

"You can call off security," Ferguson said, now standing behind his desk.

The receptionist nodded and closed the door.

"So, you know Marjorie?" Ferguson asked as he sat down.

"We both attend the governor's weekly cabinet meetings," Fallon said, turning away from her icy stare to look at Ferguson.

"What are you doing here?" Marjorie asked again.

"I'm just here to help my old partner—"

"Why'd you call in McElliot?" Marjorie asked, turning to Ferguson.

"Because he's the best detective around."

"We don't need him."

"Yes, we do!"

Fallon remained standing by the door as he studied Marjorie's stern look and her body language. She was hiding something behind that unbendable demeanor.

"This is a Corrections issue, not an issue for McElliot," Marjorie said with a stern look.

Fallon turned and opened the door. "Why should I listen to—"

"Take a breath, Fallon. Sit down!" Ferguson said.

Fallon paused a moment, then closed the door and stood silent, staring at Marjorie.

Ferguson pointed to an empty chair next to Marjorie in front of his desk. "Please, sit down."

Fallon glanced at the empty chair. "I'll stand, if you don't mind," he said. He noticed a video conference camera on the wall opposite Ferguson's desk and stepped across the room out of the camera's reach. He leaned on a bookshelf near Ferguson's desk.

"Fine!" Ferguson exclaimed.

"Let me repeat my point," Marjorie said. "The point I made before Fallon barged in." She gave Fallon a murderous look, which he returned.

"We can't afford to have Callahan on the loose," she said. "I'm having enough trouble trying to get funding from the legislature." She stood. "This fiasco at the church is your fault."

"Don't worry, I'll get Callahan," Ferguson said.

"You'd better. And soon."

"That's why I brought in Fallon."

"You and I *are* on the same team, Marjorie," Fallon said. "You know—the governor's team?"

"I've known Fallon a long time. He won't let us down," Ferguson said. "He'll find Callahan before anyone else."

"Make sure he does," Marjorie said, and slammed the door shut behind her.

Fallon sat in one of the chairs in front of Ferguson's desk. "I'm glad she's not my boss."

"She runs a tight ship."

Fallon looked at the finely appointed office with richly finished oak furniture and ornate lamps. "This is a step up from our old precinct office when we were partners."

Ferguson chuckled. "Beats those old steel desks and chairs."

"I can't believe you still have that picture," Fallon said, nodding toward a framed picture of him and Ferguson in army uniforms.

"Don't you still have your copy?"

"All my army stuff went into storage after the divorce. I haven't looked at it since."

Ferguson nodded.

"You bringing up saving my life in Afghanistan doesn't help."

"Look, Fallon—"

"For the record—this is the last time I'm doing you a favor. Call us even after this."

They sat in silence for a moment.

"Okay, I'll get to the point," Ferguson said. "This is the first prison escape we've had since that Archipelago software came online for Corrections. That software is so effective that the prisoners have to wait until they're outside the prison to escape."

"Marjorie seems very agitated about this escape," Fallon said.

"Callahan had an approved hardship release to go to his dad's funeral, but Marjorie claims she never approved it."

"Was it a software problem?"

"The approval came through the system with her e-signature."

"Sounds like she's trying to set you up as the fall guy."

Ferguson sighed. "Regardless, Callahan is still on the loose." He leaned forward. "What were you doing at the church bombing site?"

"Governor wanted eyes and ears on the ground so there would be no misinformation."

"So, what did you learn?"

Fallon leaned back in his chair, trying to assess Ferguson's intentions. He recalled their police training in the use of flash-bangs and tear gas to disperse crowds. "There was no explosion. It appears smoke bombs and flash-bangs were used as a diversion. Someone went to a lot of trouble to help that prisoner escape. He must be pretty valuable to someone."

"The only people who knew ahead of time that Callahan would be there were me and Brogan. The guards who transported him to the funeral didn't know until the morning of the funeral. We never even told the family he was coming. We took every precaution to prevent exactly what happened."

Fallon tapped his chin as he thought. "Would it be possible for anyone with access to the Archipelago system to discover the hardship release?"

"No. Only Brogan and I would have the necessary level of access to see the form." Ferguson paused and leaned back in his chair. He looked deep in thought.

"There's something else?"

Ferguson leaned toward Fallon and lowered his voice. "What I'm about to tell you can't leave this room."

Fallon crossed his legs and draped his arms over the armrests on his chair. "I'm listening."

"This afternoon the Detroit Police went to interview Callahan's family. They were looking for any clues to Callahan's whereabouts. But the police can't find them anywhere. Callahan's brother, sister, and mom are missing."

Fallon chuckled. "You can add his dad to the list."

"Stop kidding around, Fallon. This is serious!"

"I *am* serious. The casket is empty."

Ferguson's mouth fell open. "You sure?"

"I picked the lock and opened the casket. It was filled with sandbags."

"Why would someone steal the body?"

Fallon noted that Ferguson seemed genuinely surprised. "I don't think there ever was a body. The whole funeral may have been staged."

Ferguson leaned back in his chair, shaking his head.

"They planned it well. Right down to the programs," Fallon said as he pulled out the funeral program and put in on the desk in front of Ferguson.

Ferguson studied the program and handed it back. "Any theories as to who might have helped him?"

Fallon shifted in his chair and thought for a moment. He considered Ferguson's urgent call for help and wondered again why Marjorie had been there when he arrived. Best to not say much. "I'm not sure."

"I've got one. I think his brother Daniel helped him. You know he's a detective with the FBI's Detroit Bureau?"

"Daniel Callahan is his brother?"

"You know him?"

"We've worked several cases together over the years. We spent hours together on stakeouts. There's no way he would do that," Fallon said.

"Maybe you don't know him that well. The FBI contacted me just before I called you. They tried to reach Daniel after the escape. They pinged his phone and found it in a trash can at the airport."

"Where would they go?"

"I think they left the country. The FBI is reviewing border crossing video and checking passenger manifests at the airport."

"Well, then, you don't need me. I'm sure the state and the feds have everything covered."

Ferguson paused as if in deep thought. He leaned back.

"I don't like that look you're giving me," Fallon said.

"If they were shrewd enough to fake a funeral, I think they're smart enough to elude the feds. That's why I need you. I need results."

Fallon sighed. "You know I'm not a state police detective anymore."

"That's why you're the man for the job. You can work independently—under the radar. Time's a-wasting, Fallon. What do you say? Will you help your old army buddy, your old partner?"

"I work for the governor. I can't get mixed up in this."

"What happened to having each other's back?"

Fallon sighed. "Every time you need something from me, you bring up that firefight in Afghanistan."

"You wouldn't be here today if I hadn't had your back that day."

They sat in silence for a moment, regarding each other. Something about Ferguson bothered Fallon. He always liked to play on the edge. On the battlefield or on the streets of Detroit as his partner, Fallon never felt he could trust him 100 percent. But in this case, maybe there was something he could glean from him for the governor.

"Like I said, this is the last time. No more favors after this." Fallon pulled out a stick of gum and popped it into his mouth. He waved another piece at Ferguson, who declined. "So, tell me what you know about Callahan."

"Robert Callahan Junior. Everyone calls him Cally. According to the guards, he mostly sticks to himself. His family occasionally visits him, mostly his mom."

"Did he hang out with any prisoners?"

"Just one. Louis Greene. A loner serving a life sentence for murder. He used to live in Cally's neighborhood. I arrested him on my beat in Detroit a few years ago. Man hates me with a passion."

"Let me talk to him."

"He isn't saying a word. We tried to get him to talk when we first learned about Cally's escape. It's pointless."

"He'll talk to me."

"What makes you think so?"

"You know me. I have my ways."

Ferguson smiled and picked up the receiver on his desk phone. "I'm sending McElliot to the attorney visitor area. Have Louis Greene brought to him."

Fallon stood up.

"The guard at the main security station will take you to Louis," Ferguson said. "I doubt you'll get anything out of him."

"We'll see."

Fallon walked down the long corridor to the security station. Was it possible Daniel had helped with the escape? Daniel had always seemed like a solid law-and-order type.

"Fallon McElliot?" a guard asked when Fallon reached the security desk.

Fallon nodded and showed his state ID.

"Follow me," the guard said.

They walked to the attorney visitor area. Fallon sat in an uncomfortable metal folding chair on one side of a heavy metal table in a windowless room with gray walls. He squinted at the bright, overhead lights. Two guards brought in a handcuffed man with shackles around his ankles. Fallon examined the man's haggard face partially hidden by long strands of white hair. Their eyes met as the guards secured Louis's hands to the table, his feet to the floor. The guards left them alone.

Fallon sat silent for a moment on the other side of the table looking at Louis sitting across from him in his orange jumpsuit. He looked deep into his sunken and tired eyes, beyond the tough facade.

"Who are you? What's this about?" Louis asked with an annoyed look.

"First things first," Fallon said. He stood, grabbed his chair, and parked it beneath the security camera. He pulled the gum from his mouth, smashed it over the camera lens, then put the chair back at the table and sat down. "Do you like Van Halen?"

Louis looked puzzled. "Sure."

Fallon pulled out his phone and hit play on the Van Halen album he'd selected. He cranked the volume and slid the phone to the end of the table closest to the camera.

Louis smiled and moved his head in unison with the heavy metal guitar.

"Where's Cally hiding?" Fallon asked as he leaned closer to Louis, speaking just loud enough for Louis to hear him.

"What makes you think I'll tell you?"

"You will if you care about Cally."

"Cally's doing fine or else you wouldn't be talking to me."

Fallon sat silent for a moment. "Is Cally your friend?"

"I consider him a friend."

"Do you care what happens to him?"

Louis frowned.

"A lot of people are eager to find Cally," Fallon said. "If I find him first, I can make sure he's safe."

Louis remained silent.

Fallon let the silence remain as the music echoed off the cinder block walls.

"He told you, didn't he?" Fallon stated matter-of-factly as he pulled a pack of cigarettes out of his blazer and slipped it inside the pocket on the front of Louis's jumpsuit.

Louis looked at the cigarette pack in his pocket, then at Fallon.

"Where is Cally hiding?"

Louis looked at the cigarette pack again.

Fallon started to reach for it.

"He talked a lot about Beaver Island," Louis said.

"Tell me more," Fallon said.

"He told me his family camped there once and that it was the best time in his life."

"And you think that's where he's hiding?"

"It makes sense to me. He said if he ever got out of this place, that would be the first place he would go."

Fallon sat silent for a moment. He recalled Daniel saying something once on a stakeout about him having a place on Beaver Island. "Did he ever say anything about his brother, Daniel?"

Louis smiled. "He talked highly of him. He hoped someday he could go to Beaver Island with Daniel."

"Are you lying to me?"

"No. I'm telling you what I know."

Fallon pulled out another pack of cigarettes and held it in front of Louis.

"Are you telling me everything you know?"

Louis looked at the cigarette pack in Fallon's hand. "There might be one more thing."

Fallon set the cigarette pack on the table. "Go on."

"He mentioned once that his brother has a place on Beaver Island."

"Did he say where?"

"Just that it's on a lake somewhere on the island."

That matched what Daniel had told Fallon years before. Fallon put the second pack of cigarettes in Louis's pocket. "That's helpful."

Louis looked at the cigarette packs in his pocket, then at Fallon. "Cally's the only friend I have," Louis said. "I don't have any family. Cally's like a brother to me."

"I'll find him."

"One more thing. Could you put those cigarette packs inside my jumpsuit? The guards will see them in my pocket."

Fallon smiled and slipped the cigarette packs inside the front of Louis's jumpsuit. He stopped the music and put his phone back in his pocket.

"Thanks for playing Van Halen," Louis said. "I'd forgotten how good they sound."

"Guard!" Fallon called.

Two guards entered the cell, unlocked Louis from the table and floor, then escorted him out of the room. Fallon went back to the security desk where Ferguson was waiting for him. He walked past Ferguson without saying a word and headed for the exit door.

"Hey! Where are you going?" Ferguson demanded.

Fallon felt Ferguson grab his arm. He shook the hand off.

"What's with the gum over the camera lens and Van Halen?" Ferguson continued.

"You prefer Barry Manilow?"

Ferguson glared.

"I wanted some privacy," Fallon said. "You know I like to work alone."

"What did he say?"

"Not much."

"Come on, Fallon. I need to know!"

"All you need to know is that my debt to you for saving my life is paid in full after this!"

Fallon turned and continued to the exit.

"Fallon!" Ferguson yelled.

"Don't worry, I'll call you when I learn something," Fallon said as he exited the building. He walked to his car and climbed in. He hadn't thought about Beaver Island since he graduated from high school. As he drove away from the prison grounds, he pulled out his phone and called Chip.

"Keep this between you and me," Fallon said when Chip answered. "Check the parcel map for Beaver Island in Charlevoix County and see if there's a place owned by Daniel Callahan."

"All right, give me a minute."

Fallon heard Chip typing on a keyboard.

"There. I'm into the county clerk's page . . . oh hey, they're using the Archipelago software like we are."

"Spare me the technical details."

"Sorry. Now I'm on their parcel map and I'm searching by owner for Daniel Callahan. And . . . I got a hit."

"A parcel owned by Daniel Callahan?"

"Yeah. It looks like a nice place on Lake Geneserath on Beaver Island. It's on the south half of the island. The satellite image is a few years old, but it shows a plane docked on the lake in front of the cabin."

"Interesting."

"Is that where you're headed?"

"It's as good a lead as any."

Fallon hit the end call button and tossed his work phone on the seat. He pulled out the red flip phone and dialed the governor.

"Hi, Karen. I'm on my way to Charlevoix."

"What did the warden have to say?"

"Not much."

"Keep me in the loop, Fallon."

"I will."

He ended the call and slipped the red flip phone back in his pocket. He did a mental check of the contents of the go-bag he always kept in his trunk for cases such as this. Everything he needed was in the bag, including an extra gun and ammo. He rolled down his window and rested his arm on the sill. It seemed all roads pointed to Charlevoix and Beaver Island.

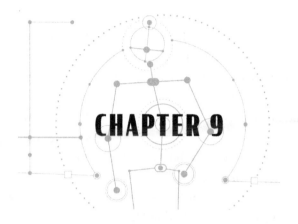

CHAPTER 9

W ho helped you with my escape, Daniel?" Cally asked. Riding with Daniel in the cab of the pickup, Cally felt anxious.

Daniel didn't say a word, eyes focused on the road.

"What are you hiding?"

Daniel glanced at Cally. "It's a long story."

"That last sign said it's one hundred miles to Charlevoix. We have time."

"Okay." Daniel gave Cally a serious look. "You can't tell anyone about this."

"Did Peninsular help you?"

"Not exactly. Through my work with Peninsular, I met Henry Massey, the CEO of Quick Connect. He's the tech guy who took down the fake Quick Connect account and traced the fake account to Ferguson. When I told him about the protesters at Mom and Dad's, he was pretty upset. That's when he hatched a plan to get revenge on Ferguson and everyone helping him."

"Why would a billionaire CEO of a major corporation do that for you?"

"Well . . ." Daniel hesitated. "When I was with Peninsular, I ran security for meetings Massey held for a group called Arpa. Every year they held a meeting in Geneva, Switzerland. Over the years, Massey and I became good friends. It made him mad that someone used his Quick Connect platform to harm my family."

"Helping me escape was his idea for revenge on Ferguson?"

"Something like that."

"Would he help us figure out the best way to handle the hard drive Chuck gave me?"

Daniel smiled. "I'm sure he would if it helped expose the corrupt people working with Ferguson."

"If we don't get the evidence on the hard drive to the right people, we're all going to prison, including Massey."

"You can't tell a soul about Massey's involvement in this."

Cally frowned at Daniel. What else didn't he know about Daniel.

"Freeing you was the right thing to do. Ferguson and the other people doing his dirty work are now sweating it out because you're on the loose. We have the upper hand. Once we get that backup drive, we can take them all down."

"And how do you plan to do that?"

"First, let's get to Beaver Island. Then we'll figure out a way."

CHAPTER 10

Cally's head jerked upright. He blinked, confused, staring at the dash of the pickup. He'd awakened thinking he was still in his prison cell. He sat up and looked out the side window at store fronts and restaurants. To his left, Daniel sat behind the steering wheel. "Where are we?"

"In Charlevoix. You were sleeping sound."

Cally rubbed his eyes and looked at the bumper-to-bumper traffic clogging the downtown. "What's with all the traffic?"

"Summer tourists."

Cally leaned his arm out the open window and looked at all the people crowded on the sidewalks walking past stores, ice cream shops, bars, and restaurants. Everyone seemed so happy, laughing and talking loudly to one another. He savored the smell of chocolate, barbecue, and fried fish wafting through his open window.

"It looks different," Cally said.

"A lot has changed since we came here as kids."

Cally looked at Daniel and smiled. With all the tourists milling around, Cally thought the town still felt the same as it had years before.

"Are you ready for a real dinner?" Daniel asked as he parked the truck.

"Here? What if someone recognizes me?"

"Just keep your fishing cap on and try to relax. A swanky tourist town is the last place people would expect to see an escaped con."

"Easy for you to say. There isn't a manhunt for you."

Daniel parked, climbed out of the truck, and reached behind the seat. "Just relax," he said as he pulled out a hacksaw. "Hold still while I cut off those nice handcuff bracelets of yours."

Ten minutes later, Cally rubbed his wrists as Daniel slipped the hacksaw and handcuff pieces into a bag and disposed of them in a nearby trashcan.

"Come on," Daniel said.

Cally followed Daniel to the main street, trying to look casual. But he couldn't help feeling paranoid. He followed Daniel across a crowded sidewalk and through a doorway beneath a sign reading "Blackbird Brewery."

"Table for two," Daniel said as a hostess greeted them.

Cally followed Daniel and the hostess to the back of the brew pub where they sat in a booth. The noise inside felt oppressive. He glanced at people seated near their booth. A man looked at him. He quickly turned his head away. "Shouldn't we keep moving?"

"Relax," Daniel said. He ordered two beers and two fish dinners.

"It's been so long since I've had a drink," Cally said as the waiter dropped off their beers and left.

Daniel took a glass and raised it. "To brothers."

"Brothers." Cally grabbed the other beer, tapped Daniel's glass and took a sip. The cool glass in his hand felt as good as the amber-colored liquid tasted. Cally smiled as he set his glass on the table. How strange—and how freeing—to have a beer with his brother.

Daniel set his glass on the table. "Sheila and I know you were framed for Chuck's murder. So, who do you think was behind it?"

Cally looked around at the other tables filled with diners. He felt uneasy talking openly about what happened at Chuck's apartment. But no one seemed to be paying attention.

"It all happened so fast. Chuck gave me a gun to protect myself, and then he gave me a computer external hard drive. He told me it was my bargaining chip—that as long as they knew I had it, they wouldn't touch our family. The next moment the police showed up and broke down the door. We ran for our lives, but . . ."

Cally sighed and rubbed his forehead. He couldn't shake the image of Chuck lying on the floor in a pool of blood.

Daniel leaned in and patted Cally on the shoulder.

Cally looked up at Daniel. "Chuck's dying words to me were to get the hard drive to you. He knew we could trust you."

"But the police intercepted you before you made it to my place."

Cally nodded and took a sip of beer.

"Why didn't Chuck put all the evidence in the cloud and send you a link to it with the password?" Daniel said.

"That's what I asked, but he told me they hacked his cloud storage and deleted everything. That's how they found out he'd made a backup copy."

"Is that the only copy?"

Cally nodded. Daniel sat quietly for a few moments, sipping his beer. "It makes more sense to me now why Ferguson made that fake Quick Connect account in Dad's name. He must be one of the corrupt people in state government who Chuck mentioned. Did you get a look at the cops who showed up at Chuck's apartment?"

"No. I escaped with the drive before they broke the door down. Chuck stayed behind to slow them down. I heard gunshots, then Chuck collapsed next to me." Cally felt his throat tighten. "Daniel, I saw three bullet holes in his back."

Daniel raised an eyebrow. "But the prosecutor said during your trial that you shot him six times in the back in cold blood. She had the pictures to prove it."

"I'm guessing they shot him three more times in the back, then used those slugs to prove he was shot with the gun Chuck gave me—the gun with my fingerprints all over it that I lost in the alley."

"They framed you."

Cally looked at Daniel. "I barely escaped with my life. The drug ring owns the apartment building. They put a hole in the wall between the two apartments as an escape route to the fire escape. I made it through the hole first . . . if Chuck had gone first, the police would've killed me! He sacrificed himself for me."

"Whatever is on that drive must be pretty incriminating."

"They want it bad enough to kill for it. That drive is the only leverage we have."

"Do you believe what Chuck told you is true?"

"The police chief was there when I was arrested. He asked me directly about what Chuck gave me."

"What about the state government? Do you think Chuck was also right about that?"

"The warden at Jackson Prison told me he was placed there to keep an eye on me. He told me he and the police chief are friends."

Daniel paused and looked at Cally. "Ferguson must have connections with someone who has enough power to make him warden at the prison where they held you. Fortunately, I have connections too. The Michigan Department of Corrections is using Massey's Archipelago software. Massey was able to access the system to create an approved hardship release for you."

"But Ferguson said you requested it for me."

Daniel smiled. "The hardship release was how we got you to the funeral. Ferguson and the others don't have a clue who they're playing with. They'll regret they ever came after our family!"

Cally didn't like Daniel's smug tone.

"You look scared, little brother."

"You seem so confident everything will work out."

"It will. Trust me."

Cally nodded, but inside he wasn't so sure.

"Two pecan-encrusted whitefish dinners," a waiter said as he set two plates on the table.

"Dig in," Daniel said.

Cally put a forkful of the fish in his mouth and nodded. "They don't serve anything like this in prison."

"I told you it's good."

Cally took a second bite. "Are we catching the Beaver Island ferry tonight?"

"We're flying to the island."

Cally raised an eyebrow as he chewed his food.

After their meal, Cally and Daniel grabbed the duffel bag out of the truck and walked to a large marina.

Cally looked at the rows of docked boats. "I thought you said we're flying."

Daniel pointed to the end of the long dock. "We're taking that."

In the direction Daniel pointed sat a red seaplane. They walked to the plane and Daniel opened the back door.

"Climb in," Daniel said, as he tossed his duffel inside the plane. "Sit up front in the right seat."

Cally looked at the plane resting on two floats. Its glossy red paint glistened in the early evening sun. He traced its white stripes with his eyes from the tail, along the side, to the large propeller on the nose. "Is this your plane?"

Daniel walked on the plane float by the dock and opened a door at the front of the plane by the cockpit. "I belong to a flying club here. I get a certain number of hours a year to use the plane. I love it. I use a lake on the island as a landing strip and dock the plane right in front of my cabin." Daniel pointed to the back door. "Climb in and let's get going."

Cally climbed in, crouching his lanky frame as he moved to the front. The door closed behind him. He sat in the right front seat as Daniel climbed into the plane through the door by the cockpit and sat next to him. He felt the plane drift away from the dock.

"Put these on," Daniel said as he handed Cally a set of headphones with a microphone. "We'll need them to talk."

The engine started; engine noise filled the plane and the cockpit began to vibrate. Cally pulled the seat belt around his waist and clicked it in place as the engine choked a few times. Puffs of blue smoke billowed past the windshield in front of them. The propeller was now a blur. Cally's pulse quickened.

Daniel inched the throttle forward and glanced at him. "First time flying?"

Cally nodded, gripping the armrest.

Daniel smiled and turned to look back at the controls. "If you need a parachute, they're under the seats."

Cally's eyes grew wide.

"Not really. I'm just teasing you."

Cally chuckled. Despite his nervousness, it felt good to be the target of Daniel's teasing. He glanced out a side window at the dock as the plane moved away from the marina. Through the windshield, he saw a large white boat docked near the drawbridge that spanned the channel to Lake Michigan. "*Emerald Isle*" was painted on the bow and a clover on the smokestack. "That must be the Beaver Island ferry. It's much bigger than I remember."

"That's the new ferry," Daniel said.

Cally turned to look out his window and saw a man standing on a nearby dock watching them leave. The low sunlight made it hard to see the man's face.

"Charlevoix traffic, this is De Havilland Beaver niner-niner-one-five-Juliet taking off from southeast Lake Charlevoix northwest bound, passing over the airfield at about fourteen hundred feet," Daniel said as the plane picked up speed.

They quickly moved across the water through a narrow passage to a wide lake where Daniel gave the plane full throttle. Cally felt himself being pressed against the seatback as they raced down the long lake, its blue, smooth, silky sheet of water spread before them. He breathed in deep, trying to calm himself. Out his side window, he saw a small wake trailing the float, glistening in the sunlight. Cally held tight as the plane lifted off. His stomach tightened as the plane wobbled a bit, then leveled out. Glancing down from his side window, he saw a few boats on the lake below. The plane tilted and turned into the sun. He squinted and looked at Daniel, who was putting on a pair of sunglasses.

"Sorry, I don't have a pair for you," Daniel said.

"It's more important for you to see where we're going."

Cally was relieved they were leaving Charlevoix, where he had felt exposed. He glanced at the gauges in front of him. The one with "ALT" on it spun as they climbed higher. Downtown Charlevoix was at first directly below, then the channel leading to Lake Michigan. He saw the waves gently washing onto the sandy beach as they passed overhead.

Before long, he could see Beaver Island ahead of them. He was surprised by how big the island, mostly covered by trees, looked from the air. The plane was approaching the south end of the island, where a lighthouse jutted from the shore. A few minutes later, he spotted a large inland lake. "Is that where we're landing?"

"That's it. My cabin is on that lake."

Cally tightened his seat belt as the plane circled and descended toward the lake. He gripped the armrests tightly, surprised he was so nervous. The treetops were now just below them. Soon they cleared the trees and landed on the smooth water. They cruised along the lake until they came to a cabin with a long dock protruding from shore. Daniel eased the plane up to the dock where a man stood waiting for them. The man grabbed the wing to guide the plane alongside of the dock as Daniel stopped the engine.

"Who's that?" Cally asked.

"One of my buddies from Peninsular."

"What are they doing here?"

"They helped with the escape. We're regrouping here."

Another man joined the first, and Cally eyed them both with suspicion as he climbed out of the plane and stepped onto the dock.

"Hey, Daniel," one of the men said.

Daniel pointed to one man, then the other. "This is Ethan and that's Logan."

"You must be Cally. Welcome."

"Looks like things went as planned," Logan said.

"Perfectly," Daniel said as he finished tying the plane to the dock.

Ethan stepped next to the plane and ducked inside the rear door. "I'll grab your bag."

"Did the cargo arrive safely?" Daniel asked as he stepped next to Cally.

"It's inside the cabin," Ethan said.

"Let's take a look," Daniel said as he walked toward the cabin.

Cally glanced at Ethan and Logan, then followed Daniel.

"I can't believe we actually pulled it off," Ethan said from behind Cally.

"It was flawless," Daniel agreed.

Shoes crunched on the stone path as they walked—the only sound breaking the quiet of the wooded lot. Cally was taken aback by the peaceful surroundings. The dark brown, rough-cut log siding on the cabin almost blended in with the tall cedar trees surrounding the cabin. Adirondack chairs set on the back porch.

"Come on in," Daniel said as he stepped onto the porch, opened the door, and stepped inside.

"This is nice. I had no—" Cally began as he stepped inside behind Daniel into a living room with rustic pine furniture. He stopped mid-sentence when he saw a man sitting on a couch.

"Surprise!" Daniel said.

"But . . . the funeral . . . the casket!" Cally stared at his dad sitting on the couch, legs crossed, holding a mug in his hand.

His dad looked surprised. "Cally!"

Cally shook his head. "But you're dead."

"Ever heard of Lazarus?" Daniel asked.

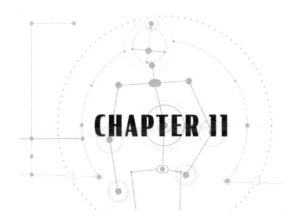

CHAPTER 11

Bumper-to-bumper tourist traffic. Some things about Charlevoix had not changed, yet so much looked different. It was hard to believe ten years had passed since Fallon had sold the family summer home after his mom's death. He let his arm drape over the sill of the open car window as he slowly nudged his car down Main Street. Along the shore of Lake Charlevoix, the marina next to downtown was filled with boats. A warm summer breeze blew through his window, along with the sound of live music and people laughing. He glanced at the people crowding the sidewalks and recognized no one. He used to know so many people here. Could there be anyone left in town who remembered his mom and dad—anyone who remembered him?

Ahead, Fallon spotted the Beaver Island ferry docked next to the channel that led to Lake Michigan. He shook off the memories and tried to focus on his purpose for being here. If Daniel and Cally were headed to Beaver Island, how would they get there? He pulled into the parking lot for the ferry and climbed out of his car. He studied the three-story-tall ferry. It would be a sizable target for a terror attack. Fallon estimated that the boat, trimmed in green and with the name *"Emerald Isle"* painted on its side, could hold at least a dozen cars and maybe a couple hundred people. He heard a plane and looked up at a red plane with floats passing overhead on its way over the channel toward Lake Michigan. Could it be Daniel? He recalled Daniel telling him he was an air force pilot.

An older woman greeted him as he entered the door to the ferry ticket office. "When does the next boat leave?"

"Tomorrow morning, eight-thirty."

"I was hoping to get to Beaver Island tonight."

"I think you could still catch a flight over tonight."

"Flying isn't my thing. Besides, I need a car when I get there."

"I could get you and your car on the 8:30 a.m. boat tomorrow."

"That would be great." If Daniel and Cally were on that plane, they would likely still be on the island tomorrow.

"What type of vehicle?"

"The Dodge Dart parked in the lot."

The woman looked out the window at Fallon's car. "That's an oldie. What year?"

"Nineteen-sixty-eight."

"That's a good year."

"It's the year I was born."

"No kidding. So was I. Can I have your name?"

"Fallon McElliot."

"McElliot," the woman said as she looked up from the computer keyboard. "Any relation to the McElliots who summered here years ago?"

Fallon smiled. "My family used to have a place here."

The woman eyed Fallon. "I remember you. Your family has quite a history here. Are you related to the McElliot with the whiskey operation on Beaver Island during Prohibition?"

"My granddad."

"No kidding. Your granddad was quite the character."

Fallon smiled. "Yes, he was."

"I have you and your car booked on the morning boat. Did you know the museum on the island has an exhibit this summer on your granddad's whiskey operation?"

Fallon raised an eyebrow. "No kidding."

"You should check it out. See you in the morning."

"Do you know where I can get a room for the night?"

"It's pretty tough finding anything this time of year. You could try Park Street Inn. Sometimes they get a no-show or cancellation this time of night. It's just up the street before the drawbridge."

Fallon thanked the woman for the tip and walked to the exit. He opened the door and paused. "Is the Raven Tavern still open?"

The woman smiled. "I haven't heard that name in a long time. That was Todd Grenshaw's place."

"Right. Is it still open?"

"Todd's son Gregg took it over a few years ago and changed it to the Blackbird Brewery. He's brewing his own beer now."

"I used to hang out with Todd when my family summered here. I spent a lot of time at the Raven when Todd's dad owned it."

"Todd's usually there at night helping his son. You should stop by."

Fallon left the ticket office and drove to the Park Street Inn. He rented a room for the night, parked his car in the lot behind the inn, and walked a few blocks to the Blackbird Brewery. He maneuvered his way along the congested sidewalk filled with the smell of chocolate, barbecue, and fried fish. When he reached the brewery, he slipped inside.

"We have quite a wait for a table. There are a few seats at the bar," the hostess said as she stood just inside the door.

Fallon made his way past tables overflowing with people and beer to an empty seat at the bar.

"What can I get you?" the bartender asked.

"Give me a short of the Raven."

The bartender returned and placed a beer in front of Fallon. He paid for the beer and took a sip as he eyed the people seated with him at the U-shaped bar. A woman at the end of the bar looked familiar to him. Their eyes locked on each other for a moment, then she quickly turned away. Could she be flirting? Did he know her? He turned his gaze to his beer and took a sip. Slowly he pulled out his phone and turned on the video camera. He put his phone to his ear and pretended to take a call as he recorded. A few minutes later he returned the phone to his pocket. He fought the urge to look at her as he took another sip of beer. He could feel her eyes locked on him. He turned and their eyes met. The dim light made it hard to clearly see her face.

"Fallon?" someone asked.

Someone touched his arm. He turned; a man stood behind the bar right in front of him. "Fallon McElliot! What are you doing here?" the man asked enthusiastically.

"Todd!" Fallon exclaimed. He glanced back at the woman. She smiled at him, then slipped away into the crowd.

"Are you meeting someone here?" Todd asked.

Fallon looked back at Todd. "No, I was hoping to find you here."

"I haven't seen you in years. What brings you here?"

"Vacation. Things sure look different up here now."

"You haven't been up here since Gregg took over?"

"It's been almost ten years since I sold our summer home." Fallon scanned the brewery packed with people but didn't see the woman. "This sure is different from the old Raven."

"Gregg's pulling in double what I did on my best summer night. In our day it was cheap long-necks of beer and fried food. Now it's organic food and craft beer for twice the money."

Fallon chuckled. "The Raven had character, though."

"If you call beer-stained carpet and garage sale furniture character."

Fallon took another sip of beer.

"Had dinner yet?"

"Not yet. I just pulled into town."

"Well, let me order you something—on the house." Todd stepped over to the bartender and talked to him. The bartender nodded.

"I ordered you a whitefish sandwich," Todd said as stepped back by Fallon. "So how long are you in town?"

"I'm taking the boat in the morning to Beaver Island."

"Beaver Island! You finally decided to go?"

"Yeah. It's on my bucket list."

"Your dad sure hated the island."

"Only because Dad felt Granddad's whiskey operation during Prohibition tainted his political career. He tried to distance himself from the island, and Granddad too."

"Too bad your dad never worked things out with your granddad."

"Yeah. I liked my granddad."

"Those were the days, Fallon. You never knew who your dad would bring into the Raven."

"What happened to all the signed pictures of the famous people my dad brought to town—the ones that used to hang on the walls in the Raven?"

"I still have them in my office in the back. No one knows who they are anymore. Would you like to see them?"

Fallon nodded, picked up his beer, and followed Todd through the kitchen to a small office in the back of the brew pub.

"My favorites are still hanging on the wall," Todd said, opening the door and turning on the light. "My son Gregg let me keep my old office the way it was before he remodeled."

"I feel like I'm stepping back in time to the Raven," Fallon said, smiling at a large, carved pineapple sitting next to a stack of papers on a worn, oak desk. "I can't believe you still have the carved pineapple that used to sit at the end of the old bar."

"I had to keep a few things from the old place."

Fallon marveled at a dozen or so black-and-white prints in black frames hanging on the wall.

"Your dad sure knew a lot of important people back then."

"Well, he was the attorney general of Michigan for quite a few years. He knew a lot of the big names at that time in the Democratic Party."

Todd pointed to a picture hanging above his desk. "I like this one signed by Bill Clinton. He sure liked our French fries. And this one of Bobby Kennedy with your dad sitting at the bar. Can you believe Bobby was in my bar a month before he was assassinated?"

"Mom told me Dad's dream of working in a Kennedy administration in Washington died the day Bobby was shot."

"Hey, how about this one," Todd said as he pulled a picture off the wall, blew off the dust, and handed it to Fallon.

Fallon smiled at the image of him as a teenager standing with his dad on the Charlevoix pier. His dad looked out of place in his gray suit surrounded by people in bathing suits and summer clothing. His dad's signature on the bottom included the title "Michigan Attorney General."

"You keep that. It's only collecting dust back here," Todd said. "Have a seat. Your food should be here soon."

Fallon sat down in an old office chair next to Todd's desk. It squeaked as he leaned back. He set the picture down next to him on the corner of the desk.

"I hear you're working for the governor." Todd smiled. "Maybe you can send me a picture of you and the governor for my wall and I'll send you a signed picture of me and Gregg."

A moment later a waiter showed up with Fallon's dinner. As Fallon ate, he enjoyed catching up on life and reminiscing with Todd. When he finished eating, he wiped his mouth. "Best fish sandwich I've ever had. I'm wondering, Todd . . . I bet you notice things around here that others don't. Have you seen anything suspicious in the last week?"

"Like what?"

"Vehicles that don't seem to fit in with the usual crowd. Maybe someone who came in here looking nervous or out of place?"

"Not really . . . except . . ." Todd tapped his chin. "Last Wednesday our bartender told me he was concerned about a couple guys sitting at the bar. He said they looked like former military and they were packing."

"Open carry?"

Todd nodded. "I took a look and they did kind of stick out from all the tourists. You can't be too careful these days. I watched them finish their meals and drinks, then they left with a sandwich to go."

"Why would they take a sandwich to go after just finishing a meal?"

Todd shrugged. "I guess they really like our food."

Fallon chuckled. "That sandwich was really good."

"Here's the interesting thing. I saw them later when I took a few kegs of beer to the Beaver Island ferry to ship to the Shamrock Bar on the island. It was the last boat out for the day. The guys were driving a shiny, new white cargo van with a rental company tag on the back. Gregg and I regularly ship kegs over to the island, and that cargo van didn't fit with the usual cargo trucks we see each week."

Fallon nodded. "Interesting."

"Why do you ask? Are you on another case?"

"Sort of."

"Mixing business and pleasure?"

"Something like that." Fallon patted Todd's shoulder. "Thanks for dinner. I should be going, Todd. I have to have my car at the dock early in the morning."

"It was really good seeing you again, Fallon."

"Thanks for dinner and the picture."

"I'll show you out the back door so you don't have to go back through the crowd."

Todd led Fallon through a storeroom and unlocked the back door for him. Fallon thanked Todd and exited the brewery into a back alley. As Todd closed the door behind him, Fallon stood a moment taking in the sights and sounds. A few revelers staggered down the alley a few yards from him. He glanced up and down the alley. As he made his way back to the Park Street Inn, he felt as if someone was following him.

Back at his car, he retrieved his duffel bag, slipped the picture inside it, and made his way to his room off the second-floor balcony of the inn. Just outside the door to his room, he paused to survey the parking lot full of vehicles. A family unloaded their van and a couple climbed into their car. Nothing seemed out of place. He unlocked the door, stepped inside, and closed the door behind him.

A musty smell seasoned with a hint of spilled beer and fryer grease filled his nostrils. Through the thin walls he heard a television droning on and people laughing. He set the duffel bag on a small table by the door and pulled out the old picture of him and his dad on the Charlevoix pier. An older man in a suit and his teenage self in nice slacks and a polo shirt. He was now the same age as his dad in the picture.

Fallon remembered the day—the press photographers had followed them as he and his dad walked the pier to the lighthouse. It was the day he told his dad he was going into law enforcement when he graduated from high school. His dad was pleased.

Fallon jammed the picture back into the duffel bag and zipped it shut. He pulled out his cell phone and opened the video he'd shot in the Blackbird of the woman watching him from across the bar. He played it over and over, finally pausing the video at a spot where he had a good look at her. There was no doubt who it was. But why was she here?

He set his work phone on the end table, pulled the red flip phone from his pocket, and dialed the governor.

"I'm in Charlevoix."

"Good. Anything to report yet?"

"No. Nothing yet. I'm booked on the morning ferry to Beaver Island."

"Good. I know you'll get to the bottom of this. I trust you."

Fallon paused a moment.

"Fallon? Are you there?"

"I'm here. Any word yet on Callahan? Did they find him?"

"Not a clue, Fallon. He's vanished without a trace. Frankly, I'm more concerned about the terror plot. Keep me updated."

"I will."

Fallon ended the call. He picked up his other phone and looked at the video again. It couldn't be a coincidence. She had to be here for a specific reason. But what?

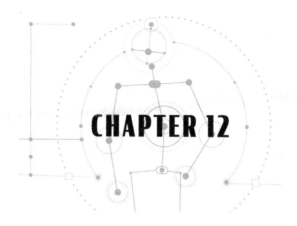

CHAPTER 12

C ally stared at his dad sitting on the couch in Daniel's cabin. Just this morning he'd seen the hearse, the casket, and the funeral program with his dad's picture. "Dad . . ." Cally said, slowly stepping closer. "Is that you? I thought you were dead!"

"So did I," his dad said, the mug in his hand trembling as he set it on the end table. "And you—I thought you were in prison!" He continued, "Would someone tell me what's going on? I woke up here with two strangers, and I have no idea where we are."

"We didn't tell him a thing," Logan said. "Just like you instructed."

"Did you have any trouble getting him here?" Daniel asked Logan and Ethan as he stepped next to Cally.

"Everything went as planned," Ethan said.

Daniel turned to Cally and said, "Dad wasn't in on our plan."

"Why didn't you tell *me*?" Cally demanded.

Daniel looked at Ethan and Logan. "Can you two step outside for a bit while we talk?"

Ethan and Logan nodded and went out onto the back porch.

"Let's all take a breath and sit down," Daniel said.

Speechless, Cally took the chair across from the couch where his dad was sitting. Daniel sat in a chair next to him.

"Will you please explain how I ended up here?" their dad asked again. "The last thing I remember is blacking out after looking at those protesters in front of our house. Next thing I know I wake up here—wherever *here* is. And what's this about a funeral and me being dead?"

"Mom gave you some sleeping pills—" Daniel said.

"She told me I needed to rest," Dad said. "Wait, she's in on this?"

"Sheila, Mom, and I worked together on it," Daniel said.

"Why didn't you tell me about this—that you faked his death?" Cally shouted at Daniel.

"We couldn't tell you until we were sure you were safe," Daniel said.

"You faked my death!" Dad exclaimed. "Why?"

"To fool those protesters," Daniel said.

"But you told me—" Cally started.

"Don't say anything, Cally."

Cally looked at Daniel, confused.

"So how did I end up here?" Dad asked.

"After those pills put you into a deep sleep, Logan and Ethan picked you up in an EMS vehicle. They were dressed as paramedics. Then they transferred you to a cargo van and brought you here."

"Why?" Dad asked.

"We wanted the protesters to think you were dead so they would stop harassing you."

"You had a *funeral* for me?"

"We wanted *everyone* to be convinced you had died," Daniel said.

"I can't believe this," Cally said.

"I still don't understand why those protesters were there," Dad said.

"The less you know, the better," Daniel said.

"But Daniel—" Cally said.

"No, Cally."

"What are *you* doing here?" Dad asked, turning to Cally.

Cally gave him a scornful look. "I got an early release."

"That's impossible! You were convicted of murder."

"We faked your funeral to help Cally escape," Daniel said.

"What have you done, Daniel! How did you fake my funeral?"

"That part was easy, actually. I used a funeral home with poor online reviews. I just told them you were killed in a horrible explosion and there was nothing left of you. They ran with it, complete with a casket, hearse, and funeral mass. They didn't care as long as I paid top dollar for everything."

Cally couldn't believe what he was hearing.

"No questions asked?" Dad asked.

"None," Daniel said. "They even posted an obituary. I also have your death certificate so we can collect your life insurance."

"How do you fake a death certificate?" Cally asked.

"I have my ways," Daniel said, giving Cally a stern look.

Cally nodded. Obviously, Massey must have helped him with the death certificate.

"I expected better of you, Daniel," Dad said.

"I did what I had to."

"The truth will come out," Dad said. "It always does."

They sat in silence for a moment.

Cally glared at his dad. Cally was right about one thing—it was better that their dad remained in the dark about what Daniel told him. But what else wasn't Daniel telling him?

"Where are we?" Dad asked.

Daniel smiled. "You're on Beaver Island, Dad. This is my cabin."

Dad looked surprised. "Where we went camping when you were kids?"

"That's why I bought a place here."

Dad was silent, looking perplexed.

Cally stood. "I need a minute to process all of this—alone. I'm going to step outside."

"Cally—"

"I'll be out by the dock," Cally said, and left the cabin. He nodded to Logan and Ethan on the back porch and walked to the end of the dock. It *was* a beautiful place. He admired the glistening water, and the pine trees lining the shore. A light breeze ruffled his hair and rustled the branches. Water rippled around the floats of the plane. Low sunlight peered through the woods. He couldn't believe he was here—and with his dad and Daniel! He took a deep breath and let the scent of the cedars permeate his consciousness. This morning he'd awakened discouraged in his prison cell and now here he was on Beaver Island by day's end. It had all happened so fast.

"Hey, Cally!"

Cally turned. Daniel was standing on the porch waving at him. "Come on in. We're getting something to eat."

"We just had dinner. I'm not hungry!"

"At least sit with us."

Cally sighed and went back inside the cabin. Everyone was seated around the table and Daniel was setting out stuff for making sandwiches.

"You have any Cheez Whiz?" Dad asked.

"We'll get some tomorrow when I take Ethan and Logan to the ferry," Daniel said.

"I can't believe you like that gross stuff," Cally said with disgust. As a kid, he had always been the one who had to run to the convenience store for his dad to fetch another six pack of beer and a can of Cheez Whiz.

"*I* can't believe you helped Cally escape from prison," his dad said, glaring at Daniel. "You threw away your FBI career!"

"Just be quiet, Dad!" Daniel said as he took a sip of cola. "There's a lot you don't understand yet. It will all make sense."

Ethan and Logan focused on eating their sandwiches.

Cally tried to ignore his dad and dumped some potato chips on a plate to occupy himself.

His dad reached across the table and grabbed the potato chip bag from Cally. They glared at each other for a moment, then Cally took a chip off his plate and popped it into his mouth.

When they'd finished eating, Dad pushed his chair back from the table. "I'm whipped. I'm going to bed."

"I'll help you to your bedroom," Daniel said.

Cally noted his dad's thinning white hair and wrinkled face as he slowly stood. He moaned as he took a step away from the table.

"I don't need your help!" Dad said, shaking off the hand with which Daniel was trying to steady him. Cally noted his dad's angry look at Ethan and Logan. "Are you going to handcuff me and lock the bedroom door like you have the last few nights?"

"Not tonight, Dad," Daniel said.

"You boys are the ones who should be cuffed," Dad said. He slammed the bedroom door shut behind him.

Cally turned to Daniel. "They cuffed him?"

Daniel shrugged.

"I have the first watch tonight," Ethan said. "Logan will take the second shift."

"We got you covered for tonight," Logan said, heading for the stairway. "Enjoy your time with Cally. I'll get some sleep before my watch."

"I appreciate all you guys have done," Daniel said.

"Anything for a fellow vet," Logan said. "I'll be upstairs."

"I'll be on the front porch if you need me," Ethan said, and headed for the door.

Cally followed Daniel to the back porch, where they sat in the Adirondack chairs facing the lake. He looked up at the darkening sky and spotted a few specks of starlight. He admired the slight tint of pink and lavender hues still present in the sky from the sunset.

"It's so peaceful here," Cally said. "So quiet."

"It is, but we have to be careful. We can't let our guard down," Daniel said.

"If we don't get that backup drive, I'll end up back in prison with you and Dad."

"Not if they don't catch us."

"We can't keep running."

"You're right. Only the truth will set us free."

"That's what some church people told me at a Bible study in prison."

"You went to a Bible study? Why?"

"It gave me something to do."

"I can think of better things to do."

"That's because you've never been in prison."

"I'd like to keep it that way."

"Me too, but that backup drive is hundreds of miles away."

"We're closer than you think. Soon they'll give up searching for us in Detroit and look elsewhere. That's when we go get the drive."

"When?"

"Let's talk about that in the morning."

Cally yawned and rubbed his eyes. The view of the glassy lake and the sound of crickets soothed him.

"You should get some sleep," Daniel said as he stood up. "Come on, I'll show you the bedroom."

Cally followed Daniel upstairs to a narrow hallway with a bedroom on each side. The wooden floor planks creaked as they walked. He heard snoring coming from Logan in the bedroom on their left.

Daniel opened the bedroom door on their right and turned on the ceiling light. "We'll sleep in here."

Cally stepped inside and saw two single beds. The room smelled musty and felt humid. He walked to the window between the beds, opened it, and looked at the lake. A chorus of crickets filled the air. He noticed a full moon rising above the trees. "Beautiful."

"Nice night," Daniel said, joining Cally at the window. "Take whichever bed you want. Bathroom is at the end of the hall. Everything you need should be in there."

"I could use a shower."

"I'll say," Daniel said with a smile. "I'll be downstairs for a bit if you need anything."

Cally turned to look at Daniel standing in the doorway. "Thanks."

Daniel smiled. "Get some rest."

Cally stepped to Daniel and gave him a hug. The two stood awkwardly next to each other for a minute.

"Sleep well, brother," Daniel said.

Cally watched Daniel go downstairs, then sat on the edge of the bed and tried to sift through his emotions. Confusion. Joy. Anger. Freedom. How long would it be before he was back in prison? The truth seemed out of reach. He had no idea how they could possibly retrieve the drive, yet something deep inside told him everything would be okay. A phrase popped into his head, "A peace that surpasses all understanding." Where did he hear that? Was it church in prison?

He went back to the window and looked at the moon. The smell of cedars filled the room as a light breeze blew over him. His mind drifted to the camping trip on the island when he was a kid—Dad passed out drunk in the tent; Mom cleaning up while he, Daniel, and Sheila sat around the fire and joked with one another. He wiped tears from his eyes. Maybe a shower would help. He headed for the bathroom, then stopped in the hallway when he heard someone talking downstairs. Could Daniel be talking to Ethan? He strained to hear above Logan's snoring, picking up a few words.

". . . as planned . . . Cally's here."

Cally carefully inched closer to the stairwell. At the top of the stairs, he peered down the dark stairwell at the light coming from the crack below the closed door.

"The drone is here . . ." he thought he heard.

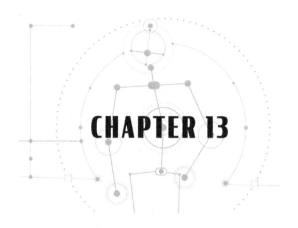

CHAPTER 13

Fallon stood along a railing in a park overlooking the loading area where the *Emerald Isle* ferry was docked. He took a sip of coffee from his to-go cup as he scrutinized the crew busily loading the boat—forklifts zipping back and forth with supplies amid trucks and cars driving into the cargo hold. Nothing stood out to him, but wasn't that the goal of a terrorist? He picked up his duffel bag and made his way to the dock area a short distance from the ferry. A crowd gathered near the stairway leading to the upper deck. He surveyed the crowd. No telltale signs of anything suspicious.

He turned his focus to a nearby parking lot and watched a couple emerge from a dusty, blue sedan. Then he froze. There, near the couple, stood the auburn-haired woman he'd seen last night at the brewery. She met his eyes with a smile. He quickly turned away, walked to a vacant bench, and set his duffel bag at his feet. He casually looked back again. His heart beat faster when he spotted her walking toward him. A man walked by with a black Labrador retriever on a leash. The dog sniffed his leg. He welcomed the interruption.

"Sorry," the man said. He pulled on the leash, but the dog resisted and moved closer.

"No problem," Fallon said as he petted the dog's head. "She reminds me of my granddad's dog."

Fallon watched the man and his dog walk away, then turned and saw the auburn-haired woman closing in on him with a look of determination. She smiled. What was Alicia doing here? It seemed unlikely to be just a coincidence.

"Now boarding the *Emerald Isle*," a speaker blared from the boat. "Please have your ticket ready before you board."

Fallon lost sight of Alicia as the crowd pressed toward the stairway. He grabbed his duffel bag and joined the crowd as they made their way to the metal stairway leading to the first level of the boat above the cargo hold. Then, standing in line to turn in his ticket, he saw her at the head of the line. Their eyes met as the attendant took her ticket, then she disappeared inside the boat. He boarded and wound his way along the first-floor deck. When he didn't find her there, he climbed to the top deck of the boat.

"Last boarding call!" a speaker blared.

Fallon moved along the outside boat railing toward the stern, looking at the people filling the rows of seats. Then he saw her sitting in an otherwise empty row of benches at the very back of the boat, facing the stern.

"Mind if I sit next to you?" Fallon asked, approaching her.

"Have a seat, Fallon," Alicia said.

Fallon sat and slid his duffel bag under the seat.

The ship's horn blew three times. Fallon felt the metal floor vibrate as the boat engines powered up for departure. Despite the clean, Lake Michigan air, Fallon could smell diesel fumes and hear the water pounded by the propellers. They sat without speaking as the boat began to move away from the dock.

The early morning sunlight reflected off Lake Charlevoix as the boat cleared the dock. A bell clanged. He turned and saw the drawbridge opening as they moved toward the channel that led to

Lake Michigan. The two halves of the bridge stood erect as the boat passed and powered through the channel toward the open water of Lake Michigan.

Houses sat on a small bluff overlooking the channel.

"Wasn't that your parents' house?" Alicia asked, breaking the silence. "The yellow one?"

"That's the one." Fallon looked at the grand old house with its massive back porch facing the channel. He remembered sitting on that porch as a kid, watching the ferry coming and going, wondering what it would be like to go to Beaver Island. As the boat powered out of the channel, the house shrank from view along with Charlevoix. The boat engines groaned as the ferry picked up speed in the open water of Lake Michigan. Fallon felt his hair ruffle in the fresh lake breeze.

"The lake is calm. We should have a smooth crossing," Alicia said. She looked at Fallon. "I was surprised to see you here."

"Likewise."

"It's been a few years," she said.

"The last time I saw you was at the detective association conference in Chicago more than ten years ago," Fallon said as he observed the fading shoreline. "Too bad I couldn't convince you to move to Lansing and join the state police as a detective."

"I like DC too much. It's my home now."

"We could've been partners."

Alicia remained focused on the distant shoreline. "I read you're working for the governor."

"I'm the governor's liaison for the state police—basically a policy advisor."

"I saw you quoted in the news. I can't believe you're working on policy. You hate politics."

"It's not what you think." He paused. "Are you still with Homeland Security?"

"Yes. And loving every minute of it."

"You're a long way from home."

"I get back to Michigan several times a year to vacation at my grandfather's house on the island." She smiled. "I remember when we were kids that you never wanted to go to Beaver Island."

"This is my first time."

Alicia looked puzzled. "Really? Why now?"

"I'm stalking you?" Fallon said with a smile.

"Very funny. But I saw how surprised you were to see me at the Blackbird. You can forget about being a couple again."

Fallon turned to look at the boat's wake on the glassy water of Lake Michigan and the thin ribbon of mainland still visible in the distance.

They sat silently for a moment.

"Seriously, what brings you here?" Alicia said.

"I heard the museum in St. James has a display about my granddad's whiskey operation, so I thought it was a good opportunity to learn more about his time on the island."

Alicia nodded. Fallon wasn't sure if she was buying it.

"That's kind of ironic," Alicia said. "Your dad tried to cover up your granddad's Prohibition-era whiskey operation and now there's an exhibit about it."

"It didn't fit my dad's tough, crime-fighting image as Michigan attorney general, but he liked the wealth it created for our family."

"Your dad was all about image."

"That's for sure."

Fallon felt uncomfortable in the quiet that followed. It appeared that Alicia was purposely letting the silence hang in the air to make him nervous. It was working.

"Things aren't always what they appear to be," Fallon said finally. "You're not here on vacation."

"What makes you say that?"

Fallon looked around them. They were alone on the back of the boat. He lowered his voice. "It's no coincidence that a transportation security detective for Homeland Security is on the *Emerald Isle*."

Alicia frowned. "Even if that's true, you know I can't talk about it."

Fallon nodded.

"And it's no coincidence you're on this boat," Alicia said.

"You know I can't talk about it." On second thought—Alicia, as the agent sent by Homeland Security, might have new information the governor didn't yet know, or maybe that she did know but couldn't tell him. "At least not now," he added.

Alicia nodded. "Okay. Let's talk about something else. How are your boys?"

Fallon smiled and updated her on his two boys and their college careers. As they talked about life since they last saw each other, he relaxed. He had forgotten how comfortable he always felt talking with her. He didn't even resist when he felt the old feelings he'd had for her rekindling. As teenagers, they'd spent hours talking as they sat on the pier in Charlevoix, watching the boats pass through the channel. He lost track of time as they talked—until the steady hum of the boat's diesel engines lessened. Fallon turned to his left and saw a lighthouse on the shore of Beaver Island. In the distance, along the shore, he spotted boat docks and a small town.

"That must be St. James?"

"That's it," Alicia said, turning to look at the shore, then at Fallon. "If you get a chance, stop by and see me before you leave the island." She scribbled something on a piece of paper and handed it to Fallon. "That's my address and cell number. I'll be here for the week."

Fallon looked at the piece of paper.

"You know—in case you want to talk," Alicia said.

"I'll think about it."

Fallon stashed the paper in his shirt pocket.

As the boat slowed, pivoted, then backed into the dock, Fallon stood and went to the railing. The boat engines went silent. A ramp was lowered, and crew members scurried to unload the boat.

Alicia joined Fallon at the railing. "Meeting someone?"

"No. I brought my car over on the boat," Fallon said as he watched vehicles and cargo unloaded from the boat.

"Don't tell me you still have that old Dodge Dart?"

"Okay, I won't."

Alicia chuckled. "That thing is like your security blanket."

"It's been reliable."

Fallon noticed that she was studying the parking lot. He scanned it and found a white cargo van that looked like the one Todd had described to him. As he watched, two men jumped out of the side door with their bags and walked around to the driver's side of the van, just out of sight. Only the tops of their heads were visible. They had that distinctive appearance of ex-military—a buttoned-down, precise, confident walk. The driver's side door opened, and another person with a cap joined them. Someone remained in the front passenger seat, but Fallon couldn't get a good view of him. The other person returned to the driver's seat and closed the door. The two military-looking men walked to the ticket office as the van pulled away. Fallon could just barely make out the license number.

"Why did the governor send you here?" Alicia asked.

Fallon kept his gaze focused on the parking lot. "The governor wants me to review security on ferry operations in Michigan so she can develop a policy plan to improve it." He turned his attention to Alicia. "Why did Homeland Security send you here?"

"I'm also looking into the security of ferries on the Great Lakes."

Fallon gave Alicia a skeptical look. "Homeland Security doesn't investigate unless there's a credible threat." He looked back at the cars coming off the boat.

"Just as the governor wouldn't send you here unless she had a serious concern—such as a credible threat."

"Think what you want to. Besides, why would terrorists bother with an obscure ferry service in a remote part of the state."

"That's the perfect reason, Fallon."

"What do you mean?"

"No one would expect a terrorist plot here. It's an easy target. Imagine the fear and economic impact on tourism if they succeeded in attacking a small ferry service on the Great Lakes. People across the country would be scared to visit small tourist sites. They would feel no place is safe."

Fallon nodded. Was that why Massey was so concerned about the drone he reported stolen? Or was he just concerned about the impact on his investment in the delivery drone business if one of his drones was used for a nefarious purpose.

"There's my car," Fallon said.

"I can't believe you brought that piece of junk here. If it breaks down, I have a truck at my house you can use."

"Thanks. Need a ride to your house?"

Alicia smiled. "A ride would be nice."

At his car, he tossed his duffel onto the back seat and climbed behind the steering wheel.

Alicia joined him on the passenger side of the bench seat. "This reminds me of when you and I used to drive around Charlevoix in the summer."

"This sure isn't like my dad's Buick."

"I don't remember why your dad didn't drive one of your granddad's McElliot cars."

"He tried to distance himself from my granddad's car company and the family fortune. As you said—always thinking about his image."

"I must say, this car isn't helping *your* image," Alicia laughed.

"I drive it because it's simple. No fancy tech stuff. Manual shift on the column, AM radio, and crank windows."

"Well, this car *does* fit in well on the island."

Fallon gave her a puzzled expression.

"A lot of people keep old cars on the island so they don't have to pay to bring their car over and back from the mainland."

Fallon nodded, started the car, and drove out of the parking lot and onto Main Street. They cranked open the windows to let the fresh breeze from the harbor blow through the car. Main Street was busy with people who'd just arrived on the ferry, but it was much quieter than Charlevoix. Alicia directed Fallon to her house a few blocks away. He parked the car on the gravel driveway behind an old yellow pickup with rust spots.

Fallon opened the door, climbed out, and looked at the small house with two dormers and faded green shingle siding. White posts with flaking paint propped up the sagging roof of a small cement porch on the front of the house. He looked at the tall trees that shaded the lot. "Nice place."

Alicia opened her door and stepped out. "It needs a lot of work."

"That truck looks as old as my car."

"Yes, but it runs great."

Fallon looked at Alicia across the roof of the car. "It was nice seeing you."

"Why don't you come in and have some lunch?" Alicia asked.

"You have food here? You're not just arriving, then."

"Very observant. Okay, so I've been here for a week."

"So, you *are* staking out the ferry."

"Why don't you come in for a minute and we can talk."

Fallon hesitated. *Not yet.* Her face was neutral. Her deep hazel eyes were focused on him. *But maybe soon.* "I think I'll go into town and get a room for tonight," he said.

"You don't have a room reservation? Everything is going to be booked this time of year."

"I'll see what I can find."

"Suit yourself. I'll have lunch ready when you come back empty-handed."

Fallon climbed back into his car.

"It was nice seeing you, Fallon. Keep in mind that I have a guest room you could use."

"Thanks, but I should be able to find something in town."

"I'll be here," Alicia said, waving.

Under a cloudless blue sky, Fallon drove past the harbor and back into town. The proximity to Lake Michigan and the fragrant, warm summer air took him back to past summers in Charlevoix as a kid. He wished he really was on vacation as he drove past shops and vacationers filling Main Street. Instead, he pulled out his phone and asked Chip to run the plate number he'd seen on the van. He ended the call just as he spotted a banner hanging on the front of a building: "Prohibition Display, McElliot Whiskey Works." He parked in front of the museum and walked to a sandwich board near the entrance that read "Check out the McElliot Whiskey Runner boat display at the municipal marina." It piqued his curiosity. Was it his granddad's boat?

Fallon crossed the street to the municipal marina near the docked ferry. There was a wooden Chris-Craft boat in the first slip that looked identical to his granddad's boat, with its rich brown wooden hull and glossy lacquer finish. On the bow a small triangular flag, with "Chris-Craft" embroidered in white-on-blue material, waved in the breeze—just as it did when he rode with his granddad on Lake Michigan.

A man standing in the boat watched Fallon walking toward him.

"Is that the McElliot boat?" Fallon asked as he neared the man.

"The actual boat Mr. McElliot owned," the man said. "It was quite the effort to restore it, but the museum had a big donor step forward last year to fund the project."

"It looks better than I remember it."

"You've seen this boat before?"

Fallon nodded. He would never forget those summer days as a kid sitting in the front of the boat with his granddad at the wheel, pushing the big V8 engine to its limits as they zipped across Lake Michigan near Charlevoix and the channel. His granddad would just laugh, his white hair fluttering in the wind, as Fallon's parents in the back of the boat pleaded for him to slow down.

"I spent a lot of summers in it as a kid in Charlevoix."

"No kidding," the man said. "Did you know Mr. McElliot?"

"My granddad. You docked the boat just as he would've—with the bow pointing out."

"We studied the pictures of your granddad's boat docked on the island." The man smiled at Fallon. "Want a ride?"

"I do, but I don't have time right now."

"Do you have time to at least climb on board?"

Fallon smiled and stepped into the front seat area next to the man seated behind the wheel. "He used to carry protection," Fallon said, reaching under the dashboard.

"It's still there," the man said.

"The old shotgun?"

The man nodded, smiling.

Fallon was inordinately pleased to feel the shotgun secured to its bracket behind the wood dash.

"No one knows that's there except the museum staff—and apparently you," the man said.

Fallon bent down and felt the floor beneath his seat.

"The shotgun shells are there as well—in the secret compartment," the man said. "Did your granddad ever use the shotgun during Prohibition?"

"I was just a kid when he showed me. He told me it was for duck hunting—and it was hidden because he didn't want Grandma to know about it," Fallon said.

"I shouldn't tell you this, but since you're obviously a relative of Mr. McElliot, we keep the keys under the seat," the man said, lifting a cushion under the driver's seat and pointing to the keys. "You can come back for a ride later or . . ." The man hesitated. "Or, if we're not giving rides, take the boat for a ride before you leave the island— at your convenience. Just shoot me a text to let me know." The man handed Fallon his business card.

"I might do that," Fallon said. He took the card and climbed out of the boat. Then he stood on the dock a moment admiring the boat. "Maybe tomorrow."

Fallon returned to Main Street and walked to the Harborview Motel. He asked the woman behind the counter if she had a room available.

"We're booked solid," the woman said. "You must be Fallon McElliot."

"How do you know that?"

"Alicia texted that you were coming by. You might as well just stay at her place. You're not going to find a room for tonight anywhere on the island."

"You can't think of any other place?"

"You could try one of those online house rental apps, but I doubt they'll have anything available."

"I'm not a fan of online bookings. I prefer to talk to people."

"Suit yourself, but Alicia's spare room is your best bet."

Fallon thanked the woman. He checked a couple of other motels in town and, as predicted, found no rooms available. He reluctantly returned to Alicia's place.

"Come on in, lunch is ready," Alicia said as she opened the door.

Fallon followed her into the kitchen. "Your friend at Harborview says hi," Fallon said as he sat down at a small metal table with a white top. The sandwiches were already made, sitting on two plates flanked by bottles of iced tea.

"She's been on the island for quite a few years," Alicia chuckled. "I hope you still like ham and Swiss cheese with brown mustard."

"I'm surprised you remember." Fallon took a bite out of his sandwich, then washed it down with iced tea.

Alicia took a bite of her sandwich. They sat a moment, awkwardly looking at each other.

"Is now the time to talk about it?" Alicia asked at last.

"About what?"

"The real reason you're here."

"Maybe." Fallon took a sip of his iced tea and leaned back in his chair.

Alicia leaned in closer. "I think we're here for the same reason."

"And what would that be?"

"Look, Fallon. The clock is ticking. I don't have time to play games. I think we're both here because there's a credible terror threat to the ferry. We both have the same goal—to stop it."

Fallon studied her, debating whether he should trust her. He didn't respond to her remark.

"You're always so difficult!" Alicia sighed and leaned back in her chair. "If the governor sent you and Homeland Security sent me, then each of us may have information the other doesn't."

"And if that's true?"

Alicia paused and took a bite of her sandwich.

Fallon watched her chew, a frustrated look on her face. "The governor told me that Homeland Security sent an agent here a couple days ago," he said. "You've been here for a week."

Alicia swallowed. "See! We don't have the same information."

"Do you have any leads?"

"Just one."

Fallon raised an eyebrow.

"I've been riding and monitoring the ferry every day. That white cargo van you were watching in the parking lot by the ferry this morning . . ." Alicia paused.

Fallon frowned. "Why are you giving me that look?"

"Don't deny it, you were watching the van too."

Fallon sighed. "Okay, but what's so important about that van?"

"That van is the same one I saw unloaded off the ferry a few days ago. I wasn't able to get a look at the license plate, but the same two military-looking men who climbed out of it today were driving it the other day."

"Did you follow the van?"

"By the time I was able to get to my truck, they were gone."

"I might be able to help you with that."

Alicia paused. "You know—the federal and state governments don't always work well together."

Fallon smiled. "You think *we* would work well together?"

"Perhaps."

"So, let's compare notes."

Alicia took another bite of her sandwich, then a sip of iced tea. "This doesn't leave this room."

"Likewise."

Alicia nodded. "A few days ago, we intercepted encrypted text messages sent between someone in Detroit and someone on Beaver Island. They were talking about a package being delivered to the island. The encryption is identical to that used by terrorists we've caught in the past."

"Were you able to pinpoint the location of whoever sent the text messages?"

"No."

"Any idea what that package might be?"

Alicia shook her head. "We speculate it may be explosives."

"Have you considered that it might be a drone?"

"That wasn't on our radar."

"Are you aware that a delivery drone has gone missing?"

"Recently?"

"It was reported missing yesterday."

"You think this missing drone could be used to bomb the ferry?"

"My gut tells me the drone is on the island."

"Another of your hunches?"

"It's more than a hunch." Fallon paused, replaying in his mind what he knew: the cargo van, the military-looking people, Cally's escape, and Daniel's cabin. Could there be a connection? Perhaps the drug ring was funding a terror group. He'd never made Daniel out to be a terrorist, but then again, wasn't that the goal of terrorists? To plant normal-looking people who don't raise suspicions? Could it be that some terror group got through to Daniel? Maybe they offered to help Daniel free Cally.

Alicia took a bite of her sandwich and eyed Fallon. "I know that look . . ."

"What look?"

"You're hiding something from me. It's the same face you'd make when we dated as teenagers."

Fallon chuckled. "You were always good at reading me."

"You're not telling me everything."

Fallon nodded. "There is something else that may or may not be connected. Yesterday Tom Ferguson called me—"

"That friend of yours I saw with you at the detective conference years ago?"

"I wouldn't call him a friend. We were partners when we were with the Detroit Police and we served together in Afghanistan."

"You've known him for a while. You talked about him when we reconnected after the conference. Isn't he a Detroit Police detective?"

"He's now the warden of Jackson Prison."

"How did he manage to get that job?"

"I'm guessing it had something to do with who he knows, not his qualifications."

"Why did he call you?"

"He wanted me to meet with him. Did you hear about the Jackson prison inmate named Robert Callahan who escaped yesterday while attending his dad's funeral?"

"Yes, the church bombing. We were on high alert until they figured out it was likely connected to the protesters, not terrorists."

"It wasn't a bombing. They were smoke bombs and flash-bangs to create a diversion for the prisoner escape. Ferguson thinks a guy named Daniel Callahan, the brother of the guy who escaped, masterminded the whole thing."

"They used their dad's funeral to help him escape? That's pretty cold."

Fallon paused, holding back what he learned at the church. "If it was Daniel, he went to a lot of trouble to help his brother, Cally, escape."

"Cally?"

"The nickname they use for him. His dad is Robert Senior. Cally's connected to a large drug ring."

"Why are you involved with the investigation? Isn't this a case for the FBI?"

"Daniel is a detective with the FBI. The FBI is concerned other people in the FBI might be involved and they might warn Daniel if they get close to finding him. They don't know who they can trust to investigate, so they talked to Ferguson and Ferguson asked me to help find Cally."

"So, Ferguson wants you to find them before anyone else."

"Exactly. He figures if I find Cally, the escaped prisoner, I'll find Daniel."

"Is that what brought you here to Beaver Island? You must have a lead."

"I interrogated a friend of Cally's in Jackson Prison. He said Cally talked about Beaver Island all the time—about a camping trip here when he was a kid."

"And you came here on a hunch that this would be the perfect hideout for them."

Fallon smiled. "Another of my hunches."

"Did you tell anyone you were coming here?"

"Only the governor knows, but she thinks I'm here looking for the missing drone."

"She doesn't know anything about you looking for this escaped prisoner, Cally, or his brother Daniel?"

"No," Fallon said, finishing his sandwich.

"And Ferguson doesn't know you're here looking for the missing drone."

"Exactly, but they seem connected to me."

"What makes you think—"

Fallon's phone rang. "Hey, Chip."

"Hey, Fallon. I ran that plate number," Chip said.

Fallon took a few notes as Chip talked, then hung up.

"Who's Chip?" Alicia asked.

"My assistant, who happens to be an excellent tech guru and policy analyst. I had him run the plate from that cargo van we saw at the ferry dock. It's a rental."

Alicia smiled.

"You knew that already."

"I had the plate number run while you were looking for a motel room."

Fallon nodded. "I should've guessed you'd be on it. So, you know who rented the van."

"Al Kaline," Alicia chuckled. "They used Trumbull Street for their address—where the old Tiger Stadium was located. They must be Tigers fans."

"What you don't know is that they used the same name and address for the rental car used to help Cally escape from the church after the smoke bombs and flash-bangs went off."

"Why would they do that?" Alicia asked. "That seems sloppy. It's almost like they want us to connect the two." Alicia looked deep in thought. "Does Chip know you're here?"

"Sort of . . . he dug into the property records for Charlevoix County and helped me locate the address of a cabin Daniel has on the island on Lake Geneserath."

"How did you know Daniel has a cabin here?"

"That's another thing . . . I know Daniel. He and I worked some cases together when I was a detective with the state police. We did a lot of stakeouts together. During one of our stakeouts, he talked about Beaver Island and told me I should go with him sometime to his cabin. Plus, I interrogated Cally's friend in prison. He told me Cally talked about his brother Daniel's cabin here on the island."

Alicia jumped out of her chair and leaned across the table. "You've had the address to his place all this time and you didn't say anything? That could be the terror cell!"

"I don't think Daniel is running a terror cell. It doesn't make sense. He's a pretty straight shooter."

"Isn't that the mark of a terror cell? No one suspects them," Alicia said as she headed for the door. "We need to call in some backup and raid that cabin before it's too late."

"No!" Fallon stood and followed Alicia. "If a bunch of feds descend on the island, they'll scare them away before we catch them."

Alicia stopped. "We need eyes on that cabin. It's the best lead I've had all week. I need to know if that's the terror cell."

"Then why don't you and I check it out?" Fallon pulled out the piece of paper with the cabin address on it.

Alicia took the piece of paper. "I know exactly where this is. It's wooded around there. We'll have enough cover to check it out without raising suspicions."

"Have any more weapons than the gun you're carrying?"

Alicia opened her jacket and tapped the gun in a holster strapped to her side. "Just this."

"There's extra ammo and another gun in my duffel on the back seat in my car," Fallon said.

"Let's go," Alicia said as she hurried out of the house.

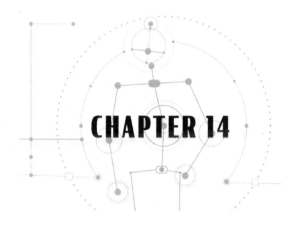

CHAPTER 14

Cally sat in the passenger seat of the cargo van as Daniel climbed out the driver's side door. Cally watched the crowd of people coming off the Beaver Island ferry, then glanced at the side mirror and saw Daniel standing next to Logan and Ethan. He could hear them talking through the open windows.

"Call if you need anything," Logan said.

Ethan punched Daniel lightly on the shoulder. "Good working with you again."

Cally watched Ethan and Logan walk in front of the van and head to the ticket office. Daniel climbed back into the van. "We shouldn't have left dad alone at the cabin," Cally said. "What if he called the police?"

"There's no phone at the cabin, and it's miles from town," Daniel said as he pulled onto Main Street.

Cally looked over his shoulder at the large crate in the back of the van. "What's in the crate?"

"Oh . . . we used that to transport dad."

"You put him in a crate?"

"Well . . . he slept the whole way. He never knew he was in a crate."

Cally studied as much as he could see of the crate, looking for air holes. "There's a Caspian logo on the side of the crate. From something big you ordered online?"

"Something like that." Daniel pulled into McDonough's Market. "I need to pick up a few things."

Cally followed Daniel into the store, pulling his cap lower, worried that someone would recognize them. Even when they left the store with a bag of groceries, Cally wondered if someone would call the police.

Daniel pulled out of the parking lot and headed toward the north end of the island. "Before we head back to the cabin, I want to stop by the campsite where we stayed as kids." Daniel glanced at Cally, then back at the road. "What's your best memory of that camping trip?"

"The nights you, me, and Sheila sat around the fire talking."

"We really bonded that week," Daniel said.

Cally paused. "I appreciate the way you and Sheila stuck with me last year after I was arrested. You did your best to try to free me."

"Sheila's a good attorney, but the deck was stacked against you. It doesn't matter now. You're free."

"For now, I guess." Ahead, Cally saw the entrance to the township campground. "Is that it?"

"That's it."

Cally scanned the campsites as they drove through the campground, trying to find the spot where they'd camped as a family so many years ago. "I remember camping near a bluff overlooking Lake Michigan."

"Right there," Daniel said. He parked the van.

They climbed out and walked to a campsite overlooking Lake Michigan. Cally stood at the edge of the bluff and watched the waves below gently washing onto the shore. There was another island in the distance. "Is that Garden Island?"

"Yes. One of several islands in the Beaver Island Archipelago."

"What's an archipelago?"

"Just a fancy name for a group of islands."

Cally breathed in the aroma of fresh lake air, musty leaves, and cedars. He turned to survey the site where they camped. He could still envision himself sitting with Daniel and Sheila around the now-empty firepit. He stood silent and listened to a light breeze rustling the leaves on the birches surrounding the campsite.

"Being here makes it easy to forget everything," Daniel said.

Cally swallowed and looked at Daniel. "I wish we could stay here forever."

Daniel nodded.

Cally took another deep breath as he fought the tears welling up inside.

"We should get back to Dad and the cabin," Daniel said.

They climbed back into the van and Daniel started the engine.

"What if we just fly to Canada and meet up with Sheila and Mom?" Cally asked as they drove out of the campground.

"Then the truth will never come out. We would be on the run for the rest of our lives. We need to get that hard drive."

"But how? Don't you think Ferguson will have his goons waiting for us at Mom and Dad's house?"

"They already searched the house. It's the last place they'd expect us to go."

"I don't know, Daniel."

"I'll fly to Detroit tomorrow night and be back before you know it."

Cally sighed. "You make it sound so easy."

"Just relax, Cally. I'll take the scenic route back on the west side of the island."

"I remember going swimming on the west side at Donegal Bay. I remember the beach there."

"Too bad we don't have our swimsuits. This would be a great beach day."

Cally smiled, put his arm out the open van window, and leaned his face into the warm summer breeze.

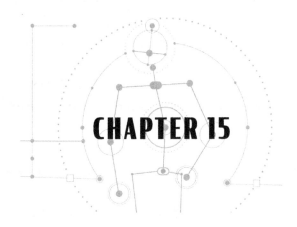

CHAPTER 15

What are you looking at?" Alicia asked, sitting in the passenger seat. "You keep looking at me."

"Nothing," Fallon said. "It's just . . . I'm used to working alone." He knew that wasn't a completely truthful answer. Somehow, he couldn't keep his eyes from drifting her way.

"Am I getting in your way?"

"No."

The car groaned as it went up an incline in the road. Fallon shifted to a lower gear.

"I've never driven a stick shift mounted on the steering column," Alicia said.

"It's the only way to have a manual transmission."

"I'm glad you're driving."

Fallon glanced once again at Alicia and noted her auburn hair glowing in the sunlight. He needed to focus. "What are your thoughts about going in?" Fallon asked.

"If there's one thing I've learned, expect the unexpected."

"You're right about that."

"The cabin is in a wooded area so we should be able to approach it undetected. I have friends who live nearby—we can park in their driveway. They're from Chicago and let me park in their driveway when I fish on Lake Geneserath. Usually, they're not here this time of year. There's a wooded lot between their place and the cabin."

Alicia directed Fallon to her friend's place and he parked the car in the driveway close to the house. "Looks deserted."

"That's good. If they were here, we'd have to spend an hour talking to them before we stake out Daniel's cabin."

They climbed out of the car. Fallon took a few steps away from the house and scanned the area. His senses came alive. Above, leaves rustled in the breeze on trees surrounding the property. Waves lapped the shore of the lake, barely visible from where they stood. The stillness of the area made him tense. He took a few more steps, slowly, automatically examining the ground for improvised explosive devices—listening for the slightest sound of enemy insurgents. He shook his head. It was hard to turn off his army training.

"Are you okay?" Alicia asked, her voice barely above a whisper.

"Yeah, I'm fine." Fallon tried to concentrate, to focus on the task at hand.

Alicia motioned to him to follow her as she stepped into the woods and carefully wove her way through brambles and saplings in the underbrush. Fallon followed, stepping cautiously. A twig snapped under his shoe. Startled, he froze and scanned the area.

Alicia stopped and looked back at him.

Fallon took a deep breath and pointed his finger forward.

Alicia resumed her slow progress toward the cabin. Fallon studied the landscape in front of them, looking for anything unusual.

"It's just ahead," Alicia whispered.

Fallon looked at the rustic brown cabin with log siding, porches on the front and back. "You're sure this is it?"

"Positive."

They stopped behind two large trees on the edge of the clearing. Fallon saw a red seaplane tied to a dock. He noted the empty driveway.

"It looks deserted." Alicia motioned toward the cabin. "Let's get closer."

Fallon followed Alicia as she crouched and hurried across the lawn to the side of the cabin. They pressed themselves against the wall, then inched closer to a window. Alicia peered inside. "No one there."

They carefully circled the cabin, peering in each window until they reached the back side of the attached garage.

"The place is empty," Fallon said as he pressed against the side of the garage by a back door.

Alicia peered through a window in the door to the garage. She looked at Fallon, nodded, and slowly opened the door. The hinges squeaked. They paused a moment in the doorway, listening.

Inside the garage, they encountered nothing but a few yard tools hanging on the wall. He motioned Alicia forward and they entered the garage together. Suddenly Alicia stopped and put her finger to her mouth. Fallon heard someone walking inside the cabin. He slowly stepped toward the door leading into the cabin, but Alicia grabbed his arm.

"Wait," she whispered. "We have no idea how many are in there. We should wait for backup."

"This could be our only chance to stop them before they flee."

They stared at each other for a moment. Alicia nodded.

Fallon cautiously opened the door a crack and peered inside—the kitchen. An older man stood at the counter with his back to Fallon, pouring steaming water into a mug. Fallon didn't see anyone else in the kitchen or the adjoining room. The man picked up his mug and left the room. Fallon signaled to Alicia that he was going in. She nodded. He slowly opened the door wide enough to enter. Fallon pulled out his gun and crouched as he entered, quietly slipping behind an island in the kitchen. Alicia followed, gun in hand.

"Daniel?" someone called.

Fallon sprang up with his gun outstretched. The old man, startled, was standing next to a couch. His mug fell to the floor and shattered.

"Don't move," Fallon said.

"Are you the police?" the man asked nervously, slowly raising his shaking hands.

"We'll ask the questions," Alicia said, gun drawn.

"Wait a minute. I recognize this man," Fallon said. He remembered the funeral program still inside his blazer pocket, pulled it out, and handed it to Alicia. "Look at the picture. This is Daniel and Cally's dad, Mr. Robert Callahan Senior."

Alicia looked at the man, then the program.

"Who else is with you, Mr. Callahan?" Fallon asked.

"No one," Mr. Callahan said.

"Looks like you've had at least a couple people here," Alicia said, gesturing toward the table with empty plates and glasses.

"Where are they?" Fallon asked.

"I don't know," Mr. Callahan said. He slowly sat down on the couch, hands still raised. "I was kidnapped. Please believe me. I don't know anything."

Fallon studied his terrified face. He looked like he was telling the truth. "You can put your hands down."

"Tell us what you do know!" Alicia demanded.

"Can you put that gun down?" Mr. Callahan asked. "I've already died once this week."

"Do what the man says," came a voice from behind Fallon.

Fallon started to turn, tightly gripping his gun.

"Keep looking forward!" the man instructed. "No sudden moves. Slowly put your guns on the floor."

Alicia slowly set her gun on the floor. The voice sounded familiar to Fallon. He kept his gun pointed at Mr. Callahan.

"Set your gun down, now!" the man yelled.

Fallon maintained his position.

"I *said* drop the gun!"

Fallon heard a gun cock behind him. He could feel sweat beginning to bead on his face. He saw Alicia's frantic stare out of the corner of his eye. "You shoot me, your dad takes a bullet."

"How do you know that's my dad?" Daniel asked.

131

"It's been a while, Daniel," Fallon said, "but I still remember the sound of your voice." He reluctantly set his gun at his feet and turned to look at Daniel.

"Fallon!" Daniel said. "What are you doing here?"

"Nice to see you again, Daniel," Fallon said. He looked at the man standing next to Daniel. "I assume this is your brother, Cally."

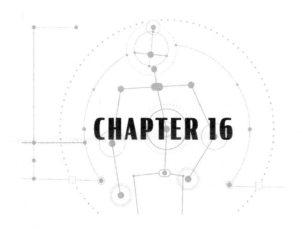

CHAPTER 16

Cally stood in the doorway of the back bedroom while his dad, asleep, lay on the bed. He watched his dad's chest rise and fall, still struggling to grasp that his dad was not dead. His emotions were jumbled. So much to think about, and now two officers show up at the cabin. He gently closed the door and walked back to the living room. "Dad's asleep," Cally said, and sat next to Daniel in a chair across from the couch.

"You gave him quite the scare," Daniel said, looking at Fallon and Alicia seated on the couch, zip ties securing their ankles together and their hands behind their backs.

How were they able to locate us so quickly? Cally wondered. *And why just two of them and not a dozen officers to raid the cabin?* Fallon's stare made Cally feel uneasy.

"Alicia is your partner?" Daniel asked.

"Yes," Fallon said.

"You're both working for the governor?"

"Yes," Alicia said.

"Why would the governor send you here?" Cally asked.

"She wanted us to find you and Cally before anyone else," Fallon said.

"Why would she want that?" Daniel asked. "Why wouldn't she just let the state police or the FBI search for us?"

How safe were they here? Cally wondered. If these two had found them so quickly, how long before others would show up?

"She felt we were her best chance to capture you and Cally," Fallon said.

Daniel smiled. "Unfortunately, now we've captured you."

"I don't think they came here alone," Cally said, standing and walking to the window. He scanned the backyard and lake. The water on the lake was calm—no sign of boats. "Why would they come here without backup?"

"I know Fallon. He likes to work alone," Daniel said.

Cally plopped back into the chair next to Daniel. "You know Fallon? How?"

"Fallon and I have worked several cases together over the years. I spent a lot of time with him on stakeouts. He's doesn't always play by the rules, but he's a good detective."

"You didn't always play by the rules either," Fallon said.

Daniel nodded. "That's why we worked well together."

"How did you find us?" Cally asked Fallon.

Fallon took a moment to answer. "Remember that stakeout a few years ago where you told me I should come to your cabin on Beaver Island?"

"And you figured this was a likely place for a hideout," Daniel said.

"Something like that."

"But how did you find the address?"

"Property records."

"Who else knows you're here?"

"The director of the state police. If I don't check back with him in an hour, he's ready to raid the place."

Cally watched Daniel eye Fallon, then Alicia.

"Is that true?" Daniel asked Alicia.

"Yes."

The room went silent. To Cally, the two detectives looked as if they were hiding something.

"Don't lie to me, Fallon!" Daniel said. "Your old Detroit Police partner Ferguson sent you here. I have proof."

The sound of Ferguson's name sent a shiver up Cally's spine. "What?"

"It's been years since I worked with Ferguson," Fallon said.

"But that doesn't mean you aren't doing him a favor. Cally, grab my laptop backpack by the door."

Cally retrieved the bag and set it in front of Daniel, who pulled out a laptop computer and set it on the coffee table between him and the couch. As the computer powered up, Cally wondered what Daniel was doing. What proof did he have about Ferguson working with Fallon?

"What you don't know," Daniel said, then paused as he ran his finger over the laptop trackpad, "is that we've been running surveillance on Ferguson. I have video of you from yesterday in Ferguson's office."

Cally glanced at Daniel, surprised. Daniel had never said a word about Ferguson being under FBI surveillance.

Daniel spun the computer around to face Fallon and Alicia. "Just watch."

Cally went to the back of the couch, behind Alicia and Fallon, to watch the video on the laptop screen. He was surprised to see Ferguson's office with Fallon sitting in a chair in front of the desk— the same chair Cally had sat in a few days ago. His body tensed as he listened.

Fallon: Well, then, you don't need me. I'm sure the state and the feds have everything covered. I don't like that look you're giving me.

Ferguson: If they were shrewd enough to fake a funeral, I think they're smart enough to elude the feds. That's why I need you. I need results.

Fallon: You know I'm not a state police detective anymore.

Ferguson: That's why you're the man for the job. You can work independently—under the radar. Time's a-wasting, Fallon. What do you say? Will you help your old army buddy, your old partner?

Fallon: I work for the governor. I can't get mixed up in this.

Ferguson: What happened to having each other's back?

Fallon: Every time you need something from me, you bring up that firefight in Afghanistan.

Ferguson: You wouldn't be here today if I hadn't had your back that day.

Fallon: Like I said, this is the last time. No more favors after this.

Daniel spun the laptop to face him and paused the video. "I know Ferguson sent you here, not the director of the state police. That's quite the favor you're doing for Ferguson."

Cally looked from Daniel to Fallon. "You're part of the crime ring?"

"Crime ring?" Fallon looked taken aback. "More than drugs?"

"No, we're not!" Alicia stated emphatically.

"True," Daniel said. "They aren't."

"But they're helping Ferguson!"

"Ferguson is playing Fallon," Daniel said. "I could show you more surveillance video, but that would only prove that I know what you know."

"Then you saw the part where I stuck up for you," Fallon said.

"Yes, I did."

"And that's true," Fallon said.

Daniel smiled. "I'd show you the video of your interrogation of Louis Greene, but I think you know there's not much there to see or hear." Daniel worked the trackpad on the computer.

"Louis!" Cally said.

"Who's Louis?" Alicia asked.

"A friend of mine in prison," Cally said. He looked at Fallon with disbelief. "You talked to Louis? Why?"

"I thought he'd know where you were hiding," Fallon said.

"He told you we were here?"

"Not exactly. He just said you talked a lot about Beaver Island. It backed up my hunch that you came here, to this cabin."

"I can't believe Louis would give me up like that. Show me the video, Daniel."

"Look for yourself," Daniel said as he spun the computer around so Cally could see the screen.

For a moment, the video showed just Louis sitting with his hands cuffed to a table. Then Fallon's face appeared followed by his hand pressing something onto the lens. A moment later, loud Van Halen music accompanied the out-of-focus blob over the lens.

"I suspect Fallon thought Ferguson might listen in on their conversation," Daniel said as he flipped the laptop screen down. "For some reason, he didn't want Ferguson to know what Louis told him."

"Louis wouldn't have told you anything," Cally said. "He's loyal to me."

"Loyalty only goes as far as two packs of cigarettes," Fallon said.

Could that be true? Would Louis turn him in for some smokes?

"Forget it, Cally," Daniel said. "Fallon already knew we were here before he talked to Louis. He just needed Louis to verify his hunch."

"You still have access to the FBI servers?" Fallon asked.

"Of course," Daniel said. "I downloaded them last night after we arrived here."

"I doubt you still have access to FBI servers now. I'm sure they suspect you helped Cally escape. They would've immediately suspended all your computer access and security clearances."

"That proves my point," Daniel said. "I still have access. We know Ferguson is part of the crime ring. Either he duped you, or you are also part of it."

"Which do you think is true?" Fallon asked.

"I don't think someone could easily dupe you—except an old army buddy of yours."

Cally noticed Alicia staring at Fallon, confused.

"Both of you need to know that we're going to bring down Ferguson and everyone else involved in this crime ring," Daniel said.

"I find it hard to believe the FBI would help you plan Cally's escape," Alicia said.

"I know the director of the FBI Detroit Bureau," Fallon said. "If I called her right now, would she back up your story?"

"You know as well as I do, she would deny everything if it's an undercover investigation."

"You're working undercover?" Cally asked. "But you—"

"Don't say anything, Cally," Daniel said.

Cally closed his mouth and clenched his fist. Everything was so mixed up right now, he didn't know what to believe. But he had to trust Daniel. His brother had brought him this far.

"Do you believe me when I say no one else knows we're here?" Fallon asked.

"You could've still called Ferguson," Daniel said as he opened the laptop again and called up another video. "But I know you like to work outside of the rules. I think you didn't tell Ferguson you were coming here because you want to get to the bottom of this first. That way you will know who you can trust. Let me show you why you should trust the governor and me."

Cally's head was spinning.

Daniel spun the computer around so the screen faced Fallon, Alicia, and Cally.

"You have video of Brogan talking to Ferguson?" Fallon asked.

"Who's Brogan?" Cally asked.

"She's the director of Corrections. Just watch." Daniel said.

Cally tensed when he saw Ferguson appear on the screen with a woman sitting in the chair in front of the desk. Could this be the state government person Chuck mentioned who is involved in the crime ring?

CHAPTER 17

How long have you been running surveillance on Ferguson?"
Fallon asked.

"For a while," Daniel said.

Fallon fixated on the laptop screen, eager to hear what Brogan
and Ferguson were discussing—wondering if this had been taped just
before he burst into the office:

> **Brogan:** If Cally gets that evidence to the feds before we find it,
> we're finished.
>
> **Ferguson:** Cally isn't going to get the evidence.
>
> **Brogan:** How can you be so sure? Captain Peters said, yes,
> Chuck's laptop was wiped clean—but he thinks Chuck downloaded
> the evidence to a hard drive. And we have no idea where he hid it.
> We've been searching for it for the last year. We monitored Cally
> every minute in prison—and you still don't know where it is. For
> all we know he already has it.
>
> **Ferguson:** If he somehow got hold of that drive, he would've
> already gone to the feds to cut a deal.

Brogan: I still can't believe Chuck betrayed us like that. We should have never let him maintain our computer servers and network. Who knows what he collected? He had access to everything.

Ferguson: I looked at his personal cloud storage account before we wiped it clean. It was filled with records from our entire drug operation, including bank records and those warehouse logs. That's probably what he copied to that drive.

Brogan: Where do you think Cally hid it?

Ferguson: I'm not sure. We scoured Chuck's apartment, Cally's parents' house, and his car. We've searched his sister's and brother's places. That drive is so small, it could be anywhere.

Brogan: They should have killed Cally right then and there. Then we wouldn't be in this mess.

Fallon turned to look at Cally staring wide-eyed at the screen, then returned his gaze to the laptop.

Ferguson: When Chief Peters spotted Cally running down the alley, he was out of range. At least we caught him and kept him locked up for Chuck's murder so we could keep an eye on him.

Brogan: Smart of Chief Peters to frame Cally by shooting Chuck with Cally's gun that they found in the alley. But now Cally's on the loose. If he gets that drive to Daniel and the FBI, we're all finished!

Ferguson: Not if we find Cally first.

Brogan: And just how do you plan to do that?

Ferguson: I have a plan . . .

Brogan: I hope it's better than your plan that let Cally escape.

Ferguson: He was very upset when I told him I was going after his family. I know he was about to break and tell me where he hid it.

Brogan: Really? Looks more like he was about to break out of prison!

Ferguson: I'll get him.

Brogan: Do that. Whatever it takes. You take care of Cally and I'll handle the governor.

Ferguson: Do you still think you can take her down?

Brogan: I'm surer now than ever. After we tie her to the drug ring, her career will be over and we'll take out all her cronies, including McElliot. That will open the door for me to run for governor.

Ferguson: And for me to be lieutenant governor?

Brogan: Only if you take out Cally.

Just then, on the video, Fallon saw himself burst through the door into Ferguson's office—and registered with satisfaction the startled faces of Ferguson and Brogan.

"And that's where you came in," Daniel said as he spun the computer around and stopped the video.

"I told you Ferguson is corrupt!" Cally exclaimed.

Cally was right, Fallon thought. The video verified his suspicions about Ferguson.

"Now do you believe you're being played?" Daniel asked.

"How could Ferguson *not* know his office is under surveillance?" Fallon asked, looking first at Alicia, then Daniel. "He's the warden!"

"We tapped into the video conference camera in Ferguson's office and used Archipelago software to run our surveillance."

"You need a warrant to do that," Fallon said.

"Of course we had a warrant."

"Really? If you did, the governor would know about it."

"Because Brogan is part of the governor's administration, we couldn't tell her or anyone else in state government. The FBI doesn't know who else might be involved."

"But how could you tap into the video conference software without the state knowing about it?"

Daniel smiled. "We have our ways."

Fallon nodded. "Of course."

"You think the governor is involved in the crime ring?" Alicia asked.

"I don't think so, but we can't be sure," Daniel said. "Everyone is a suspect for now."

Fallon recalled how Karen had taken him into the secret room up in the Capitol dome to avoid the video conference equipment. For some reason, she knew she had to be careful when she talked to him. Fallon looked at Daniel. When they had worked together on stakeouts, he had always trusted Daniel. He had never given Fallon any reason not to trust him.

"There's one more thing I want you to see," Daniel said as he moved his finger on the computer trackpad, then spun the computer around. "I want you to understand why I felt compelled to rescue Cally."

The laptop screen showed Cally sitting in Ferguson's office:

Ferguson: You have no idea who I am.

Cally: Thomas Ferguson?

Ferguson: So, you can read. Do you know why you're here? Remember Chief Peters? The man who arrested you on the freeway about a year ago. The chief and I are buddies. I've kept an eye on you since I started here as warden last month. You know where something is that we want.

Cally: I don't know what you're talking about.

Ferguson: We think Chuck gave you a hard drive with lots of information on it. Where did you hide it?

Cally: All Chuck gave me was trouble.

Ferguson: We scoured your parents', brother's, and sister's place. We searched their digital footprint online. We've exhausted all options. Except for beating it out of you! This prison is run by a private firm. The guards who brought you here are my special guards. They answer only to me. Where is it, Cally?

Fallon recognized the familiar look on Ferguson's face—the look before his anger exploded. Just as he expected, Ferguson leaped across the desk and smacked Cally across the face.

Ferguson: We've been watching you, listening to every conversation you've had since you were arrested. We're tired of waiting for you to say something. We're coming for your family.

Cally: You leave my family out of this!

Ferguson: Too late. We've already started.

Cally: The Quick Connect posts! You're the one.

Ferguson: You're catching on. I was surprised how quick it went viral. It doesn't take much these days to incite a mob. Nobody cares about the truth. They only know what they see online.

Cally: You!

Ferguson: Your dad said a lot of hate-filled things online and now he's paying for it. The stress is slowly killing your parents. When they're gone, we'll destroy your sister, Sheila, and brother, Daniel. Soon we'll post embarrassing things. They'll be so humiliated—who knows what could happen.

Cally: What do you want?

Ferguson: We know Chuck downloaded a bunch of stuff from his cloud account. We suspect he dumped it on a small backup drive that he gave you at his apartment. Tell me where you hid it and save your family.

"You get the picture," Daniel said. He swung the computer back around and closed the screen.

"What did Chuck give you?" Fallon asked.

"Just what Ferguson said, all kinds of evidence on a hard drive," Cally said.

"Chuck must have known they were on to him if he gave you the drive," Alicia said.

"That's what he told me," Cally said. "He gave me the drive right before they showed up at his apartment. We ran for our lives, but . . ." Cally choked.

"It's okay, Cally," Daniel said. "We know what happened next."

Fallon paused, looked at Cally, then said, "A hard drive would be easy to hide."

Cally didn't respond. Fallon watched him walk to the window facing the lake. He was visibly upset.

"You didn't shoot Chuck, Cally—they did," Fallon said.

Cally's head whipped back toward Fallon. "They broke the door down in a surprise raid. The police killed Chuck, not me!"

"Our family was next on their list," Daniel said.

"Now I understand, Daniel," Fallon said. "If someone was after my family, I'd do whatever was necessary to protect them."

"Me too," Alicia said. Her face looked angry.

The room went silent except for the faint noise of Mr. Callahan snoring in the back bedroom.

"You're good at what you do, Fallon," Daniel said. "When I go down to get that backup drive, I want you to come with me."

"You can't go get it now!" Cally said. He sat down in the chair next to Daniel. "They'll be waiting for you."

"Where is it?" Fallon asked.

"Detroit," Daniel said.

"I don't think that's a good idea." Alicia said, frowning. She looked at Fallon and gave her head a slight shake no.

"How can you trust him, Daniel?" Cally asked.

"I've known Fallon for a while," Daniel said. "It'll be okay."

"But why risk getting it now?" Alicia asked.

"You saw the videos," Daniel said.

"Yes—but I don't think we're getting the whole story," Alicia said.

"I've laid it all out for you," Daniel said.

"How *did* you get access to those videos?" Alicia asked. "It seems strange to me that the FBI is tapped into the State of Michigan computer system without them knowing about it."

"No way we could let them know," Daniel said. "It's a federal corruption investigation into state officials."

"But how *did* you tap into the Archipelago system?" Fallon asked. "The CEO, Henry Massey, told us in the governor's cabinet meeting that their software is an impenetrable lockbox."

"We had a warrant. Massey was very cooperative," Daniel said.

"Wait," Alicia said. "Massey the tech billionaire? You served him a warrant?"

"We did everything by the book," Daniel said.

"Legally?" Fallon asked.

"You doubt me?"

Fallon and Daniel locked eyes for a moment, then Fallon looked at Alicia. She flashed Fallon a look of skepticism.

"Fallon," Daniel said, then hesitated a second. "Do you remember the Montreux Case about seven years ago?"

"That was the first time we worked together."

"And do you remember when we were on stakeout together—when the suspect tried to flee?"

Fallon nodded, recalling the tense moment when they pursued the suspect into a dark alley.

"I ran into the dark alley first. I didn't see the suspect hiding in that doorway. Somehow you knew he was there and you shot him before he shot me."

"Anyone would've done the same."

"But not everyone has your instincts or your quick reflexes. You saved me. I know you would do the same for me now."

The room went silent. Fallon thought about what Daniel had said. Never before had he questioned Daniel's integrity as a law enforcement officer. He processed what he'd seen on the videos and what Daniel had told him. "There's one thing I can't quite figure out," he said. "Henry Massey's name keeps popping up in all of this. Why?"

"Well . . . " Daniel paused. "I guess his software touches a lot of things."

"It seems that way," Fallon said.

Fallon noticed Cally shifting in his seat the way a suspect does when he's hiding something.

"If we team up with Daniel, we're complicit," Alicia said as she glared at Fallon.

"If we get the hard drive into the right hands, I believe we will all be cleared," Daniel said.

"And just who do you think are the right hands?" Fallon asked.

"The FBI."

"I'd feel better taking it to the state police."

"You can't trust them!" Cally said. "Chuck said there are people in state government who are corrupt, who are involved in the crime ring—and that could include the state police."

"He's right," Daniel said.

"What if we make a copy so we each have one?" Fallon asked.

"We can do that," Daniel said.

"How do you know the drive isn't blank?" Alicia asked. "Did you get a look at it?"

Cally shook his head. "But Chuck told me the drive had everything needed to put away a lot of people for a long time. He said it had dozens of videos, recorded phone calls, text messages, emails, even bank records. Chuck sacrificed his life to get the truth out. He wouldn't have done that just to give me a blank drive!" Tears were forming in Cally's eyes.

Fallon said to Daniel, "Why don't you take these zip ties off us so we can go get the drive?"

Cally nodded. "We've gotten this far," he said to his brother. "We have to get the drive. It's the only thing that will help us."

Daniel cut the zip ties off Alicia and Fallon. They sat a moment in uneasy silence as Fallon rubbed his wrists.

"Here," Daniel said, handing Alicia and Fallon their guns. "A sign of trust."

Fallon slipped his back into his side holster. Alicia held on to hers for several seconds, looking at Daniel, then put it back into its holster as she said, "So . . . where in Detroit is this drive hidden?"

"You must have been fairly certain no one would find it where you hid it," Fallon said, looking at Cally, "someplace you know well but others don't, someplace between Chuck's place and where they arrested you. . . . I'm guessing it's at your parents' house."

"What makes you say that?" Daniel asked.

"It's the only place that makes sense."

"And if you're right?"

"Let me get it."

"Alone?"

"Yes."

"No way. We go together."

"I'm going with you!" Alicia said.

"I think you should stay here," Fallon said. "You know this island better than anyone." Fallon looked at Daniel. "Alicia summered here as a kid."

Daniel nodded. "That could be useful if someone from the crime ring shows up here."

Alicia raised an eyebrow. "What makes you think they'll show up here?"

"I don't. But we can't take the chance that I'm wrong," Daniel said. "Besides, Fallon and I have worked together before." Daniel looked at Fallon. "We make a good team."

Fallon smiled. "We do work well together."

"But I—" Alicia said.

"Remember," Fallon said, "they're still looking for Cally."

"Don't remind me," Cally said.

"Take us with you," Alicia said.

"We can't risk taking him back to Detroit," Daniel said. "There's an army of police looking for Cally by now."

Alicia pointed out the window. "There's room in that plane for all of us."

The room went silent. Fallon looked at Daniel, then Alicia. "I trust your instincts, Alicia. We need you here."

Alicia sighed. She didn't look pleased. "Okay."

"We all have the same goal," Daniel said.

"To get to the bottom of all of this," Fallon said.

Daniel smiled at Fallon. "I guess we're working another case together. We should eat something, then leave."

"What's your plan?" Fallon asked.

Daniel pointed out the window toward the lake.

Fallon turned and looked out the window at the shadowy shape of the seaplane in the early evening light. "And I suppose you know how to fly that thing."

"Yes," Daniel said. He headed into the kitchen. "I'll unload these groceries and get some stuff out of the fridge so we can make some sandwiches."

Mr. Callahan entered the room, rubbing his eyes.

"How are you doing, Dad?" Cally asked.

"Better," Dad said. "I see your friends are still here."

"It's nice to meet you in person," Fallon said. "Sorry about pointing our guns at you."

"Forget it. I understand—you didn't know me." He picked up the funeral program from the kitchen table. "You know—I hate that picture of me they used on the funeral program."

"It's not that bad," Alicia said.

"You don't need to be nice about it." He tossed the program onto the table with disgust. "I'm kind of hungry."

"We were just about to make some sandwiches," Daniel called from the kitchen.

"Did you get my Cheez Whiz?" his dad asked.

"Sure did, Dad," Daniel said, tossing the Cheez Whiz can to his dad.

His dad caught the can, opened the top, and sprayed a portion into his mouth. "It's best straight from the can."

"Disgusting," Fallon said.

"It's better if you don't watch," Daniel said, approaching with an armload of sandwich fixings. "Let's sit and have something to eat."

Fallon sat at the table across from Daniel. Alicia sat next to him, looking tense. Cally sat next to Daniel, and his dad sat at the head of the table.

"Dig in," Daniel said, reaching for the loaf of bread.

"Wait a minute," Mr. Callahan said. "We need to say a prayer of thanks first."

Fallon looked at their dad, then at Cally, who rolled his eyes but bowed his head. Was this a thing for their family? Fallon never prayed before meals—not since he was kid. Fallon bowed his head and stared at the worn wooden tabletop. He turned his head slightly and looked at Alicia.

"Don't go," she mouthed at him.

Fallon mouthed back, "I need to."

"We're grateful, Lord Jesus, for this moment where we can sit around this table and enjoy your blessings," Mr. Callahan said. "I pray you'll give us wisdom and safety. I pray we would all know your peace in a powerful way. Thank you, Jesus. Amen."

Fallon raised his head and looked at their dad, who smiled at him.

"I wish Sheila and Mom were here," Cally said.

"And why aren't they?" Fallon asked, grabbing a couple slices of bread.

"They're in a safe place. That's all you need to know," Daniel said.

"Where?" Mr. Callahan asked. "I need to know if they're safe. I'm worried about Liz."

"Who's Liz?" Alicia asked.

"My wife," Mr. Callahan said. "I'm worried about her. I want to see her."

"They're fine, Dad. Sheila's taking good care of Mom," Daniel said. "It's safer for them that we split up for now until we can get things sorted out."

"Then let's get things sorted out! I'm still not sure why you brought me here," their dad said.

As they ate, Daniel explained to his dad what he had missed while he slept. Fallon watched as Mr. Callahan's face seemed to show more confusion rather than less. It apparently didn't make sense to Mr. Callahan, and not everything was adding up for Fallon either. There were a lot of pieces to this puzzle. He suspected that the missing hard drive was the key piece that would fill in some of the blanks.

When they finished eating, Daniel slipped his computer into a backpack and headed for the back door. Fallon tensed. In the past, he'd trusted Daniel with his life on stakeouts of hardcore criminals. Now things seemed to be in flux.

"We need to get going before it gets too dark to take off," Daniel said.

Mr. Callahan sat down on the couch. "Wait—you're going back to Detroit? I'm not following what's going on here."

"Just stay put, Dad. That's all you need to know," Daniel said. He opened the back door. "You ready, Fallon?"

Fallon looked at Alicia standing next to him by the kitchen table. They had not anticipated this awkward situation, where they would have to split up and one of them would have to babysit an escaped convict.

"When you get back to the house . . . can you check to make sure the coffee maker is unplugged?" Mr. Callahan asked.

Daniel chuckled. "Sure, Dad."

"Fallon?" Alicia asked.

"Don't let your guard down," Fallon said, and followed Daniel.

"Stay here, all of you," Daniel said. "We'll be back in the morning."

"What if someone finds us?" Cally asked.

"They won't," Daniel said.

"But what if they do?"

"Alicia's a seasoned detective. She'll take care of you," Fallon said, giving Alicia a look.

After a short pause, she said, "I'll make sure we're safe." She stepped close to Fallon and said, "Be careful."

"I will," Fallon said.

"We're part of this now. We need the evidence on that drive," Alicia said. "Make sure you come back with it."

"Don't worry, we'll get it," Daniel said.

CHAPTER 17

"We all need the truth to come out," Cally said, as he and his dad joined Alicia by the back door.

Fallon followed Daniel through the back door, then stopped and looked back at the odd trio in the open doorway. He felt a tinge of apprehension as he turned to follow Daniel to the plane.

CHAPTER 18

C ally stepped onto the back porch of Daniel's cabin and watched Fallon climb into the plane through the back door. He should be the one going with Daniel to Detroit, but the fear of getting caught and going back to prison stopped him. He watched Daniel untie the rope securing the plane to the dock, then climb into the plane. Daniel waved at Cally through the small window in the door as the plane slowly drifted away from the dock. Cally gave a half-hearted wave back as the engine started and the propeller began to spin. A puff of blue smoke rose from the front of the plane as the engine sputtered.

"Where did he get that plane?" Mr. Callahan asked, joining Cally on the porch.

"Some flying club he belongs to in Charlevoix."

"They better return with that hard drive or we're all in big trouble," Alicia said, joining them.

Cally watched the plane taxi away from them on the water until it disappeared around the point of a small peninsula in the lake. For a moment the plane was barely audible, then the sound of a revving engine filled the air. Cally stepped down from the porch and walked to the end of the dock. A moment later the plane emerged from behind the trees, rising above the lake with a small stream of water trailing off the floats. It banked east toward the mainland and disappeared from sight beyond the treetops. He returned to the porch where his dad and Alicia stood looking at the sky.

"I'm going inside for a cup of tea," his dad said.

Alicia followed him inside.

Cally stood a moment on the porch. He took a deep breath and relished the smell of cedars as he looked at the tree-lined shore. The setting was so serene, yet he felt unsettled. The nagging fear of someone catching him was never far from his mind. He went back inside, where Alicia was sitting on the couch while his dad stood by the stove watching the tea kettle on the burner.

"I have a bad feeling about this," Cally said.

"What do you mean?" Alicia asked.

"You saw Ferguson in those videos," Cally said. "He'll do whatever it takes to find me."

"If you and Fallon found us," Mr. Callahan said, "what's to stop Ferguson from doing the same?" He poured steaming water into two mugs.

"Fallon knew Daniel had a cabin here. Ferguson doesn't," Alicia said.

"But Fallon used public records to locate it. Ferguson could do the same," Cally said.

"He would first need to know Daniel has a cabin here," Alicia said.

"I don't know . . ." Cally sighed as he walked toward the windows facing the lake. "It just seems it didn't take much for you to find us, and pretty quickly."

"Fallon is good at what he does," Alicia said.

"That just proves it can be done. So you can't assure me that Ferguson won't be able to do it. I'm feeling uneasy staying here," Cally said.

"Still," Mr. Callahan said, "Daniel said we should stay here." He set two mugs of hot tea on the table by the couch and sat in a chair across from the couch.

Alicia stood up, looking uneasy. "I have to admit," she said, "I'm feeling a little uncomfortable staying here myself." She came to stand next to Cally and looked outside. "Ferguson may find the cabin, but he doesn't have to find us."

"What do you mean?" Cally asked.

"We leave the cabin and hide someplace else," Alicia said.

"But where?" Mr. Callahan asked.

"I know this island. Ferguson doesn't," Alicia said.

Cally looked at his dad, then Alicia. "Where can we go that's safe?"

"I have an idea," Alicia said. "But first let's pack some supplies."

Cally sighed and looked at Alicia. "Is *any* place on this island safe?"

Alicia walked back into the kitchen. "You can stay here, but I'm not waiting for Ferguson to find us."

"I'm with you," Mr. Callahan said.

Cally nodded and followed her into the kitchen.

"Grab one of those plastic grocery bags and toss dry food into it, stuff that doesn't have to be refrigerated," Alicia said as she opened cupboards. "He has to have matches around here somewhere."

Cally began to fill a bag with food, then spotted the Cheez Whiz on the table. He sighed and slipped it into the bag.

"Thanks," Mr. Callahan said.

"Found them!" Alicia said, holding up a box of matches. She sealed them into a plastic bag. "Come on. Let's get out of here."

"But Daniel has the keys to the van! We don't have a vehicle," Cally said.

"Fallon's car is parked down the road at the neighbor's place," Alicia said. She stepped onto the front porch.

"Where we going?" Mr. Callahan asked.

"Just follow me," Alicia said. "I'll explain in the car."

Cally grabbed a jacket from a hook by the door and followed Alicia, with his dad right behind him, a jacket draped over his arm. A short distance down the road, they came to a driveway where an old car was parked. "We're taking that?"

"It's all we have," Alicia said.

"Shush, you two. Listen," Mr. Callahan said, his finger to his lips.

Through a gap in the trees, Cally saw two small boats on the other side of the lake moving in their direction. "Maybe someone is fishing?" Cally said, hopefully.

"Let's not wait to see," Alicia said, hurrying toward the car. "Come on!"

The sound of the boat engines grew louder. Opening the car door, Cally took another look through the trees at the boats closing in on Daniel's cabin. "Do people fish with rifles?"

"What?" Alicia stopped halfway into the driver's seat.

Cally pointed toward the boats.

"That's a rifle, all right," Mr. Callahan said.

"Quick, get in!" Alicia said. Once behind the wheel, she reached up to the visor, then threw her hands up. "Fallon usually keeps a spare key in the visor. It's not there."

"You don't need keys," Mr. Callahan said. "Hit the hood release. This car is easy to hot-wire."

"How do you know how to hot-wire?" Alicia asked.

Mr. Callahan shrugged. "Oh . . . let's just say it came in handy when my parents were gone and we didn't have the car keys. See if there's a screwdriver or something else metal in the glove box."

Cally nodded. He found a screwdriver in the glove box and handed it to his dad.

"That'll work," his dad said. He leaned under the hood.

The boat motors cut to a lower roar as they neared the shore. Cally walked toward the back of the cabin and peered around the corner. Two boats were easing up to Daniel's dock. "Hurry, Dad!" Cally called, jogging back to the car. "We have company."

"You better get this thing started!" Alicia said.

A second later, the engine started. Mr. Callahan closed the hood and handed Cally the screwdriver. "Don't lose that. It's our key."

Cally climbed into the back of the car and sat next to the food bag as Alicia sat behind the steering wheel.

"Let's hope I can drive a column shift without stalling it out," she said. "Our lives depend on it!"

"When you put it like that, slide over, I'll drive," Mr. Callahan said. "I've driven a stick shift a good portion of my life."

Alicia slid across the bench seat to the passenger side, and Mr. Callahan climbed behind the wheel.

Alicia pointed down the road. "Head that way. Turn right at the end of the road."

The car fishtailed as his dad accelerated down the road. Cally noticed a duffel bag on the seat next to him. "There's a duffel back here."

"That's Fallon's," Alicia said. "He has a gun and extra ammo in there. We may need that. Toss the food bag in it too."

"Where are we going?" Cally asked, unzipping the bag. The butt of a gun protruded from beneath some folded clothes. He reached for it, but hesitated as thoughts of Chuck flooded his mind. He set the food bag on top of the folded clothes and closed the zipper.

"To the lighthouse on the south side of the island," Alicia said. "Anyone behind us?"

Cally turned to look out the back window. A cloud of dust from the gravel road rose up behind them. "There's too much dust to see anything."

"Let's hope they didn't see us leave."

At the end of the road, Mr. Callahan ran the stop sign and turned right. Cally slid on the vinyl seat as his dad accelerated into the turn.

"Sheeesh, Dad!" Cally said, clinging to the back of the front seat.

"How far is it?" Mr. Callahan asked.

"Just a few minutes from here," Alicia said.

Cally leaned back in his seat. A sudden rush of fear took hold. He didn't want to go back to prison. "What if they follow us? This island isn't that big."

"If that's Ferguson, what would he do if he caught us?" Mr. Callahan asked.

"I think he would kill us all!" Cally said.

"That's not going to happen," Alicia said.

In the rearview mirror, Cally could see his dad's face—and how scared he looked. "What makes you so sure?"

"They may have found Daniel's cabin, but he won't have a clue where to find us after that," Alicia said. "I know this island like the back of my hand; Ferguson doesn't."

"Well, it wouldn't take long to get to know the back of your hand!" Mr. Callahan said. "There aren't a lot of places to hide on this island."

Cally's eyes met his dad's in the mirror. "He's right."

"They won't catch us!" Alicia said. "Stay calm."

Cally took a deep breath. "Fine, but what do we do if Fallon and Daniel don't get that hard drive?"

"One thing at a time," Alicia said. She looked over her shoulder at Cally. "Right now, we need to stay one step ahead of whoever is after us."

CHAPTER 19

F allon tightly gripped the airplane seat. The cockpit felt warm. He wiped beads of sweat from his forehead. The plane bounced slightly up and down. Was that normal? He tried not to panic.

"Thermals," Daniel said over the headphones. "We'll land in a few minutes."

"Good," Fallon said. He glanced out the window at Lake Michigan below. Large waves were cresting, sunlight shimmering off them.

"You look like you have a question."

"When we . . . Well, I'm thinking about those stakeouts we did together. We talked about a lot of things."

"I remember—like my cabin."

"You never told me what you did between the time you left the Air Force and before you joined the FBI."

"I told you I worked for a security company."

"But you never gave me any details."

"Pretty sure I told you I can't talk about it because of confidentiality agreements." Daniel glanced at Fallon. "What's eating you, Fallon?"

"You didn't pull off that stunt at the church by yourself."

Daniel kept his eyes focused forward and didn't respond.

"What aren't you telling me?" Fallon asked.

"I don't want to implicate anyone else."

"Who helped you?"

"A couple of my Air Force buddies who still work at the security company."

Fallon nodded, not quite satisfied with the answer, wondering what Daniel was leaving out.

"We're about to land," Daniel said. "I need to focus now."

"Land?" Fallon looked ahead. "That's an airport, not a lake."

"The floats have wheels for a runway landing," Daniel said. "I need to refuel before we head to Detroit."

Fallon thought about Daniel's answer as the plane slowed and began to descend. Daniel's Air Force buddies would have the tactical know-how, but what kind of guys would help break someone out of prison?

The plane touched down with a hard impact. Or at least it seemed hard to Fallon. He watched Daniel adjust the throttle as he maneuvered the plane toward a hangar and a set of fuel pumps. A woman walked toward them as Daniel shut down the engine.

"We'll refuel and then head to Detroit," Daniel said. He opened the door by his seat. "Might as well step out and stretch your legs."

Fallon unbuckled as Daniel climbed out of the plane. As he stepped toward the back of the plane, Fallon noticed an automatic rifle lying on the back seat. On the floor was the backpack containing the laptop. What other secrets might Daniel be hiding on his computer? He opened the back door and stepped outside.

"I see you have some protection back there," Fallon said.

"Hopefully, we won't need it," Daniel said.

"Hey, Daniel," a woman said, approaching.

Daniel smiled. "I need a fill up."

The woman nodded and retrieved a wheel of wire. Fallon watched her attach the end of the wire to the plane's exhaust. "What's that?"

"Static line to ground the plane in case there's a spark," Daniel said.

"Well, I'd hate to have a spark ignite the fuel," Fallon said as the woman put a stepladder next to the wing and began to refuel the plane.

"I should give Ferguson a call," Fallon said. "He has to be wondering about me."

"What will you tell him?"

"That I have a lead I'm planning to pursue in the morning."

"Don't tell him where you are."

"Why would I do that? You saw the gum on the lens. I've kept him in the dark since I left the prison."

As Fallon reached into his pocket to grab his work phone, he bumped the flip phone the governor had given him. It reminded him that Ferguson and Brogan wanted to discredit the governor. A flash of anger surged through him. He took a few steps away from the plane and called Ferguson.

"Fallon!" Ferguson answered.

Fallon heard a lot of commotion in the background. Someone shouted, "They're not here!"

"Who's that shouting?" Fallon asked.

"Oh . . . yeah . . . a couple prisoners are missing from a work detail. I'm out with the search team. Any leads on Cally and Daniel?"

"Yes. I have a lead I'll follow up on in the morning," Fallon glanced at Daniel and nodded.

Daniel smiled.

Ferguson didn't respond. Fallon thought he heard someone near Ferguson say, "They must be close. There's hot tea in these mugs."

"Are you there?" Fallon asked.

"Yeah," Ferguson said.

Fallon heard someone in the background say, "I have a signal."

"It sounds like you're busy. I'll call you back."

"No! Where are you, Fallon?"

Fallon hesitated.

"Fallon? Are you there?"

"You're breaking up. I think I have a bad signal."

"Fallon!"

"I'll call you back when I have better reception."

"Fallon!"

Fallon ended the call and stared at the screen. When he looked up, the woman was again climbing the stepladder, this time next to the other wing, to refuel.

"What's wrong?" Daniel asked, walking closer.

"Ferguson seemed preoccupied."

"What makes you say that?"

"There were people with him. It sounded like they were searching for someone. He claimed they were looking for a missing work detail."

"Do you think they're onto Cally and Alicia?"

"I'm not sure. But if Ferguson is on Beaver Island, this is the perfect time to get the hard drive."

"But if he gets Cally and my dad—"

"He won't. Alicia will see to that."

"Call Alicia and warn her."

"No. If they're hiding, her phone might ring and tip them off."

"You're fueled up and ready to go," the woman said, sliding the stepladder away from the plane.

"Put it on my account," Daniel said.

The woman nodded and hooked the hose back to the fuel pump.

Daniel turned back to Fallon and pulled out his phone. "I'll check the security video in my cabin."

Fallon watched as Daniel scrolled through video images of his cabin. Fallon shook his head when he saw two men dressed in black exit the cabin and head for two boats moored at the dock. One man turned to look back, his face clearly visible to the camera.

"Ferguson!" Fallon muttered. "How did he find us so fast?"

"We need to go back!" Daniel exclaimed.

"Wait! Go back to the views inside your cabin."

Daniel scrolled through the other views.

"The cabin is empty. Alicia and the rest must have fled before Ferguson got there."

"But where would they go?" Daniel asked as he slipped his phone into his pocket.

"Alicia knows the island. She'll find a safe place."

"I can't leave my brother behind," Daniel said.

Fallon gestured impatiently. "We know Ferguson is on Beaver Island. It's the perfect time to get the drive. If we wait, it may be too late."

Daniel stared at Fallon.

"Alicia will protect them," Fallon said.

"It could also be too late for Cally and my dad if we go to Detroit."

CHAPTER 20

C ally watched the dust cloud behind the car as they raced along the gravel road away from Daniel's cabin. They had left the cabin just in time. It had to be Ferguson, or at least his men, on those boats. Who else would show up with rifles? He turned. Alicia was sitting on the passenger side of the front bench seat of the car. "Do you think that was Ferguson on those boats?"

Alicia turned to look back at him. "I don't know . . . I sure didn't want to stick around to find out."

"How much further should I drive?" Mr. Callahan asked.

"Drive past the lighthouse," Alicia said. "There's an abandoned summer camp just ahead on the left. Pull in the drive and park there."

Cally saw a clearing in the woods just ahead. On a small hill stood a tall, brick lighthouse. "I remember this," Cally said as they drove past the tall brick cylinder capped with a circle of windows. "Is this the same lighthouse we visited when we camped here?"

"That's it," Mr. Callahan said.

Cally and his dad exchanged a look in the rearview mirror. He turned to look at the lighthouse as they passed. He could still see himself as a kid piling out of the minivan with Sheila and Daniel and running up the small hill to the lighthouse, Mom and Dad shouting after them to wait.

"It looks more overgrown and rundown," Mr. Callahan said.

"It needs a lot of work," Alicia said. She pointed to an approaching driveway beyond the lighthouse. "Turn in there."

They pulled into a gravel driveway just past the lighthouse and parked near an abandoned building. Suddenly the car jerked and the engine stalled.

"What was that?" Cally asked as he and Alicia climbed out of the car.

"I had to pop the clutch to stall the engine since we don't have a key to turn it off," Mr. Callahan said, joining them.

Cally looked at the abandoned campground. "What is this place?"

"An old summer camp for teens," Alicia said. "They used to bring kids here for the summer to work on the lighthouse."

"Looks like it hasn't been used in a while," Mr. Callahan said.

"It's been closed for years," Alicia said. "If Ferguson and company did follow us, our car will be hidden here."

"This old car will look like it was abandoned here," Mr. Callahan said.

Alicia chuckled and pointed to a trail. "We can take that to the lighthouse. Grab Fallon's duffel from the back seat."

"So we're hiding in the lighthouse?"

"Yes," Alicia said as she headed to the trail.

Cally grabbed the duffel and followed Alicia and his dad to the lighthouse.

"I never thought I'd make it back here," Mr. Callahan said.

Cally looked up at the tall brick tower. "Me either."

"When were you two here?" Alicia asked. They were approaching the back entrance to a building attached to the lighthouse.

"About twenty years ago," Cally said. Alicia, standing at the door, pulled a key ring from her pocket. "You have a key?"

"I'm chair of the volunteer group restoring this lighthouse," Alicia smiled as she unlocked the door. "Overnight stays are a perk I get."

Cally heard the surf pounding. He stepped to the edge of a bluff and looked at the beach and Lake Michigan below. To his right, he saw the roof of another building on the shore. "What's that building?"

"An old signal station and boathouse." Alicia unlocked the door and stepped inside.

Cally followed Alicia inside, with his dad behind him. "Do you have a cabin on the island?"

"I inherited my grandfather's house in St. James," Alicia said. She locked the door behind them.

Cally scanned the room. The dim, evening sun, through a single window, lit only a small square on the worn linoleum floor. He spotted a light switch and reached for it.

"Wait," Alicia said, grabbing Cally's arm. "We don't want to tip anyone off that we're here. We have to be careful. We can't let our guard down."

In the kitchen, Cally set the duffel on a small table with four chairs. He stepped up to the old metal kitchen sink and looked out the window at the vast expanse of Lake Michigan. "That's quite the view."

His dad joined him at the window. "Beautiful."

Alicia mumbled something. Cally turned to see her holding a framed picture over the open duffel bag. "What's that?" he asked.

"A picture of Fallon as a teenager and his dad standing on the pier in Charlevoix," Alicia said. "I've seen this picture before. It used to hang in the Raven Tavern in Charlevoix."

Cally chuckled when he saw the boyish picture of Fallon. "What's up with his dad wearing a suit on the pier? He looks out of place."

"It's signed, 'Nicholas McElliot, State Attorney General,'" Mr. Callahan said, looking over their shoulders at the picture. "I didn't know he was Fallon's dad."

"His dad was kind of a big deal," Alicia said.

"Did you know Fallon back then?" Cally asked.

Alicia smiled. "His family summered in Charlevoix. The summer after I graduated from Charlevoix High School, I met Fallon on the beach."

"Ah, summer love," Mr. Callahan chuckled.

"You two were a couple?" Cally asked.

Alicia blushed. "Only for a year. It didn't work out."

"You've known Fallon a long time," Mr. Callahan said.

Alicia looked uncomfortable with the conversation.

"And now you're partners?" Cally asked.

Alicia set the picture on the table. "Enough small talk." She pulled a gun and a box of ammo from the duffel.

Cally tensed. The handgun looked too familiar—like the one Chuck slid across the coffee table to him the day he gave Cally the computer drive.

"You expect one of us to use that?" Mr. Callahan asked.

"Only if necessary," Alicia said. "You know how to use it?"

"I've used a shotgun for hunting, and that's about it," Mr. Callahan said.

"How about you, Cally?" Alicia asked.

Cally squeezed his hands into a fist and bit his lip.

"Cally?" Alicia asked again, after a pause.

He took a deep breath and looked at Alicia's concerned face. "Not since I ran from Chuck's place."

Alicia looked at him with compassion. "Well, it's here if we need it."

Mr. Callahan walked toward a door on the other side of the kitchen. The worn wooden floor creaked as he walked. "What's in that room?"

"A living room. There are also bedrooms on this floor and upstairs," Alicia said.

Through the kitchen window, Cally watched the waves gently breaking on the sandy beach at the bottom of the bluff. "It's stuffy in here," he said as he opened the window, letting in a light breeze and the sound of the surf.

"That breeze feels good," Mr. Callahan said. He sat at the table and rested his head in his hands. "I'm wiped out."

Cally sat across from his dad at the table. He noticed how old his dad looked.

"Why are you staring at me?" his dad asked.

"Nothing, Dad," Cally said. He looked at Alicia. "What's your plan if they follow us here?"

"They're not going to find us here," Alicia said.

"You sound overconfident," Mr. Callahan said.

"What if they *do* find us?" Cally asked.

"We'll do some island hopping," Alicia said. "There's a boat in the signal station down by Lake Michigan. North Fox, just south of here, is the closest island."

"Run away? That's your plan?" Cally asked.

"Yes," Alicia said as she sat at the table. "If we have to face Ferguson and his thugs, I don't want to do it until Daniel and Fallon come back. But for the moment we can rest."

Mr. Callahan put his head back down on his arm.

"Are you okay, Dad?" Cally asked.

"Just tired out."

"Why don't you lie down for a while in one of the bedrooms?" Alicia suggested.

His dad pushed himself slowly to his feet. "That sounds good."

Cally observed his dad closely, maybe for the first time ever: bags under his eyes, wrinkled skin, rumpled white hair, and white beard stubble.

"I'll show you to the bedroom," Alicia offered.

After the two of them left the room, Cally went to the window by the door. Outside, leaves vibrated in the breeze. The sky was turning orange and yellow. He relaxed to the sound of crickets—until he realized that the sound was gradually being overpowered by the growl of an approaching vehicle. A truck passed the lighthouse driveway, slowed, then stopped and backed up. Cally's pulse quickened when the black truck pulled into the parking lot.

Cally jumped away from the window. "We have company!"

Alicia joined Cally, and they crouched by the windowsill as they watched the truck.

"Maybe just sightseers?" Alicia suggested hopefully.

"I sure hope so," Mr. Callahan said, crouching behind them.

The truck parked, the doors opened, and two men and a woman, all of them wearing all black, climbed out. They quickly slipped out of sight behind the truck, then a moment later reappeared carrying rifles. Slowly, they approached the lighthouse, rifles pointed forward.

"The guy on the right—that's Ferguson!" Cally remarked.

"How do they keep finding us?" Alicia asked. She ran to the table, slipped the food bag back into the duffel, and zipped it closed. "Come on," she said. "Out the back door to the lifesaving station and the boat—and try to be quiet."

"Right behind you!" Cally followed Alicia out the door and down a short flight of stairs. He glanced to his left and right and saw no one; then he looked over his shoulder—his dad quietly closed the door behind him, turned, and stumbled down the stairs to the ground. Cally hurried back. He took his dad's arm and helped him up. They stood a second as Cally steadied him.

Down the trail, Alicia was stopped, waving at them. "Come on!" she mouthed, then turned and continued running along a path that led down the bluff.

"We need to hurry, Dad," Cally said as he turned and hurried after Alicia.

"I'll try to keep up."

Cally continued down the path after Alicia. After several steps, he looked over his shoulder. His dad was falling behind. He rushed back, draped his dad's arm over his shoulder, and struggled to move the two of them along. Ahead, he no longer saw Alicia, but the path was clear.

"Go without me," Mr. Callahan said. "I'm slowing you down. Just set me over in those bushes. Maybe they won't see me."

"No way, Dad!"

Together, they hobbled along the path and down the slope into a clearing by the beach. Waves pounded the shore as Cally helped his dad to a big brick building with a wide, open doorway. Inside, Alicia was scurrying around.

Cally helped his dad through the open door and over to a large, fiberglass boat perched on a trailer-like structure with wheels that rested on a track like a train car. The tracks inclined toward the water. The boat looked fairly new, with a large motor mounted on the stern. Alicia was opening two large doors in front of the tracks near the bow of the boat.

Alicia pointed to a small stepladder propped against the boat's side. "Hurry, get in the boat!"

Cally helped his dad climb the ladder. Mr. Callahan stumbled on the boat's gunwale and fell to the floor next to Fallon's duffel. Cally quickly climbed into the boat and helped his dad up and onto a seat in the back of the boat. He turned to look at Alicia now standing next to the boat. "Can I help?"

"I've done this a few times to show how the Coast Guard used to launch their rescue boats to aid a ship in trouble. Now I'll pull the wheel chocks away. Brace yourselves." She disappeared.

Cally heard something sliding on the cement floor under the boat. Suddenly the boat started to coast forward toward the water, picking up speed as it moved down the inclined ramp. He heard the stepladder fall to the floor as the boat moved closer to the water. A moment later, with the boat still moving down the ramp, Alicia somehow hoisted herself inside.

Cally sat with his dad and watched Alicia slip behind the wheel. A second later, the boat hit the water with a loud splash, jerking them all forward. Alicia turned a key on the dash by the steering wheel. Behind them, a motor roared to life. As the boat floated onto the lake, outside the boathouse, waves thrashed them, turning the boat sideways. The floor vibrated beneath Cally's feet, and a moment later the boat lurched forward.

"Hang on!" Alicia shouted as the boat powered away from the shore and into the rough waters of Lake Michigan. Cally gripped his dad's arm as the boat pounded the waves. Water spray blew into his face as waves crashed over the bow. Cally looked back at the shore and saw three shadowy figures running toward the boathouse in the failing sunlight. One raised a rifle.

"Get down!" Cally shouted as the rat-a-tat-tat of automatic weapon fire rang out. He pulled his dad to the floor of the boat and laid on top of him. He glanced up at Alicia just as she disappeared below her seatback. A split-second later, bullets pierced the dash and shattered the windshield. Shots rang out again, and more bullets hit the back of the boat.

"They're trying to shoot out the motor!" Alicia yelled.

The engine groaned as the bow of the boat cut through each large wave. Cally felt the impact of each wave as it echoed against the fiberglass boat bottom. Their bodies thumped the floor with each wave they hit. Cally heard the faint sound of more gunshots and waited for more bullets to hit the boat, but nothing happened. He slowly raised his head and peered back toward shore. They were now some distance from the three people on the beach.

"I think we're out of range," Cally said, and helped his dad back onto the seat. He sat next to him.

"That was close!" Alicia said with relief.

"I'm glad you had a backup plan!" Cally responded.

"I'll pretend to head to the mainland," she said. "Once we're out of view, I'm heading to North Fox Island."

The boat picked up speed as they bounced across the waves on Lake Michigan. Mr. Callahan was hunched over on the seat, staring at the floor of the boat, head bobbing with each wave they hit. Cally looked back and could no longer see the boathouse. He felt the boat turn. Ahead, he saw the silhouette of an island against a bright orange sky from the setting sun. "Is that North Fox?"

Alicia nodded.

The constant wind generated by the boat's speed swept back Cally's hair. Cally glanced at his dad; the orange light on his face from the setting sun began to fade. To the west, the sun was disappearing behind some black, menacing clouds, and toward the horizon a bolt of lightning shot down. Several seconds later, there was a low rumble of thunder. The air was growing colder. The water spray off the bow grew larger as the waves intensified.

"This weather doesn't look good!" Cally observed.

Alicia glanced at the horizon as another bolt of lightning shot out of the dark clouds. "That should stop them from following us!" she shouted over the roar of the motor.

The sky grew darker. Cally gripped the seat as the boat crested each wave, then slammed into the trough, spraying water over them. The boat motor groaned as they rode up the next wave. Alicia's knuckles were white on the wheel, straining to hold the boat on course. The ride became rougher and rougher, as each wave tossed Cally and his dad up, then slammed them down again. Cally struggled to see the island ahead as rain began to pelt them. North Fox Island did not appear to be any closer.

"Help us, dear God," Cally called out. He felt his dad's eyes on him and turned to look.

"Amen," his dad said.

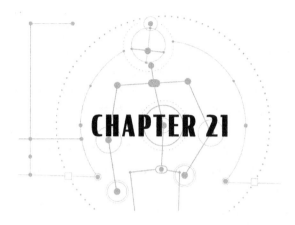

CHAPTER 21

T
he landmarks on the east side of Detroit were familiar to Fallon. Driving along the Jeffries Freeway brought back memories of patrolling the area as a police officer with Ferguson. Even then, he hadn't trusted him.

"Riding with you here reminds me of all those stakeouts we did," Daniel said.

Fallon smiled at Daniel riding shotgun. At the time, he'd enjoyed working with Daniel. They shared a common approach to law enforcement and seemed to understand each other. He looked at the road ahead. "How far yet to your parents' house?"

"A few more miles."

Fallon checked the rearview mirror. Not a car in sight.

"You worried someone is following us?"

"Can't be too careful."

Daniel sighed. "Well, I'm still not sure landing at Coleman Young Airport and parking the plane at the State of Michigan hangar was such a good idea."

"They're used to me doing that—coming in at all hours of the night and using the kiosk to get a state car."

"But landing there with a seaplane seems a bit obvious."

"They know I'm a bit unorthodox. Besides, where else would you land the plane?"

"Maybe the Detroit River."

"And that wouldn't draw attention?"

"Okay, so maybe Coleman Young Airport was a good idea, but you used your State ID to get this car."

"It was the quickest way to get a car. We have to retrieve that hard drive ASAP—no time to waste. Besides, it's unmarked." Fallon saw Daniel look out his window at the side mirror.

"Now *I'm* nervous about someone following us," Daniel said.

The two were silent for a moment. Fallon caught a glimpse of Daniel's face as they passed under streetlights illuminating the inside of the dark car. Daniel looked upset. "What's eating you?"

"This whole thing is bothering me. We should have gone back to the cabin. Who knows what Ferguson would do if he caught Cally and my dad?"

"You saw that the cabin was empty. I'm sure they made it out before he arrived. Alicia will take care of them."

"You're putting a lot of faith in her."

"I just don't get how Ferguson found the cabin. You saw the gum on the security camera lens. I didn't tell anyone I was going to Beaver Island."

"Except the governor."

"I've known her since I was a kid. She wouldn't betray me like that."

"You should know as well as I do that we don't always know the truth about the people closest to us."

Fallon glanced at Daniel, then back at the road. "I still don't get how you tapped the State of Michigan computer to run surveillance on Ferguson. Massey seems too willing to cooperate without the governor's consent."

"We had a warrant. He had to comply."

"Massey doesn't seem like the cooperative type."

"How do you know him?"

"I met him a few times at the governor's Archipelago software implementation meetings," Fallon said. "He seems pretty full of himself."

"Actually, he's pretty generous. Did you know he sponsored the restoration of a Prohibition-era boat for the Beaver Island Museum?"

"What! How do you know that?"

"I saw that the museum on Beaver Island has a display about a McElliot who had a whiskey operation on the island during Prohibition," Daniel said. "Any relation to you?"

"That was my granddad's boat."

"No kidding. Did you know about the display?"

"I heard about it," Fallon said. "Why would Massey pay for the restoration of that boat?"

"Apparently he has some connection to Beaver Island."

"What kind of connection?"

"I'm not sure."

"Massey seems to be more than an acquaintance to you."

"He was personally involved when we set up the surveillance. I think you know he likes to talk a lot about himself."

Fallon chuckled. "That's for sure."

Daniel pointed at an approaching sign. "That's our exit."

Fallon exited the freeway. Daniel directed him to an old, two-story house barely visible in the glow of a nearby streetlight.

"Drive past the house," Daniel said. "We can park in the alley."

Fallon drove down the alley, scanning the parked cars and trash cans, looking for anything suspicious.

"Park there," Daniel said as he pointed to a spot next to some tall hedges. "We can cut through the hedges to the house."

Fallon parked the car and shut off the engine. He looked at Daniel. "You know they have to be watching the house."

"If they are, they won't bother us until we reveal where the drive is hidden."

"But then we'll be trapped inside the house. They'll get us and the drive."

Daniel pulled a small gray box about the size of deck of cards from his coat pocket and showed it to Fallon. "That's not going to happen."

"What's that?"

"It's a blank drive. If we run into trouble, we can use it as a decoy."

"But they'll still capture us."

"There's a secret passage in Cally's room they don't know about."

"And that's where the drive is hidden?"

"Yes."

"You're always a step ahead," Fallon said. "That's what I liked about working with you on those cases."

"Follow my lead," Daniel said as he slipped the decoy drive back in his pocket and opened the car door.

Fallon climbed out of the car and stood next to Daniel, now standing by the tall hedges. Only the distant sound of traffic on the nearby freeway broke the silence.

Daniel pulled out his gun as he parted some branches on the hedges. "We used to sneak out of the house and slip through these hedges when I was a teenager."

Fallon followed Daniel through the hedges into a small backyard. He pulled out his gun as he scanned the backyard and the darkened windows on the back of the house. He kept close to Daniel as they moved toward the house, then followed him up the three steps to the back porch. Fallon watched Daniel tilt a flowerpot next to the back door, pull out a key, and unlock the door. The door squeaked as they entered the house.

Quietly, they moved through a laundry room, then stepped through a doorway into a dark kitchen. Fallon's pulse quickened as he kept pace with Daniel. He moved carefully in the dark room around shadowy shapes of furniture. He thought he heard something. His hand gripped the gun tighter. His body tensed. When Daniel looked back at him, Fallon put his hand to his ear to indicate he thought he heard something. A clock on the stove glowed, casting a dim blue light over the floor and table. He watched Daniel turn his head left and right, shrug his shoulders, then motion with one hand for Fallon to follow him, gun pointed forward with the other hand. They stepped into a small entryway by the front door and started up a long stairway. Steps creaked beneath them as they ascended.

Daniel stopped when they reached the top step. He pointed to the end of the hallway.

Fallon nodded and followed Daniel. A lone night-light plugged into an outlet in the middle of the hallway cast a dim light. Floorboards squeaked as they slowly walked to the end of the hall and stood in front of a wood-paneled door with flaking white paint. Daniel opened the door and they carefully stepped inside. A wave of hot, humid air greeted them. Streetlights outside cast squares of light on the floor of the dark bedroom. The room was trashed. Fallon stepped over clothes strewn on the floor and an empty dresser drawer as he followed Daniel to the closet. Wiping sweat from his brow, he watched as Daniel opened the closet door and stepped inside. Daniel slipped his gun into his pocket and turned on the flashlight on his phone as he knelt on the floor of the closet and traced his hand along the floor trim. A moment later he pulled out a loose piece of trim. There, between the wall studs, sat a dusty hard drive.

Daniel smiled at Fallon, grabbed the drive, and slipped it into his jeans pocket.

"Let's get out of here," Fallon said in a hushed voice as he turned to leave. He felt Daniel grab his arm and turned to see him with his hand to his ear.

They stood by the closet door, wide-eyed, listening. A steady sound of creaking floorboards seemed to be getting louder.

"The stairway. They *were* waiting for us," Daniel said in a whisper as he pulled out his gun, quietly left the closet, and slipped behind the open bedroom door.

Fallon joined him, gun ready.

The creaking boards stopped for a moment, then resumed. Fallon gripped his gun tightly. There was silence for a minute. Fallon could sense someone on the other side of the open door.

Abruptly, Daniel thrust the bedroom door shut. Fallon heard someone on the other side of the door hit the floor.

"Quick!" Daniel started to push the dresser next to them toward the closed door. Fallon helped—and just in time. A second after they got it into place, someone tried to push the door open.

"I know you're in there, Daniel!" someone shouted. "The police will be here any minute. We know you have it. Hand it over."

Instead, Daniel fired a couple shots into the ceiling, then opened a window.

Confused, Fallon started to move toward Daniel at the window, but Daniel motioned for him to follow. As they slipped back into the closet, shots rang out from the hallway. He heard splintering wood and falling plaster, then someone pushing on the door. The dresser screeched on the floor with each thud against the door. Daniel was on his knees now, with his phone flashlight pointed at the floor.

"The secret passage?" Fallon asked.

"Yes," Daniel said. He opened a trapdoor in the floor and quickly climbed into the hole. "Close the trapdoor behind you."

Fallon quickly and quietly closed the closet door and watched Daniel disappear down what appeared to be an old chimney. He slipped his legs into the hole and felt ladder rungs beneath his shoes. He climbed down far enough to carefully close the trapdoor without a sound. As he descended into the darkness, he heard the dresser screech across the floor, then several people rushing into the bedroom. He carefully rested his feet on each successive rung of the ladder. The sounds above became more muffled and the air cooler. Looking down, he saw Daniel's shadowy shape with his flashlight pointing down in one hand, his other grabbing each rung. Fallon could feel clumps of protruding mortar against his back. Soon he saw Daniel reach the bottom and walk out of sight. He heard the faint sound of approaching sirens.

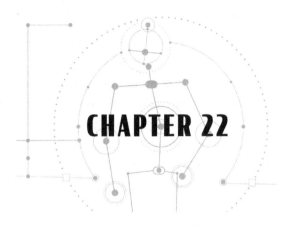

CHAPTER 22

Cally gripped the boat's seat. The shore of North Fox Island was barely visible, framed by dark clouds above the treetops. Thunder and flashes of lightning punctuated the dimming daylight as rain continued to pummel them. His body jerked back and forth with each wave that pounded the boat. He looked at Alicia, who held a death grip on the steering wheel. "We're not going to make it!"

Alicia shouted something inaudible above the sound of the groaning boat motor, crashing waves, and thunder. Cally's dad flashed him a terrified look, water dripping from his soaked hair and across the stubble on his face. Another wave crashed over the boat, soaking their already soggy clothes. Cally tried to wipe the water from his eyes, watching Alicia struggle to keep the boat pointed toward shore. Another flash of lightning illuminated several rocks protruding from the water. Cally's hands locked onto the seat as the boat lurched sideways, hung precariously balanced for just a second, and then began to tip. A second later he was overboard, caught below the surface in a swirl of churning, shockingly cold water.

Instantly his lifeguard training kicked in. He swam as hard as he could toward the dim light above him until his head popped up above the surface. Where were Alicia and Dad? He turned his head and spotted the half-submerged boat coming toward him with its motor racing and thrust his arms forward to get away from it. The boat surged past him, just missing his legs. Wave after wave continued to pound him. A minute later he saw Alicia's head emerge from the water, but still no sign of his dad.

"Dad!" Cally searched the crashing waves, straining to keep his head above water. Looking over his shoulder, he saw his dad flailing in the water behind him. Cally swam to him, secured him with one arm, and swam toward shore. When his foot touched bottom, he stood and strained to drag his dad's limp body onto the sandy beach strewn with large rocks, away from the water and crashing waves, then collapsed next to him. His father stirred weakly. Cally rolled onto his back, panting as sheets of rain pelted him.

Alicia staggered out of the water. "Is he okay!" Alicia asked. She bent over his dad as he began to cough.

"I was afraid you'd drowned," Cally said, rolling onto his side to glance at his dad, who was looking up at Alicia.

"Thank God, you saved me," his dad said to Alicia between coughs.

Cally shook his head. "I was the one who saved you, Dad!"

His dad looked at him, then Alicia.

Alicia nodded. "He saved you," she said, then plopped down next to Mr. Callahan.

Cally concentrated on catching his breath. He jumped as a clap of thunder echoed in the trees along the beach, their faces illuminated by a flash of lightning against the darkening sky.

"Daylight's fading fast," Alicia said, as she stood and grabbed Mr. Callahan's hand and pulled him to his feet. "Follow me."

Cally stood, startled suddenly by a loud thud nearby. It was their boat, crashing into the shore, propelled by powerful waves, a portion of its hull ripped open.

Cally and his dad stood side by side, staring at the boat. He reached for his dad's arm to steady him.

His dad shook off Cally's hand. "I'm okay."

Just past his dad, on the beach, the waterlogged duffel washed up on shore. Cally retrieved it and returned to his dad and Alicia.

"Glad you saw that," Alicia said, and walked toward the woods lining the shore. "I was afraid we'd be stuck here without food. Come on, follow me."

"Where to?" Cally asked.

"There's a trail right there leading to an old homestead not far from here."

Cally reached again for his dad's arm.

"I don't need your help, I said."

"Suit yourself." Cally followed Alicia as she stepped into the woods and started down a narrow, overgrown trail.

Cally had to push branches aside. He glanced back and saw his dad following a few paces behind him.

"Do you know this island too?" Cally asked.

"I've been here a few times with our lighthouse volunteer team," Alicia said.

They wound through the darkening woods on a barely visible trail. The waterlogged duffel felt heavy, and the cool air chilled Cally's wet body. Leaves rustled above them as rain continued to fall. Flashes of lightning occasionally illuminated the trail.

"The log house should be right up here," Alicia said.

"I hope so," Mr. Callahan said.

Cally turned; his dad was stumbling along the trail several steps behind him. "Dad, you need—"

"I told you, I don't need help!" his dad shouted.

Cally sighed and pressed on, branches slapping his body as he followed Alicia. Soon he spotted a clearing ahead.

"There," Alicia said as she stepped into the clearing.

Cally joined her. A dilapidated log house sat in the middle of the clearing, barely visible in the encroaching darkness.

"Is it safe?" Cally asked as he eyed the sagging, moss-covered roof, broken windows, and rotten door half off its hinges.

"It's all we have," Alicia said. She stepped inside.

Cally shrugged. He stopped by the front door and looked back at his dad emerging from the woods and hobbling toward him.

Cally joined Alicia inside the cabin.

"I'm glad I had a waterproof case for my phone," Alicia said as she used the flashlight on her phone to survey the contents of the log cabin.

There was a gaping hole in the roof; water dripped onto the rotted floor below. "Doesn't look like much protection from the weather," Cally said.

"The roof is better by the fireplace." Alicia propped her phone against the fireplace to light the area around her. She gathered some branches and logs from a pile next to the fireplace. "Grab the matches from the duffel bag."

Cally set the duffel down by the fireplace and rummaged through it. He found the plastic bag with matches and handed them to her.

Alicia took out a match, struck it, and lit some kindling in the fireplace. "Let's hope the food is as dry as the matches."

Cally pulled plastic bags with crackers and cheese from the duffel. "Looks like some of it survived, along with Dad's Cheez Whiz."

"Well, that's good news," his dad said.

Cally looked up as his dad, entering the cabin, immediately tripped over the doorsill and tumbled to the floor. "Dad!" Cally exclaimed, and hurried to him.

"That last step is a big one," his dad said.

"Come over by the fire and get warm," Cally said, helping his dad toward the growing flames in the fireplace.

This time, his dad didn't resist. He promptly sat on the floor by the fireplace, sighed, and rubbed his forehead. His tired face was highlighted by the orange glow from the fire.

Cally looked up at the hole in the ceiling. The rain was letting up. "I don't hear thunder anymore."

"I think the storm has passed," Alicia said, placing another log in the crackling fire. "I'm glad we made it here before dark."

"I'm just glad we made it here!" Cally affirmed. He was beginning to feel the warmth of the fire.

Alicia turned off the flashlight on her phone. "Better save the power."

"Are you going to call for help?" Cally asked.

"There's no phone service on this island. No one lives here."

"We're stranded?" Mr. Callahan asked.

"You saw the boat," Cally said. "I don't think we'll be taking that back to Beaver Island."

"At least that storm stopped Ferguson from chasing us," Alicia said.

The room went silent. Cally looked at his dad with his head buried in his hands, then Alicia. "Now what?"

"We might as well eat something, then try to get some rest," Alicia said.

"Hand me that Cheez Whiz," Mr. Callahan said.

"Enjoy," Cally said, glad that his dad at least had an appetite, even if only for artificial cheese. He handed the can to his dad, then tried to ignore the fizzing sound as his dad squirted the liquid into his mouth.

Alicia winced. "Gross! What else is in the bag?"

"Granola bars and apples." Cally placed the food in front of the fireplace.

"How about an apple to go with that cheese?" Cally asked. When he got no answer, he looked at his dad, who was now lying on the floor, his chest gently rising and falling, Cheez Whiz can still in hand.

"I think that's a no," Alicia said. She put some cheese on a cracker and popped it into her mouth.

"We're stuck here," Cally said. "No one knows we're here. What's the plan?"

"Hope someone rescues us."

"Anyone except Ferguson," Cally said, grabbing a cracker. He put a slice of cheese on it.

"I hope they think we went to the mainland," Alicia said. She looked at Mr. Callahan snoring. "Right now, I think your dad has the right idea."

Cally nodded as he ate another cracker, then lay on his back near his dad. For a moment he watched the dancing shadows on the ceiling from the fire and listened to the crackling logs in the fireplace. His mind drifted as sleep overtook him. He saw a fuzzy image of Daniel sitting next to him by a campfire. They laughed together as they shared stories.

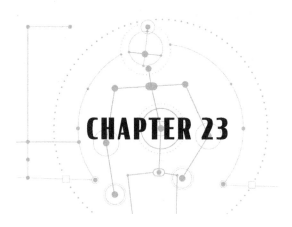

CHAPTER 23

F allon stepped down onto the floor, easing himself out of the old chimney. Daniel stood a few steps away, shining his flashlight on a large metal door mounted to the basement wall. It looked just big enough for them to crawl through. "What's that?"

"An old coal chute," Daniel said. The metal door's hinges creaked as he propped it open. "When we were teenagers, we used this to sneak out of the house." He reached into the chute, grabbed a stout metal handle welded onto the chute's wall, and hoisted himself up. A moment later his legs disappeared into the chute. Fallon grabbed the first handle and hoisted his lanky frame through the chute. At the top, he grabbed Daniel's extended arm and stood up. They were now outside, on the side of the house by the alley. The approaching sirens grew louder. Flashing blue and red lights were growing brighter around the house. There was a light on in a bedroom upstairs.

"Let's go," Daniel said. He slipped through the hedgerow next to the alley. Fallon squeezed through right behind him. As he emerged, someone called, "Hey, Danny!"

"Hey!" Daniel said casually to a man standing next to a garage in the alley. He pointed toward Fallon just behind him and said, "This is my friend."

Fallon exhaled deeply as he brushed some mortar from his hair. He nodded at the man.

"What's going on?" the neighbor asked. "I heard gunshots and now police cars."

"Not sure. We were upstairs when we heard noises down on the first floor," Daniel said. "We started downstairs and I think maybe we startled some intruders. They took a couple of shots at us."

"Are you okay?" the man asked.

"Yeah, we're fine. I called the police before we slipped out through the basement."

The man smiled. "The old coal chute. I remember you and Cally using that to sneak out of the house at night." He shook his head. "The police sure have been at your folks' place a lot. They were there for hours the other day."

Daniel nodded. "Mom's staying with Sheila. We're headed there now."

"We should get going," Fallon said as he anxiously glanced back at the hedge.

"Yeah, sure," the neighbor said. "Hey, sorry about your dad, Danny."

"Thanks. I appreciate that," Daniel said.

They slid into their car. Fallon started the engine and drove to the opposite end of the alley away from the house.

"He calls you Danny?" Fallon asked as he pulled onto a side street a block from the house.

"Ever since I was a kid. It was always Cally and Danny."

As they drove through an intersection near the house, Fallon glanced down the street and saw several police cars parked in front of the house with flashers going.

"That was close," Daniel said.

Fallon checked the rearview mirror. A police car a few blocks back was heading their way, flashers going. "Someone is on our tail."

Daniel looked over his shoulder.

"How do you want to handle this?" Fallon asked.

"Pick up speed and see if he's after us."

Fallon pressed the accelerator. After a block, he checked the rearview mirror. "Now there are two. And they're gaining on us."

"See if you can shake them."

Fallon immediately jerked the steering wheel, and the car squealed around a corner. His body leaned into the turn, both hands gripping the wheel. He checked the mirrors. Both police cars missed the turn and skidded to a stop.

"That bought us a little time," Fallon said, squealing around a turn onto another street.

"All we need is enough time to get the plane airborne," Daniel said.

They wound their way through the neighborhood to a freeway on-ramp. As they accelerated onto the freeway Fallon checked the mirrors. "I think we lost them."

"Don't be so sure."

Sure enough, a few minutes later Fallon spotted flashers in the distance behind them. "They found us." He wove in and out of traffic on the freeway, trying to maintain their distance from the police cars pursuing them. "Should we avoid the airport?"

"I think we should go there while we have the chance. If we get to the plane before they catch up to us, won't the security fence keep them out?"

"Maybe. If they're Detroit Police, they won't have access to the State of Michigan hangar."

"Go to the airport!"

Fallon nodded and punched the accelerator. "It's all or nothing now." A few minutes later, with the police cars slowly gaining on them, they reached the airport exit. Tires squealed as they headed into the exit curve to the road that led to the airport.

"Sheesh!" Daniel exclaimed. "Where did you learn to drive?"

"My dad knew Jack Roush," Fallon said. "I did some racing in my day."

They pulled into the airport and drove toward the State of Michigan hangar. Fallon parked in a lot next to the hangar. The two of them ran to the entry gate embedded in the tall security fence that surrounded the airport. He waved his state ID card over a sensor on the latch. The gate opened and they stepped inside the fenced area. Fallon closed the gate and they sprinted to the plane. Daniel opened the door by the cockpit and climbed in. The engine sputtered, then roared to life. A puff of smoke flew past Fallon as he slipped into the plane through the back door and dropped into a seat in the back of the plane next to the open door. The plane vibrated beneath his feet. Instinctively, he grabbed the automatic rifle from the back seat and held it across his lap as he braced himself with his legs against the seat mounts and the fuselage. How had he gotten caught up in this? Was he really ready and willing to fire on patrolmen just doing their job, not knowing whether they were corrupt or not? What if he killed someone?

He held the door open with his foot as the plane began to move. Three police cars squealed to a stop next to the access gate. Two officers ran to a larger, vehicle gate in the perimeter fence.

"Get us in the air!" Fallon yelled.

"I don't have clearance for takeoff!" Daniel replied.

"Get us in the air now or we're finished!" Fighting a fierce battle within himself, Fallon raised the rifle as he watched the large vehicle gate in the security fence begin to slide open. *Fire only if necessary*, he urged himself. The plane shook as the engine sputtered, then revved louder. Another puff of smoke blew past the open door. Fallon tried to steady the rifle as he took aim at the cars. The plane's engine screamed as they taxied toward a runway. It was getting harder to hold the door ajar. The access gate began to open.

"This isn't going to be a smooth takeoff!" Daniel warned.

Fallon felt the plane abruptly pivot, throwing him toward the open door. He grabbed the seatback with one hand and tightly gripped the rifle with the other. The engine raced as the plane lurched forward, throwing him against the seatback. As the plane accelerated, he steadied himself against the seat, watching the police cars speed through the now-open gate, flashers going. Fallon raised the rifle and pointed it through the open doorway toward the police car leading the pursuit. *Shoot only if necessary.* He looked ahead. Not much runway left. The plane began to lift off the ground.

Fallon saw a flash from the police car, then heard gunshots. Bullets pierced the fuselage. Fallon kept his finger on the trigger—praying he would not have to squeeze it. *Shoot only if necessary.* He sighted in on the lead police car—and then the cars veered abruptly off the runway. Daniel screamed an expletive. Fallon whipped his head toward the front just in time to see a blinding light from an incoming plane closing in on them. Fallon swore and braced himself for a mid-air collision. The rifle dropped to the floor as he grabbed the seatback. The plane abruptly banked hard to the right. The force of the turn pressed Fallon's body toward the floor. He lost his grip and slid across the seat. His body hit the door on the other side with enough force that it popped open. He grabbed one of the brackets holding the seat in place as he felt himself falling out of the plane. He hooked his foot on the edge of the doorway to stop his fall. A second later, he was tossed back inside as the plane suddenly leveled out, then went into a steep climb. Fallon pulled himself onto the seat.

"Are you still with me?" Daniel shouted.

"Barely," Fallon said, trying to pull himself together. Still feeling the downward pressure of the climb, he strained to close the doors on each side of the plane.

"Wasn't that fun!"

"Fun? I almost fell out!" In a crouch, Fallon used the rear seatback to pull himself toward the front of the plane and climbed into the seat next to Daniel. He rubbed his bruised legs.

Daniel touched Fallon's shoulder and then pointed at the headphones over his ears.

Fallon slipped on his set of headphones and buckled his seat belt.

"My fighter pilot instincts just kicked in," Daniel said.

Fallon looked out the side window at the receding city lights below them. "I'm glad they did or else we would be toast right now."

"Burnt toast."

Fallon rubbed his forehead. His body began to ache as the adrenalin rush eased. "I felt like I was in a rock tumbler."

"That's what I love about this plane! It's so responsive."

Fallon looked at Daniel sitting at the controls like he was out for a Sunday drive. "How can you be so calm?"

"Experience. The tower sure gave me an earful. They told me to immediately return to the airport."

"I assume we're not doing that?"

"No way. Those guys are after us and my little brother needs me."

"I'm glad you thought to refuel the plane before we went to the house."

"I've learned to always be ready."

They sat silent for a few minutes in the cockpit.

"We still make a pretty good team," Fallon said.

Daniel smiled and nodded at Fallon.

"Let's hope I'm wrong about Ferguson being on the island," Fallon said.

"Well, at least we now have the hard drive." Daniel patted his jeans pocket.

"Hey, earlier I saw a computer bag in the back," Fallon said. "Do you have a laptop in there? We should make a copy of the hard drive."

"Good idea. Why don't you do that now."

Fallon climbed into the back seat and looked first under the seats and then anywhere else the computer backpack might have landed. Frustrated, he returned to the seat next to Daniel and slipped on the headphones.

"It's not there," Fallon said. "I think it fell out the open door when you made that evasive maneuver."

Daniel stared at Fallon with wide eyes.

"I guess we go in with no backup," Fallon said.

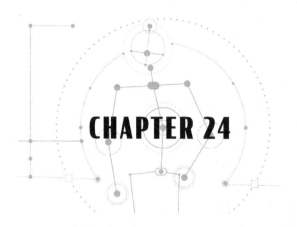

CHAPTER 24

Cally opened his eyes slowly, then sat up and squinted at the warm sunlight filling the ramshackle room. His arms hurt as he stretched. His clothes were mostly dry, still damp in some places. To his left his dad lay asleep. The fire crackled in the fireplace as Alicia poked at the logs. "How did you sleep?" she asked.

"Not that well."

"Me either."

They sat silent for a moment, staring at the fire. Cally rubbed his head. How would Daniel know where they were if he and Fallon returned to the cabin? What if Daniel and Fallon had been captured, unable to get the backup drive? Then Cally would remain a fugitive with no hope of the truth coming out.

Alicia handed Cally an apple. "Here's breakfast. Sorry we don't have any bacon and eggs."

Cally took a bite out of the apple. "We don't even have enough food to get us through today. What are we going to do about that?"

"I'll think of something." Alicia took a bite of her apple.

As they finished their apples, Cally heard a faint buzzing sound. He tossed his apple core into the fire and stood, looking through the hole in the ceiling at the blue sky.

Alicia stood and looked up. "I hear it too."

"Maybe it's Daniel," Cally said. He ran out into the open area around the cabin and scanned the sky. The buzzing grew louder.

Alicia joined Cally and pointed just above the treetops. "There it is. I don't think that's Daniel. I don't see floats on the plane."

"Then who is it?"

"I don't know whether it's friend or foe." Alicia turned and ran toward the cabin. "Quick, get inside before they spot us."

Cally followed Alicia. "But what if it's a search plane? They could alert someone to pick us up with a boat."

"Or what if it's Ferguson?"

"He'd still need a boat to get us."

Alicia stopped just inside the doorway of the house. "Maybe not. There's a grass airstrip on this island."

Cally looked up and saw the plane fly over the house. "You think they're landing here?"

"It may just be passing by."

"It's flying awfully low for that."

Alicia went back down the steps and stood a moment, listening. "It sounds like they're coming in for a landing."

Cally's dad joined them on the step, rubbing the sleep from his eyes. "Is that a plane?" he asked.

Alicia nodded. "Might be Ferguson."

"If that's him, how does he keep finding us?" Cally asked.

The plane's engines grew quieter, as if it were slowing down.

Alicia frowned. "I've been wondering the same thing. I wonder . . ." She went back inside the cabin.

Cally followed and watched her dig through the duffel, feeling the sides and the bottom.

"Here!" Alicia pulled out a small black box about the size of a deck of cards. "A satellite tracker!"

"We've had that bag with us the whole time!" Cally stated.

"Now what?" Mr. Callahan said from the doorway. "We have no way to get off this island and away from them."

Alicia looked at Cally as she tapped her finger on her chin. "Except their plane."

"Do you know how to fly?" Cally asked.

"Not exactly."

"What does that mean?" Mr. Callahan asked, stepping closer.

"I took flying lessons but never got my license."

"You want to steal a plane that you *might* be able to fly?" Mr. Callahan said.

They all stood in silence a moment.

"You know," Mr. Callahan said, "they can only know where the tracker is, not us. If we leave the tracker here, they'll come here looking for us."

"And where would we go?" Cally asked. "There can't be many places to hide on this island."

"We go to the airstrip and take their plane while they're here looking for us," Alicia said.

"But how do we get to the airstrip without running into them?" Mr. Callahan asked. "Won't they take the same trail we took here?"

"I know another trail to the airstrip," Alicia said

The plane engine sputtered. "Are they landing?"

"Sure sounds like it." Alicia said as she tossed the tracker across the room and grabbed the duffel. She ran toward the trail. "Come on!"

Cally followed Alicia into the woods along a trail. He glanced back—his dad seemed more stable than the day before as he trotted along. They wound their way through the woods along a narrow trail. The plane's engine sounded as if they were taxiing. It became louder as they moved closer to the airstrip.

Alicia gestured for Cally and his dad to hurry. "We need to get there before they get out of the plane and hear us."

Cally pushed aside branches and brush as they moved along the trail. He looked back.

"I'm coming!" Mr. Callahan said.

"Stay low," Alicia said in a hushed tone as she crouched behind some dense brush along the edge of the grass airstrip.

Cally crouched next to her. The plane taxied to the end of the grass airstrip and turned to position for takeoff. As his dad approached, Cally gestured for him to stay low.

Three people, dressed in black and carrying automatic rifles, climbed out of the plane. One of them pointed toward where they crouched behind the brush, and Alicia slipped back a little deeper into the underbrush. Cally pressed into the thicket, feeling prickers from raspberry canes scratch his exposed arms. He tried to push them away as his dad joined him, rustling leaves. Alicia held her finger to her mouth as the three people from the plane walked along the edge of the airstrip toward their hiding spot. Cally tried to ignore the pain from the scratches on his arm as he peered up through the leaves and brush. When the three armed people were close enough, Cally recognized Ferguson. He was following a woman in the lead; another man walked behind them.

"Are you sure they're here?" Ferguson asked.

"I have a lock on the satellite tracker," the woman said. "It's stationary. They're close."

"You saw the wrecked boat on the beach. They're stuck here," the man said.

"This island isn't that big," Ferguson said. He swore. "I can't wait to get my hands on Cally. And Fallon. That traitor."

"The trail is up there," the woman said.

The sound of Ferguson's voice made Cally tense. His pulse quickened as Ferguson walked by only a few feet away. Cally sensed movement; his dad, kneeling next to Cally, wobbled a bit. Cally grabbed his arm and steadied him, rustling some leaves.

Ferguson stopped. "What's that?"

Heart pounding, Cally stared at Ferguson from the underbrush as Ferguson scanned the area, rifle raised.

"What?" the man asked.

"I think I heard something," Ferguson said.

"Stop being so jumpy," the woman said. "Come on."

Ferguson stepped closer, now nearly in front of them, scanning the woods. "I know I heard something."

"The tracker tells me they haven't moved since we landed," the woman said, "and they're still a few hundred yards off. Let's go."

"I saw smoke from the chimney when we flew over that house," the man said. "They must be there."

Cally watched Ferguson scan the woods one more time, then turn and follow the woman as she moved toward the trail. He heard branches crack and leaves rustle as they entered the woods.

"We can just leave their bodies at the cabin," Ferguson said as his voice faded. "It'll be a long time before anyone finds them."

Cally's body ached. His legs were growing tired. When he could no longer hear Ferguson and the other two moving through the woods, he looked at Alicia, one eyebrow raised.

Alicia nodded. "To the plane!" She pressed through the underbrush to the airstrip.

Cally jumped to his feet, then helped his dad up. "We need to hurry, Dad." He ran after Alicia through the underbrush onto the airstrip. He looked behind—his dad was running, but falling behind. Cally jogged to a stop.

Ahead, Alicia opened the door to the plane and flipped the pilot's seat forward. "Hurry!"

Cally glanced back at his dad and saw him trip over a rut. He ran back to his dad and helped him stand.

"I'm too old for all this excitement," his dad said.

Cally put his dad's arm over his shoulder and helped him to the plane. Alicia guided Mr. Callahan into the rear seat, flipped her seat down, and climbed in. The plane's engine coughed to life and the propeller began to spin as Cally joined Alicia in front. The engine revved and the plane began to move down the airstrip.

"Buckle up!" Alicia shouted as she slipped on her headset.

Cally buckled his seat belt and turned to his dad. "Are you buckled?"

His dad nodded, breathing hard, face covered with a sheen of sweat.

"Hang on!" Alicia said as the plane wobbled and bounced on the grass strip, picking up speed.

The plane went airborne for a second, then dropped back onto the airstrip. "You said you knew how to fly!" Cally stated nervously, watching the fast-approaching trees at the end of the runway.

"It's been a few years."

Out his side window, Cally saw Ferguson emerge from the trees and step onto the airstrip, followed by the man and woman. Ferguson raised his rifle just as the plane became airborne. Even above the roar of the engine, Cally could hear the gunshots, and bullets began to hit the plane. Ducking, Cally looked back at his dad, crouching low in his seat. A bullet ripped through the side of the plane, inches from his dad. Cally turned forward, peering over the plane's instrument panel, just as the plane barely cleared the treetops at the end of the airstrip. He heard the landing gear brush the leaves on the treetops. The automatic rifle fire became more distant, then stopped.

Alicia's eyes were fixed forward, one hand gripping the yoke, the other on the throttle.

"That was close," Cally said.

"Flying came back to me like riding a bike!" Alicia said excitedly. She let go of the throttle long enough to flash a thumbs up.

Cally nodded. He looked at his dad, who was still breathing hard. The corner of his dad's mouth raised a bit as if he was trying to smile.

"Glad they didn't hit the engine," Alicia said.

"Don't be so sure," Mr. Callahan said, looking over his shoulder. "Looks like a trail of white smoke."

Cally looked back; white smoke trailed the plane. Suddenly the plane's engine sputtered. The plane hesitated, then revved back to life.

"Bad news," Alicia said. "We're losing oil pressure and the oil temperature is rising."

Cally looked out the side window at Lake Michigan below. Ahead he saw Beaver Island.

The engine sputtered and quit.

Alicia swore. "I don't know if we can make it to Beaver Island Airport. I may have to put us down on the beach!"

The engine sputtered to life again and the plane shuddered. Cally looked out the window and saw that they were now flying over Beaver Island. He stared at the beach lining the west side of the island. It didn't look wide enough to accommodate a plane.

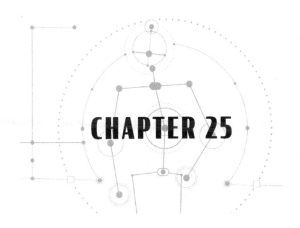

CHAPTER 25

A strange buzzing sound stirred Fallon. He slowly opened his eyes and realized he was in the cockpit of an airplane. He pulled his slumped body upright and looked at the tinge of orange and yellow in the sky.

"Good morning, sleepyhead," someone said.

He turned in his seat and looked at Daniel sitting at the controls. He shook his head, recalling the panicked takeoff from Coleman Young Airport. "I'm still tense from that takeoff," Fallon said as he cracked his neck and looked out the side window. "Aren't you tired?"

"The adrenaline hasn't worn off yet," Daniel said.

"Where are we?"

"Almost to Beaver Island," Daniel said as he pointed toward the windshield.

Fallon craned his neck and spotted the island to his left. The plane slowed and began to bank. A large inland lake became visible. "Is that Lake Geneserath?"

Daniel nodded. "I wish we'd gotten here sooner."

"We know they weren't in the cabin when Ferguson arrived. I'm sure Alicia handled it."

Daniel sighed. "I'll land on the opposite side of the peninsula, away from my cabin in case Ferguson is still there."

They descended toward the lake. Fallon tightened his seat belt. They cleared the trees, then dropped lower until the floats skimmed the water.

"I'll beach the plane there," Daniel said, pointing toward shore. The engine sputtered, then stopped. Fallon's body jerked forward as the plane abruptly stopped, floats scraping the pebbly beach. Daniel grabbed a rope from under the seat and climbed out of the plane through the door by his seat. Fallon exited through the back door and followed Daniel, walking on the float to the shore. The morning air was cool. A light fog hung over the lake. Birds chirping their morning song broke the silence as the sky lit up from the rising sun.

A light breeze ruffled Fallon's hair as water gently sloshed along the shore. Fallon looked at the wooded peninsula. He felt uneasy. "Where's your cabin?"

"On the other side of the peninsula. Follow me." Daniel began to walk down the shoreline, his shoes crunching on the gravelly beach.

Fallon eyed the dark cabins nestled in the woods lining the shore as they walked. They looked empty and lifeless. Not a single light on in any of the windows. "I don't like the feel of this. It's too quiet."

"We can approach along the shore and stake out the cabin first."

Fallon stepped carefully behind Daniel. The beach gravel crunched under their shoes. His body tensed. Not a soul in sight.

Daniel stopped. "Did you hear something?"

Fallon listened and scanned the shore. "No. Nothing."

Daniel nodded and continued along the shore, then slipped into a wooded lot. A few minutes later he stopped and pressed his body against a large tree along a road.

Fallon stepped next to him. He recognized the house where he'd parked his car. "My car's gone!"

"Let's hope they used it to escape," Daniel said. He crouched and scurried across the gravel road, slipping into the wooded lot next to the house.

Fallon followed. He recalled taking the same route with Alicia.

Daniel stopped just before the clearing surrounding his cabin. They both stayed quiet and still, studying the cabin from behind large trees. "I don't see any activity."

"There's a Jeep parked in the driveway next to your cargo van."

Daniel pulled out his gun. "Ferguson may be here." He crouched and began to move across the clearing toward the cabin.

Fallon sprinted across the lawn to the wall of the cabin, his gun at the ready. He pressed his back against the cabin next to Daniel. He looked toward the front of the cabin, then the back, then the dock. Daniel peered through the cabin window next to them, then motioned for Fallon to follow him toward the back.

Fallon carefully looked through the window as he passed. The kitchen was dark. A night-light on the far wall cast a dim light around the table and chairs where yesterday they sat for a meal. Was Alicia still hiding somewhere on the property with Cally and Mr. Callahan? Daniel motioned for Fallon to follow him. Carefully, Fallon moved to the back porch where Daniel quietly climbed the steps, crouching low as he moved toward the back entry door. His body tensed; his eyes darted back and forth, looking for danger, looking for someone hiding, looking for anything. On the video from the security camera, they'd seen Ferguson leave the cabin, but maybe he had returned.

Daniel eased himself against the wall next to the door. He motioned for Fallon to open the door. Fallon carefully twisted the doorknob, eased the door open, and slipped into the cottage with his gun pointed forward.

A floor lamp clicked on next to the couch.

"Don't make a move!" Fallon snapped, pistol aimed at the man sitting on the couch with his back to them. "Hands in the air!" He moved closer to the couch. The man raised his hands, but otherwise remained motionless. From the back, he didn't resemble Ferguson.

"Oh, put that gun down and join me for a drink," the man said, keeping his head turned away from Fallon.

"How do you know I have a gun?"

"I know the great Fallon McElliot always comes prepared for the worst," the man said, and turned to look at Fallon.

Fallon was shocked. It was the last person he expected to see sitting on the couch in Daniel's cabin.

CHAPTER 26

Fallon stood in front of the man seated on the couch with his legs crossed, holding a drink, as relaxed as if he were at a cocktail party. He despised his arrogant look as he kept his gun pointed at Massey.

Daniel still stood by the open back door. He shrugged his shoulders, seemingly unfazed. But he still held his gun in his hand.

Massey smiled. "Put that gun away and join me for a drink, Fallon."

But Fallon didn't move, suspicious of Massey's intentions.

Massey chuckled. "Are you really scared of me? I'm a nerd, not a sharpshooter."

"How do I know you're not armed?"

"Do you see a gun?" Massey said as he raised his glass and showed his other empty hand.

Fallon studied Massey's smug look. "Why are you here?"

"I'll explain everything. Just put the gun away and have a seat."

"No!"

"Give me the gun," Daniel said.

Surprised, Fallon turned back to Daniel.

"I *said*, give me the gun!"

Fallon locked his eyes on Daniel. He didn't like the determined look on Daniel's face. "What's going on here?" He tried to get a read on Daniel. Was he serious?

"Better listen to Daniel," Massey said.

Fallon studied Daniel's face, trying to read his intent, gun pointed at Massey. Would Daniel actually shoot him if he didn't hand over his gun?

"Just give me the gun and take a seat, Fallon," Daniel said. "Massey will explain everything."

"I thought—"

"Sorry, Fallon, but I'm not giving you a choice here. Give me the gun and sit down."

Was this the terror cell Alicia talked about? Was Daniel part of the crime ring after all? Fallon felt foolish having trusted Daniel this far. And what role did Massey have in all of this?

"Have a seat," Massey said, pointing to an empty chair facing the couch.

Fallon looked at Daniel. "So if this was your plan, why did you take me to Detroit with you?"

"You're an experienced detective. I needed your help to get the hard drive."

"Are you working with Massey?"

"Sort of."

Fallon looked at Massey. "Who else is here with you?"

"No one."

Daniel pulled the drive from his pocket and tossed it to Massey.

"Good work," Massey said as he caught the drive and set it on the end table next to the couch.

"What are the two of you up to?" Fallon asked.

"Give Daniel the gun and sit down," Massey said.

"Before someone gets hurt," Daniel said.

"You shoot me, I shoot Massey."

"I don't believe you'd shoot an unarmed man," Daniel said.

That was true. Fallon tightened his grip on his gun. He could make a break for it and risk a gunfight with Daniel, but his instinct told him that he needed to know what was going on. He sighed. Reluctantly, he set his gun on the floor and shoved it toward Daniel with his foot. He sat in the chair across from Massey. "I'm listening."

Daniel slipped Fallon's gun into his coat pocket and sat on the couch next to Massey, his own gun in his lap.

Massey poured some whiskey into a snifter and handed it to Fallon.

Fallon took the snifter and examined the golden liquid as he swirled it in his glass. "And I suppose you spiked this with something to knock me out."

Massey laughed. "If you drink too much of it, yes, it will knock you out. But I wouldn't think of ruining a fine whiskey like this by adding some drug to it."

Fallon looked at the glass in his hand to cover the whirlwind of thoughts running through his mind. Why would Daniel "sort of" work for Massey? Daniel had told him that his old Air Force buddies had helped with Cally's escape. If that was true, why would he need Massey? The facts about the escape at the church ran through his mind. What had he missed? Clearly, he didn't know Daniel as he'd thought he did.

"Nothing like a fine whiskey," Massey said as he took a sip, leaned back, and looked at Daniel seated next to him. "Need a drink, Daniel?"

"No. We'll be flying soon," Daniel said, his expression stoic.

Fallon set the snifter on the table next to him.

"You're not going to take a drink?" Massey asked.

"Maybe later."

Massey chuckled as he looked at the snifter in his hand. "Your grandfather made a pretty good whiskey."

"How would you know?"

"I make it a point to know everything I can about people I work with."

Fallon leaned back in his chair. "I don't work for you."

"But you know I would like you to."

Fallon smiled. "I remember. You offered me a job a few months ago."

Daniel frowned at Fallon.

"Your loyalty to the governor impresses me," Massey said.

Daniel looked at Massey. "You offered him a job?"

"Oh, it was after one of my Archipelago software presentations to the governor's cabinet a few months ago. Fallon peppered me with probing questions. I like skeptics like him."

"Why do you have such an interest in me? I know nothing about software."

"Our grandfathers knew each other."

What! Fallon thought.

"My grandfather helped your grandfather with his whiskey operation on Beaver Island."

Fallon made no attempt to hide his surprise.

"Apparently you don't know much about your family history—about your grandfather's whiskey operation."

"All my dad ever said to me was that Granddad made whiskey on Beaver Island during Prohibition."

Massey took another sip of whiskey and set the snifter back on the end table. "In the 1920s, my grandfather was struggling to keep his farm—until he started providing grain for your grandfather's distillery. *Your* grandfather started making whiskey to save his faltering car company. They both did what they had to do to save their businesses."

The pieces were coming together. Fallon smiled. "You're the big donor who paid for the restoration of my grandfather's boat."

Massey nodded. "That's how they brought the grain to Beaver Island and whiskey back to the mainland. They don't make boats like that anymore. Fast, powerful, and beautiful. Your grandfather knew how to stay one step ahead."

"Ahead of the law," Fallon said.

"Maybe so, but he was a smart businessman. Both our fathers benefited from that whiskey operation. It made them wealthy, and that gave us opportunities we wouldn't have had without it."

"What's your point?" Fallon asked.

"I know a lot about you, but what do you know about me?"

"You started Quick Connect. You're the richest man in the world. And you're pretty full of yourself."

Massey laughed.

"And Quick Connect's Archipelago software is popular with state governments."

"Correction. The software is from the venture capital firm Arpa."

"What's the difference? It's still your thing."

"Quick Connect is *my* company. Arpa is the combined force of several tech entrepreneurs—a powerful force to reckon with. Together, we run the world with our technology. Our combined wealth is greater than most countries." Massey leaned forward and looked at Fallon with his beady eyes. "There's a lot you don't know, Fallon."

"Enlighten me."

"After Prohibition, my dad took over my grandfather's farm and provided high-quality grain to the new distilleries that opened. He loved his Massey tractor because it bore our name. Did you know he named me after the founder of Massey tractors, Henry Massey?"

"I'm sure it will be in your autobiography," Fallon said.

"Oh, so you know about the book I'm writing!"

"Lucky guess."

"And your name, Fallon. It's different. What's the story?"

"Apparently you didn't find *that* on the internet?"

"Ah, what's *not* on the internet is the most fascinating. What's your story?" Massey asked as he took another sip of whiskey.

"My uncle had a law firm in Detroit that he started with his friend whose last name was Fallon. It was called Fallon and McElliot. My father liked the sound of Fallon McElliot, so reluctantly my mom agreed to name me Fallon."

"Fascinating," Massey said. "I'm always interested in the story behind people's names."

Fallon sighed. "Let's stop the history lesson. Why are you here?"

"Always to the point, Fallon." Massey leaned back in his chair and crossed his legs. "The reason I'm here—the reason you're here, Fallon—goes back to our childhood. My father taught me to work hard, to be innovative, to overcome barriers that get in the way of being successful. Like your dad, my dad was embarrassed by what my grandfather did during Prohibition, but he still used the wealth it generated to benefit our family. Because of that, my dad was law-abiding like your dad—like you. But that's where we differ, Fallon. I think my grandfather had the right idea. Governments get in the way of business. In some ways you're the antithesis of me."

"I'm the government?" Fallon asked.

"You are part of a system that is a barrier to my success."

"But you're already successful despite the government."

"Maybe so, but the government is threatening my success with their regulations and inquiries into whether my business is too big."

"Enough of your babble." Fallon looked at the hard drive on the table next to Massey. "What do you plan to do with that drive?"

Massey chuckled. "You just can't turn it off, can you, Fallon? You're a detective at heart, always trying to get to the point. Tell him, Daniel."

Daniel leaned back on the couch. "When those fake posts appeared with my dad's name and address, I went to Massey to help me take them down."

"You've known Massey for a while," Fallon said.

Daniel nodded. "Massey was a client of the international security company I worked for, Peninsular."

"I've heard of that company. They do a lot of top-secret security for high-level executives." Fallon looked at Massey. "Like tech CEOs."

Massey nodded. "Daniel coordinated security for a lot of our Arpa meetings in Geneva. We became good friends."

Fallon looked at Daniel. "So that's what you did before you joined the FBI."

"Now you know," Daniel said. "I knew Massey could quickly take down those Quick Connect posts."

Fallon nodded. "Of course. Being the founder of Quick Connect."

"Wouldn't you do the same? Help a friend in trouble?"

"But Massey didn't just help me take down those posts, he helped me free Cally. Plus, he's going to help me take down Ferguson and everyone else connected to the crime ring that framed Cally."

"What's the catch?" Fallon asked.

"I agreed that, if we succeeded in freeing Cally and getting the hard drive, I would work for Massey."

"You're joining him at Quick Connect?"

"No," Massey said. "He's now my personal bodyguard."

"After all this, I can't go back to the FBI," Daniel said. "He agreed to hire me."

"I'll take care of Daniel," Massey said as he picked up the drive. "I'll make sure this evidence is spread all over the internet along with the surveillance video we have. It will be like my own WikiLeaks. Ferguson and every corrupt official working with him will go to prison."

"When that evidence goes public, Cally will be a free man," Daniel said.

"But you still helped Cally escape," Fallon said. "You could still be locked up for what you did at the church."

"No one saw my face at the church. I had a gas mask on. There's nothing that ties me to Cally's escape—maybe Al Kaline, but not me."

Fallon smiled. "That Kaline thing and the Trumbull address was clever. But if no one can connect you to the escape, then you could go back to the FBI."

"Let's just say the FBI knows things that aren't public," Daniel said. "I'm sure they know what I did even if they can't prove it."

"You're better off with me," Massey said.

Fallon rubbed his chin, thinking. "The videos you showed us," he said to Daniel. "They came from Massey and his Archipelago software, not FBI surveillance."

Daniel nodded.

"One of the add-ons to the Archipelago software is prison security management as well as video surveillance," Massey said. "It just happens to be tied to the video conference software. The contract company running the prison uses our software so it syncs with the State of Michigan computer system."

"And you used it to get access to Ferguson's video conference camera," Fallon said. "I don't recall you mentioning that in your presentation to the governor's staff."

Massey smiled. "My mistake."

Fallon's mind was racing, trying to figure out Massey's interest in Daniel, Cally, and the crime ring.

"Government has gotten in my way for too long," Massey said. "I'm tired of being hauled into Congress to be berated by senators and representatives. That's why a few tech entrepreneurs and I formed Arpa about ten years ago. It's our secret tool to fight back. We named it Arpa after the Defense Department project that started the internet in the 1960s. It's a new beginning for the internet."

"I take it this is more than a computer programming club," Fallon said.

Massey smiled. "Much more. We turned Arpa into a venture capital firm to fund software that would more efficiently operate governments. It was a way for us to combine the collective power of all us tech entrepreneurs—the power of our private fortunes and brain power." He stood and walked to the row of windows on the far wall with a view of the woods.

"Why are you telling me this?" Fallon asked.

Massey turned away from the windows and looked at Fallon. "Because you need to understand Arpa's mission—to make government dependent on our services." Massey walked back to the couch and sat down across from Fallon. "We want to prove to them the value of our innovation—to show them why they shouldn't get in our way."

Fallon laughed. "I don't think the government is getting the message. They sure aren't backing down on their scrutiny of tech companies."

"In time, they'll get it."

"But what if they don't?"

"Well, I'm planning a little beta test down the road in case they need further convincing."

"What sort of beta test?"

"Just a small demonstration of our ability to use force if necessary to get our way."

"I don't like the sound of that."

"Something to also show how inept our governor is at protecting the citizens of Michigan."

A picture sprang into Fallon's mind. "You're the terror cell!"

Daniel chuckled and looked at Massey.

Massey laughed. "Hardly. Rather, I would say there's a digital revolution coming and your analog state government is ill-equipped to stop it."

The gravity of what Massey was telling Fallon began to set in. "You . . ." He paused a moment. "You could hold the Michigan state government hostage with Archipelago!"

"No . . . at least not yet," Massey said. "First I'll win the governorship."

"You seem pretty confident of that."

"Quick Connect is the largest social media platform in the world. More than half of the planet uses it. It's pretty easy to control public opinion about me and my opponent."

"You mean the current governor, Karen Bauer."

"Your friend since childhood."

"So, your plan is to manipulate social media posts?"

"Only if necessary to help me win the election next year."

"Why does a tech billionaire like you want to mess with something as small-time as state government?" Fallon asked. "I would think you would want to be president of the United States."

Massey laughed. "The federal government is a bloated bureaucratic mess that just consumes resources. It's not worth my time. A state government like Michigan's is a much more manageable target. When I'm governor, I'll easily prove that tech leaders like me are much more effective at running government. It won't take long for me to win the hearts of the people, and before long every state in the nation will want us to run their state. After that, the people will beg Arpa to run the federal government. When that happens, we'll subpoena the leaders of Congress and force them to acknowledge, in their testimony before our committees, how inept they were in running the government."

"Again—why are you telling me this? I can report you to the state police or the feds."

"Do you think they would believe you? It would be your word against mine, and of course I would deny anything you tell them. They'll accuse you of believing all those conspiracy websites—websites I helped generate, by the way. What better way to make something less credible than to paint it as a conspiracy theory from the first time people hear about it."

Fallon played through his mind several options for blowing the whistle. Regrettably, he was forced to concede Massey was right. No one would believe him, except . . . He recalled Karen taking him up inside the capitol dome to tell him about Brogan. She said something about being concerned with surveillance. Why? He glared at Massey. "I find it reprehensible that you would use force."

"I don't think it will come to that, but . . ." Massey leaned back in his chair and took another sip of whiskey. "But that is a nice segue. I think you're aware that the world's largest online retailer, Caspian, is in the process of rolling out a massive fleet of commercial drones for deliveries. They've been flying test drones in Detroit. Drones are great for instant delivery of most anything like shoes, food or . . ." He paused as if waiting for Fallon to provide the word, but Fallon was in no mood to play games.

"Or what?"

"Let's just say something more damaging."

Fallon's heartbeat sped up. "Like a bomb?"

"Possibly."

"As I said—you're nothing but a terrorist."

"I prefer to think of us as revolutionaries."

"It's all the same," Fallon said. He was growing nauseated. "You're going to use the Caspian drone!"

"Good detective work, Fallon," Massey said. "You're catching on."

Fallon looked at Daniel. "When you asked Massey to help your family, did you know about all of this?"

"Not until I approached Massey about taking down those posts. That's when he filled me in on the bigger scheme and offered to help me free Cally."

"You knew about this and you didn't tell the FBI or the CIA?"

"It's pretty simple, Fallon." Daniel leaned forward. "They would've told the FBI I helped Cally escape and tied me to the crime ring."

"Massey threatened you into working for him?"

"No, not at all. Massey cares about my family."

"Which brings me to another topic," Massey said. "We have a loose end. Where is Daniel's dad and Cally?"

"What makes you think I know?" Fallon asked.

"When I arrived here, the cabin was empty," Massey said. "The plan was for Cally and Robert Callahan to leave Beaver Island with us."

"I don't know," Fallon said. "That's the honest truth. We left them here when we went to Detroit to get the backup drive."

"I don't believe you," Massey said.

"Ask Daniel."

Massey turned to Daniel, who shook his head. "I don't have any idea either. I left my dad and Cally here with Fallon's partner."

Massey looked surprised. "You had a partner with you, Fallon?"

"A woman," Daniel said.

Massey gave Fallon a skeptical look. "Who is this woman?"

"Your research wasn't as good as you thought," Fallon said with a smirk.

"Her name is Alicia Chalmers," Daniel said.

"I don't believe Fallon is telling the truth," Massey said. He pulled out his phone and typed something. "Let's see what the internet has to say about her."

They waited as Massey's requested information loaded.

"Says here there's an Alicia Chalmers with Homeland Security, Transportation Security Administration," he said.

"So, they sent her here to investigate the terror cell!" Daniel exclaimed.

Fallon nodded.

"So where did Alicia take Daniel's dad and Cally?" Massey asked.

"I told you, I don't know."

"I'm a pretty patient man, but I'm starting to lose that patience," Massey said, walking closer and standing over Fallon.

Fallon remained seated and looked up at Massey. He looked a bit overweight and out of shape. "And what are you going to do about it?"

"Don't listen to him," Daniel said to Massey as he stood up.

Fallon smiled at Massey. "You're just a harmless nerd. A geek."

Massey leaned in and grabbed him by the collar.

Just the response Fallon had been hoping for. He promptly kicked Massey in the groin.

Massey immediately crumpled in pain. As he fell backward, he tumbled against Daniel. They both fell to the floor, knocking the gun out of Daniel's hand. Fallon grabbed the gun as it hit the floor. Daniel quickly wrestled himself free of Massey and lunged for the gun, but Fallon fired the gun at the floor. Daniel stopped, crouched on his hands and knees as he looked up at Fallon while Massey moaned on the floor next to him, swearing.

"The next shot takes out your knee," Fallon said. "I'll keep shooting higher if I need to. Now, give me my gun. Slowly."

Daniel sat up on the floor, gently pulled Fallon's gun from his pocket, and tossed it at his feet.

Keeping his eyes on Daniel, Fallon crouched, picked up his gun, and slipped it back into his side holster while keeping the other gun pointed at Daniel. "Why would you align yourself with someone as shifty as Massey?"

"I did what I had to do," Daniel said.

"Now I have to hand you both over to the police." Daniel and Fallon locked eyes.

"There's two of us, Fallon," Daniel said. "And one of you. Think you can take us?"

"I'll wound you if I have to," Fallon said, trying to convince himself. Could he really shoot Daniel, a longtime friend, even if he had broken the law?

"You're wasting time, Fallon," Massey groaned. He winced as he tried to stand upright. "A lot of people are about to get hurt if you don't act soon." He looked at his watch. "Soon the *Emerald Isle* will be boarding passengers."

Suddenly Fallon heard what sounded like a giant mosquito outside the cabin, but loud enough to hurt his ears. "What's that?"

Massey smiled as he straightened. "That's our drone. With a special delivery for the *Emerald Isle*."

CHAPTER 27

Massey winced and bent over again, hands on his hips. "You have a choice, Fallon."

"There's only one choice," Fallon said, keeping the gun pointed in their direction. "I'm taking you both to the police."

"The *Emerald Isle* will be boarding in a few minutes," Massey said. "Then it will depart for Charlevoix. When it clears the harbor and enters the open water of Lake Michigan, the drone you hear hovering outside will deliver its payload to the boat."

Fallon studied Massey's face. "You're serious."

Massey gave Fallon a smug look. "That drone is carrying explosives. It's preprogrammed to rendezvous with the *Emerald Isle*."

"None of this makes sense. Why would you kill innocent people?"

"We're not going to kill anyone."

What did that mean? Was the drone unarmed—simply a demonstration of the potential threat? Something to discredit the governor by showing her inability to prevent terror plots?

Massey smiled. "I was just waiting for you to show up here with Daniel. It's been my plan all along to have you stop the drone before it reaches the *Emerald Isle*."

"Is this a bluff?"

"How well do you know my poker face?"

Fallon studied Massey's facial expressions. He was usually able to read people's real intent, but Massey had such an aura of confidence about him that it was hard to tell if it was just arrogance or if the drone actually had a bomb on it.

"It's a simple choice, Fallon," Massey said. "We can keep talking here, or you can go save the lives of the people on that ferry."

Fallon glared at Massey. "You act like this is some sort of game."

"It is. A high-stakes poker game. How much are you willing to bet that I'm bluffing? There are children on that boat." Massey looked at his watch. "You don't have much time left."

The buzzing sound grew louder.

Fallon looked at Daniel. "Daniel, do something!"

Daniel shook his head.

"Stop this insanity!" Fallon pleaded.

Fallon and Daniel locked eyes.

Massey smiled as he hobbled to the end table by the couch, grabbed the hard drive, and slipped it inside his blazer. "Don't listen to him, Daniel." He turned and limped back to Daniel.

Fallon kept the gun pointed at Massey. "Are you willing to bet your life that I won't shoot?"

"You wouldn't shoot an innocent man," Massey said.

"Innocent?"

"Of course. Unless you've been recording this entire conversation, you have no evidence that I've committed any crime."

Fallon desperately searched his mind, but it was true. There was no evidence tying Massey to anything.

"Come on, Daniel, let's go," Massey said.

"Sorry, Fallon," Daniel said. He turned to follow Massey.

Fallon fired a shot at the floor in front of them.

Massey and Daniel both jumped and looked down at a brand-new bullet hole in the floor.

The buzzing drone outside now sounded like it was over the roof of the cabin.

"You know what you need to do," Massey said, looking at Fallon.

"Think about what you're doing, Daniel!" Fallon said. "The feds will have no problem pinning this attack on you and Massey. They'll hunt you down."

"Actually, none of this will be connected to me or Massey," Daniel said.

Fallon frowned, confused.

Daniel continued, "All of this will be pinned on Ferguson."

Fallon shook his head. "What do you mean?"

"It's really a perfect plan," Massey said. "Ferguson will be framed as the mastermind of the attack. It will appear that his crime ring is not only funding terrorism but also carrying out domestic attacks."

"But . . ."

Daniel smiled. "Ferguson isn't just going to prison for drug dealing and corruption. He'll be convicted of domestic terrorism."

"How?" Fallon asked, incredulous.

"We've already created a digital footprint with his fingerprints on everything," Massey said. "He's the perfect cover we need for our drone beta test. All the evidence from this attack will point to Ferguson stealing Caspian's commercial drone from Detroit and using it for a terrorist attack on the *Emerald Isle*. The explosives we're using will trace back to Ferguson. We even have video footage showing him loading the drone into a van."

"I'll get my revenge on Ferguson for coming after my family," Daniel said.

"How is that possible? Ferguson didn't steal the drone."

"Anything is possible in the digital era," Daniel said.

"We even planted some phony chatter on the internet about this attack using terrorist signatures," Massey said. "We knew Homeland Security would pick it up and look into it—that they would send someone like Alicia Chalmers to look into it, and that the governor would likely send you to investigate."

"The chatter . . . that's you?" Fallon asked.

Massey nodded.

"The hard drive we now have will take down the rest of the crime ring," Daniel said. "Everyone involved from the Detroit Police and the state to their suppliers," Daniel said. "We're going to right the wrong done to Cally."

"The terrorist attack on the *Emerald Isle* will make Governor Bauer look incapable of protecting the citizens of Michigan—just a few months before I announce I'm running for governor," Massey said. "It's a really nice package all wrapped up with a pretty bow."

"Even if that happens, you're seriously underestimating the governor's political skills."

"But you're biased, Fallon," Massey said. "Of course, you would say that. She's your friend."

"I ask again—why are you telling me all of this?"

"Sometimes the best way to discredit a story is to put it out in the open," Massey said. "Plus, when you couple it with the conspiracy theories I've planted on the internet about big tech companies wanting to take over the world . . . well, nothing you say will be believable. You'll just sound like you're agreeing with the conspiracy theorists."

Still looking for flaws in Massey's plan, Fallon said, "But this is your cabin, Daniel. They'll trace the drone back here. You'll be a suspect."

Daniel shook his head. "It's not my cabin, Fallon. This cabin is now owned by Ferguson."

Confused again, Fallon said, "County Clerk records show that you've owned this cabin for years."

Massey smiled. "Not any more. Our Archipelago software manages the county clerk offices for Charlevoix County and hundreds of other counties across the country."

Fallon's anger grew as he looked at Massey's smug face. Every hole he tried to punch in Massey's plan—every effort he made to convince Daniel not to go with Massey—Massey had already outmaneuvered him. It seemed Massey had indeed made the perfect plan.

"You know what you have to do, Fallon," Massey said. "Come on, Daniel."

Fallon stood silent, with the gun pointed at Massey and Daniel as they walked to the front door and opened it. The buzzing sound grew louder.

"What about Cally and your dad . . . your family?" Fallon asked as he lowered the gun. "You said you wouldn't leave without them."

"Unfortunately, we have to leave now," Massey said.

"I'm sure you and Alicia will see to it they're okay," Daniel said.

Fallon and Daniel looked at each other for a second, then Massey said, "Let's get to your plane and get out of here." He stepped through the door.

Daniel followed Massey out the door and down the front porch steps.

Massey stopped on the driveway and looked back at Fallon. "Oh—feel free to use my Jeep parked in front of the garage. The keys are in it. And I left you a present on the passenger seat, something to help you."

"Gee, thanks," Fallon said.

"We want you to at least have a fighting chance," Massey said. "And no use trying to warn the captain of the ferry or anyone else. All radio and cell coverage in and around St. James will be jammed until the *Emerald Isle* clears St. James Harbor."

Daniel turned and continued to the end of the driveway, with Massey following. They crossed the gravel road, heading for the seaplane moored on the other side of the peninsula. Twigs snapped and leaves rustled as they stepped into the underbrush. Fallon walked through the open doorway, down the porch steps, and to the end of the driveway. He looked up toward the buzzing sound and spotted a large drone hovering above the cabin.

"Daniel!" Fallon called.

Daniel stopped, head still visible above the brush, and turned to look at Fallon. "Good luck!" Daniel said with a wink, then continued toward the seaplane with Massey in tow.

Fallon wasn't sure what Daniel meant by the wink. It was as if he was telling him to play along with a joke, but nothing seemed funny about the situation. The buzzing sound intensified. Fallon looked at the drone. It tilted and moved out of sight. No time to waste—he raced to the back of the cabin and the dock, just in time to see the drone hovering over the lake for a moment. He aimed his gun at it—and fired just as it tilted and zipped toward St. James, flying barely above the treetops. A moment later he heard the seaplane start.

Fallon swore as he ran to Massey's Jeep and climbed in. He found the keys in the ignition and started the engine. Next to him on the floor, propped against the passenger seat, he saw the present Massey left him—an automatic rifle with a large note taped to it: "Good Luck!"

"That should help," Fallon said. He punched the accelerator and tore out of the driveway, throwing gravel. He left a giant cloud of dust in his wake as he raced toward St. James. How could he stop the *Emerald Isle* if it had already left the dock? Would he try to shoot down the drone from the dock as it pursued the ferry?

Then he remembered his grandfather's Chris-Craft docked in the harbor—and something Massey had said to him: "They don't make boats like that anymore. Fast, powerful, and beautiful."

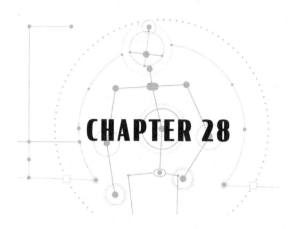

CHAPTER 28

C ally saw the coastline of Beaver Island below through the window
of the plane. The engine sputtered again and the plane vibrated.

"Do you see the airport?" he asked Alicia, at the controls of the
plane.

She pointed as the plane began to bank. "Just ahead!"

Cally heard a phone ringing. Alicia pulled hers from her pocket and
handed it to Cally. "See who it is."

"It's Fallon," Cally said a few seconds later, and put it on speaker.

"Alicia! Where are you?"

"Almost to Beaver Island Airport," Alicia said.

"What?" Fallon said. "No! You need to—"

Cally cut in. "Did you get the hard drive?"

"We did," Fallon said.

Cally felt a flash of relief. The truth would finally come out. "Is
Daniel with you?"

"No."

"Where is he?"

"I can't explain now. We have something far more pressing—"

"Where is Daniel?" Mr. Callahan shouted from the back seat.

"We don't have time for—"

"Why isn't Daniel with you?" Cally asked.

"Just listen! Don't land at Beaver Island Airport. You need to meet me at Welke Airport."

The engine sputtered again.

"I don't think I can," Alicia said.

"That's too far away," Fallon said. "You need to meet me at Welke."

"Where are you?" Alicia asked.

"I'm on King's Highway approaching St. James," Fallon said.

Alicia glanced at the gauges.

Outside Cally's window, the Beaver Island Airport came into view. "We won't make it to Welke," Cally said.

"Find a way. We need to stop the *Emerald Isle* from leaving the harbor!" Fallon exclaimed.

"What? Why?" Alicia responded.

"It's the target for a terrorist attack. Meet me at Welke," Fallon said. "If I drive all the way to Beaver Island Airport to pick you up, we'll be too late."

Alicia's eyes were focused on the landscape ahead. She moved the throttle and the plane sputtered again, then jerked from a sudden burst of acceleration. Cally looked at the airport passing below them.

"Don't say a word," Alicia said, hands tightly gripping the yoke.

"What's going on?" Fallon asked.

"No time to explain," Alicia said. "I need to focus."

"We have engine trouble," Cally said, craning his neck. He spotted Welke Airport ahead. A second later the engine sputtered. He felt the plane lose altitude. "Alicia—"

"Are you in trouble?" Fallon asked nervously.

"Mayday! Mayday! Mayday!" Alicia shouted. "Cessna five, five, seven. Emergency landing at Welke."

Cally looked out his window at the treetops getting closer. "I don't think we'll make it to—"

"I see you!" Fallon shouted. "Put her down on King's Highway."

The wide, two-lane road was just ahead as the plane tilted to line up its landing. They buzzed a Jeep heading north.

"You just flew over me," Fallon said. "You got this, Alicia."

The engine quit. Wind passing by the wings and cockpit was the only audible sound. Cally looked back—his dad's head was bowed and eyes closed; his hands were clasped together. The smell of burnt oil began to fill the cockpit.

"Dad?" Cally asked.

His dad opened his eyes and looked at Cally. "Pray, Cally." Then he closed his eyes again.

Cally looked out the side window just as the plane dropped below the treetops. Ahead, a car approached them on the road.

"Please, Lord," Cally heard himself saying as the plane shuddered, then touched down. The car veered off the road just in time to let them pass. They coasted down the road until Alicia could maneuver the plane onto an area of grass between the end of the runway at Welke Airport and King's Highway. "Nice landing!" Fallon exclaimed, approvingly. "I'm almost there."

The phone disconnected and Cally handed the phone to Alicia.

Alicia sat frozen in her seat, hands still gripping the controls, staring out the windshield. She looked at Cally, smiled, then took off her headphones and took the phone from Cally. "Are you okay?"

Cally nodded and unbuckled his seat belt. He turned—his dad looked pale and tired. "You okay, Dad?"

"I didn't think we would clear those trees," he said.

Alicia was flipping switches on the instrument panel. "Now what?" Cally asked.

"Let's get out of here." She opened the door and jumped out.

Cally climbed out, flipped the seat forward, and helped his dad out of the plane. They joined Alicia, standing at the front of the plane watching smoke rise from the vents in the engine cowling. The side of the plane was streaked with oil now dripping onto the grass.

Cally heard a siren and looked up. A fire truck pulled out of a building on the far end of the runway and headed toward them with lights flashing. A car with flashing lights followed the fire truck.

Cally turned to see Fallon running toward them, Jeep parked behind the plane.

"That was some landing," Fallon said.

The fire truck roared to a stop next to the plane as firefighters jumped out. "Is everyone okay?" a woman in firefighting gear asked.

"We need to go, Alicia," Fallon said, tugging at Alicia's arm.

"What happened?" another firefighter asked. Two other firefighters walked to the front of the plane and carefully opened the engine cowling. A cloud of white smoke rose.

"Engine trouble," Alicia said.

Cally hoped they wouldn't see the bullet holes in the side of the plane.

"You're lucky," the firefighter said.

"I'd say my prayers were answered," Mr. Callahan said.

"We need to leave right now," Fallon said.

"You're going to have to stay here," a firefighter said.

"This is urgent police business," Fallon said, flashing his state police ID. "We'll come back later to file all the paperwork."

Cally saw a firefighter examine the bullet holes in the plane. He felt someone tug his arm.

"Let's go, Cally," Fallon said.

They all climbed into the Jeep.

Cally had barely closed the Jeep's back door when he was thrown against the back of the seat as the Jeep accelerated back onto the road. He was surprised when he saw Alicia hold up a rifle.

"What's this?" Alicia asked.

"We may need it," Fallon replied.

Alicia looked at Fallon, then the rifle.

"What's going on?" Cally asked.

"The *Emerald Isle* is in danger," Fallon said.

"Terrorists?" Alicia asked.

Fallon nodded.

Suddenly Cally felt sick. "Where is Daniel?"

"I'll explain everything," Fallon said, "but right now, we need to focus on stopping the ferry."

"Did you try to contact the ferry office?" Alicia asked urgently.

"I couldn't get through," Fallon replied.

"Did you call the sheriff?"

"I did. He said he knows you. He's on the other side of the island, so we'll likely beat him to the docks."

"What if we can't stop the ferry?"

"If it leaves before we get there, we'll have to chase it."

"With what?"

Cally saw Fallon turn and smile at Alicia.

A moment later they were in the tiny town speeding toward the ferry dock—just in time to hear a loud boat whistle. The ferry was leaving the dock.

Fallon shouted an expletive.

Alicia pulled out her phone. "We have to warn them." She paused a moment, then said, "That's strange. I have zero bars."

"That's what I've had for several minutes," Fallon said. "Cell service seems to be out near town."

The *Emerald Isle* whistle blew again as they raced past the ferry dock to the marina next door. The Jeep screeched to a halt in the marina parking lot. As they climbed out, Cally spotted the ferry boat moving slowly away from the dock.

"We can run to the ferry dock and tell the workers!" Mr. Callahan said, standing beside Cally in the parking lot.

Fallon shook his head. "By the time they respond, it'll be too late." Then he surprised them all by telling Alicia, "Grab the rifle."

"Why do you need the rifle?" Cally asked, wide-eyed.

"You stay here with your dad," Fallon said.

"But—"

"Come on, Alicia!" Fallon called, running now toward a wooden boat docked in the first slip of the marina.

Alicia grabbed the rifle and ran after him.

Cally felt helpless watching the two of them hop into the wooden boat. The sound of the *Emerald Isle*'s engines grew fainter as the ferry boat powered away from the docks, creating a large wake in the calm water of the harbor. Why wasn't Daniel here helping Fallon stop the terrorists? Where was he? He squinted at the morning sun reflecting on the water, glistening on the waves. He looked at the top deck of the ferry where passengers lined the rear rail on the top deck, waving as they departed the island.

"Look at all the people on the ferry," Mr. Callahan said. "If there's a bomb on board . . ."

A police car pulled up next to them. The sheriff jumped out, stood next to Cally and Mr. Callahan, and pointed at Fallon and Alicia in the Chris-Craft. "Is that them?" he asked Cally.

Cally nodded.

The sheriff swore and ran toward the marina docks with his phone to his ear. Cally wished Daniel was with him now. Whatever Daniel's absence meant, it wasn't good.

"I pray they make it in time," Mr. Callahan said.

CHAPTER 29

F allon grabbed the keys hidden underneath the cushion and started his grandfather's boat. "Hang on!" He shouted as he hit the throttle.

"No kidding!" Alicia replied as the boat powered out of the boat slip.

The sound of the V8 engine at full throttle, the feel of the wheel in his hand, the way the boat glided over the calm water in the harbor— he felt reassured riding again in his grandfather's fully restored Chris-Craft. Ahead, the *Emerald Isle* was barely visible through the thin morning haze drifting across the water. Fallon glanced back at the disappearing marina and saw the sheriff's boat pull out in pursuit with flashers going.

"Looks like the sheriff is joining us!" Alicia exclaimed.

"He won't be able to keep up with us with that boat," Fallon said. He stood now behind the wheel, eyes fixed on the *Emerald Isle* as it cleared the harbor and sped up in the open water of Lake Michigan toward Charlevoix. He squinted at the sun rising higher in the eastern sky, wishing he had brought his sunglasses.

He pressed the throttle again to make sure they were going full speed as they skimmed over the harbor's glassy water. One hand clamped to the steering wheel, he blocked the sunlight glaring off the water with his other hand. He could see the silhouette of the ferry and the churning water behind it as it picked up speed.

"The sheriff is falling further behind us!" Alicia noted.

Fallon nodded. "We're on our own. Watch for a drone. It should be here soon."

Alicia looked surprised. "How do—"

"Shoot it out of the sky when you see it!"

Alicia nodded and clutched the rifle.

The red phone in Fallon's pocket buzzed. He opened the flip phone with one hand while keeping his other hand on the steering wheel.

"Fallon! I need an update," Karen said.

"Can't talk now, Karen. Got to go."

"Fallon! Where are—"

"You'll get an update soon."

Fallon closed the flip phone and slipped it back into his pocket. It buzzed again, but he ignored it and checked the position of the throttle one more time.

"Come on, baby," Fallon said. An arch of water sprayed out on each side of the bow. He glanced up to his right at the clear, blue southern sky, looking for the drone. "Do you see anything?" Fallon asked, shouting over the sound of the roaring engine.

"There!" Alicia exclaimed. "Coming out of the south."

Now Fallon saw a small black dot in the sky, quickly approaching.

Alicia braced herself in her seat with her legs and snugged the rifle into position. She used it to track the approaching drone.

"You know how to use that?" Fallon asked.

Alicia glared at him. "Of course!"

"How's your aim?"

"I always beat you in skeet shooting."

Fallon smiled. "That's why I'm driving."

They were closing the gap on the *Emerald Isle* now. He heard a buzzing sound faintly over the roar of the engine, first distant, then louder. He whipped his gaze skyward, searching for the drone.

"There!" Alicia announced. "Directly south of the *Emerald Isle!*"

Fallon looked to his right and saw a large black object zipping along about fifty feet above the open water. It was identical to the drone he'd seen disappear over the treetops at Daniel's cabin. He eased the throttle a bit as they approached the stern of the *Emerald Isle*, relieved that they'd caught up with it. He pulled alongside the ferry at a safe distance and then matched the bigger boat's speed. The ferry towered above them, intrigued passengers lining the railing along the two levels. He looked at the approaching drone, now clearly audible above the sound of the boat engines, then glanced at Alicia bracing herself against the seat with the rifle pointed skyward.

He heard screaming above him. He glanced up at the *Emerald Isle* and saw that the passengers were disappearing from along the railing. There was the captain, next to the pilothouse toward the front of the ferry. The captain looked at him, then the sky. Fallon followed the captain's gaze and spotted the drone quickly closing in on the ferry. "Incoming!" he shouted.

"In my sights!" Alicia responded.

Fallon glanced at the few curious passengers still lining the railing. He gripped the steering wheel with one hand, keeping his boat near the side of the ferry while waving his other hand at the passengers, trying to get them to move away. Some people waved back at him; others pointed their phones. Suddenly Fallon heard the repeated firing of an automatic weapon. Instinctively, he crouched. Then he heard screams. The passengers along the railing scurried back and dropped to the deck. He turned—Alicia was still pointing the gun skyward. The drone was hovering almost directly above them. It wobbled for a moment as if to shake off the gunfire. The drone began to gradually fall behind the two boats, and Fallon felt a tinge of relief as he watched the drone continue to wobble. Then he saw the drone begin to speed up again, and close the gap. Fallon swore and looked at Alicia. "Get it!"

She mumbled under her breath and fired again.

Fallon clenched his teeth and waved again at the few passengers still standing along the railing, phones pointed at them, filming the unfolding events. He couldn't believe they were still standing there as the drone closed in on the ferry. It all seemed surreal to him. The sound of Alicia's automatic weapon fire echoed off the water and the side of the *Emerald Isle*'s metal hull. Fallon looked behind them; the drone sputtered and shook as it approached the ferry. Suddenly it jerked sideways, then buzzed overhead and raced out over Lake Michigan ahead of them as if to circle for another approach. A moment later, a small stream of smoke began to spew out of the drone as it circled and headed straight for them.

Unsure of the drone's next move, Fallon kept the boat on a collision course with it as it descended and closed in on them. "Now or never!" he yelled at Alicia.

Alicia swore and fired again.

A few pieces flew off the drone as it was struck by bullets, but it continued to fly.

"It must be armor-plated!" Alicia called.

The drone was close enough now that Fallon could see the Caspian logo imprinted on its front. An odd thought came to Fallon: Was the drone really loaded with explosives? Or was Massey merely testing Fallon's ability to stop him? Maybe Fallon had been the real target all along. Could Massey have planted a homing device on his granddad's boat?

Fallon jerked the steering wheel hard right and jammed the throttle lever all the way forward, hoping to outrun the drone. As he gripped the steering wheel, leaning into the turn, he heard something hit the floor. Alicia was down, holding on to the seat, and the rifle was sliding toward the back of the boat. He looked back—the drone was making a wide turn to pursue them. Within seconds, it was so close, and accelerating so quickly, that there was no way they could evade it.

"Jump, Alicia! Jump!" he shouted.

She looked at him, and then they both looked at the drone, nearly on top of their speeding boat. She pulled herself up and grabbed Fallon's arm. "Come on!"

"Go! I'm right behind you!"

She jumped into the water. He cranked the steering wheel hard left, then realized he was now circling back toward the *Emerald Isle*. The buzzing from the drone now was deafening. He was out of time. He jumped overboard.

The cold water shocked his body. Because of the speed at which he'd been traveling, at first he tumbled across the surface of the water. Then he swam deeper and deeper, as hard as he could. Above he heard the muffled sound of boat propellers. A bright flash of light illuminated the water above him, followed by a deafening noise and a shock wave that engulfed his body. As he churned helplessly in the water, he cursed Massey. Suddenly he felt excruciating pain in his leg, then his side. Something hard slammed into his head. Everything went black.

CHAPTER 30

Thoughts swirled in Cally's head as he stood by the empty slip in the marina from which Fallon and Alicia had sped away more than an hour ago in the wooden boat. Across the small harbor, at the empty ferry dock a few hundred yards away, a crowd of emergency workers stood beside vehicles with flashing red and blue lights. Where were Alicia and Fallon? Were they safe? Why wasn't Daniel here? He stood alone, squinting against the sun glistening off the water as he watched a large boat crowded with emergency workers power out of the harbor. The boat passed the lighthouse and headed toward the spot in the open water of Lake Michigan where Cally had seen the explosion.

He turned and walked along the empty slip to rejoin his dad, still sitting on a bench by the marina office. He pressed his way through the crowd of people gathered in the marina parking lot since the explosion. The Jeep Fallon had driven was still parked where he left it. Cally felt self-conscious as he pushed past people, hoping no one would recognize him. He could feel their eyes on him. He spotted his dad and sat next to him on the bench. His dad's face was pale and his body slumped with his head in his hands and elbows on his knees. "How you doing, Dad?"

His dad turned his head slightly to look at him. "Okay, I guess. Any word on Fallon and Alicia?"

"No."

Mr. Callahan rubbed his forehead as he eyed the gathered crowd, then looked at Cally. "We have nothing to prove you're innocent."

"Shhh," Cally said as he glanced at the crowd of people. He made eye contact with a man staring at them, then quickly turned to look at his dad. "You believe I'm innocent?"

"I saw the videos, but we don't have a copy. We have no proof."

Cally felt sick inside.

"You're still wanted."

Cally nodded and dipped his head. He stared at the ground. Why had Daniel abandoned them? Without the hard drive or Daniel's videos, he would go back to prison.

They sat in silence. His dad gradually slumped further down.

"How are you feeling, Dad?" Cally asked, gently.

His dad glared at him. "I'm fine!"

Cally tried to stifle his anger. For all they had been through in the past twenty-four hours, he still couldn't relate to his dad. He still felt distant from him, yet for some reason he felt concern. "Suit yourself."

A plane buzzed overhead. Cally looked up, expecting to see the red seaplane, but it was only a small white plane.

"Where's Daniel?" his dad asked again as he too looked up to check the plane.

"I wish I knew."

They looked at each other for a moment, then Mr. Callahan rested his head on his hands again and closed his eyes.

"I'm going into the marina office to see if they have some aspirin for you," Cally said as he stood up.

His dad nodded.

Cally pushed his way past several people huddled in front of the marina office and went inside. "Do you have aspirin?" he said to a man standing behind the counter.

The man looked at him for a moment. "Weren't you with those two who took the museum boat?"

"No."

"You sure look like him."

"I don't know what you're talking about. Look, my dad's sitting on the bench just outside the door with a pounding headache. Do you have some aspirin?"

The man glanced out the window, then looked at Cally. "Sure." He reached under the counter and handed Cally a small packet with two aspirin. He continued to eye Cally.

"Thanks. Something wrong?" Cally asked as he slipped the aspirin into his shirt pocket.

The man shook his head. "Hey, let me give you two some coffee."

"What do I owe you?"

"Nothing," the man said. A moment later, he set two cups of coffee on the counter with two granola bars.

Cally thanked the man and returned to his dad on the bench. Mr. Callahan promptly washed the aspirin down with coffee.

"I guess we missed breakfast," Mr. Callahan said. He opened the granola bar and took a bite.

As Cally sipped his coffee and ate his granola bar, he listened to the commotion around them. "I saw on Quick Connect that someone bombed the *Emerald Isle*," he heard someone say.

Cally tried not to make eye contact with anyone. He looked at the ground—until he heard an approaching boat and looked toward the harbor.

"Maybe it's them," Cally said. He set his coffee cup on the bench and stood. He craned his head to look over the growing crowd of people and spotted the sheriff's boat motoring toward the empty slip from which Fallon and Alicia had left. A woman, wrapped in a blanket, was sitting in the back of the boat.

"Stay here," Cally said. "I'm going to get a closer look."

He pushed his way through the crowd toward the docks. A deputy standing at the entrance to the docks held up a hand, palm out. "No one is allowed in here," he said.

Cally could now see Alicia standing in the back of the boat, looking down at something. "But that's my friend on the sheriff's boat."

"You'll have to wait here," the deputy said.

Then Cally heard the sound of helicopter rotors beating the air. He looked up and saw a medevac helicopter descend over the marina. Deputies pushed the crowd back, clearing a large area on a lawn next to the parking lot. The medevac touched down a moment later. Two paramedics jumped out with a stretcher and hurried to the dock and the sheriff's boat. Cally tensed as he watched the sheriff help Alicia step out of the boat with a blanket wrapped around her. Her hair was wet. One paramedic talked to her as the other paramedic and the sheriff lowered the stretcher into the boat. A moment later they hoisted the stretcher onto the dock. Someone was lying on the stretcher covered with a blanket as they wheeled it down the dock toward where he stood.

"Is that Alicia?" Cally heard his dad ask.

"I told you to stay on the bench," Cally said.

The paramedics wheeled the stretcher off the dock toward the chopper. Cally felt himself go cold when he recognized Fallon's bloody face. A hush fell over the crowd.

When Alicia limped off the dock, guided by the paramedic, Cally called, "Alicia!"

The deputy held him back. "Please, step back."

Alicia stopped and looked up at Cally with a dazed look.

The sheriff walking next to Alicia stopped and studied Cally, then said to Alicia, "You know them?"

She nodded.

"We need to get these two to the hospital," the sheriff told Cally. "Wait here. I'd like to talk to you."

The sheriff and the paramedic guided Alicia unsteadily to the medevac. They loaded Fallon's stretcher into the helicopter as the blades continued to spin. He shouted after Alicia, "How's Fallon?"

She stopped and looked back, then shook her head. Tears filled his eyes as he watched the sheriff help her climb inside.

"He looked horrible," Mr. Callahan said.

Cally took a couple steps toward the helicopter. The sheriff closed the door and stepped away from the helicopter. They all watched it rise into the air and fly toward Charlevoix.

"Daniel must have flown Fallon back to the island," Mr. Callahan said. "So maybe he's still on the island somewhere."

Cally shrugged. He watched the helicopter disappear from sight, then turned to his dad. "How's your headache?"

"The aspirin is helping," Mr. Callahan said, but his eyes were focused on something behind Cally.

Cally turned and saw the sheriff walking toward them.

"What if he's recognized you?" his dad asked.

In his concern for his dad, Fallon, and Alicia, Cally had forgotten for a moment that he remained a fugitive. His stomach tightened. He had no hard drive to prove his innocence, no videos. No idea where Daniel was. The sheriff was still halfway across the parking lot. There was still time to run. He started to slowly move away from his dad, trying to seem casual.

"Stop, Cally," Mr. Callahan said.

Cally stopped.

"Everything will be okay."

"How do you know?"

"Have some faith."

"Easy for you to say."

"Trust me."

Cally turned and started once again to walk away, but something inside of him caused him to stop. He was tired—tired of running. He wasn't sure anymore what he was running from. Anyway, the sheriff was nearly there.

"I'd like to chat with you two," the sheriff said. He looked at the crowd around them. "Ride with me back to my office. We can talk privately."

Cally nodded and took hold of his dad's arm to help him. Their eyes met for a moment, then they followed the sheriff to his patrol car. The sheriff opened the car door and Cally helped his dad sit in the front seat. The sheriff closed the door and opened the back door. Cally took a deep breath and climbed inside. The door slammed shut, jolting him and reminding him of all the other times he'd been arrested. The feeling of freedom he'd felt over the past few days slipped away.

A few minutes later they parked at the sheriff's office just outside of town. The cruiser's back door opened. Cally and his dad stepped out and followed the sheriff to a simple one-story building that looked like a ranch-style house. A sign mounted to the siding on the front read "Charlevoix County Sheriff." They went inside and followed the sheriff to an office at the end of the hallway.

"Have a seat," the sheriff said as he pointed to two chairs facing the front of a cluttered desk. He closed the door.

The chairs creaked as Cally and his dad sat down. Overhead, a fluorescent light hummed. A picture on the wall behind the sheriff's chair caught Cally's attention. It looked like a family picture with the sheriff sitting in the middle of a group of people, older and younger. The woman on the end looked a lot like Alicia, only younger. He remembered Fallon saying that the sheriff knew Alicia.

"Sorry about the mess," the sheriff said as he waved his hand over stacks of papers on his desk. "I'm not here every day, but I'm sure glad I was today."

Someone knocked on the door.

"Come in," the sheriff said as he sat down.

The door opened and a uniformed man poked his head in. "You want me to pick up some sandwiches for all of you?"

"That would be great," the sheriff said. "Thank you, Deputy."

The door closed. There was a moment of awkward silence as they sat looking at each other.

Cally shifted his body in his chair, trying to get comfortable. The chair creaked. He felt uneasy.

The sheriff stared at Cally. "What brings you to Beaver Island?"

Cally looked at his dad.

"My son has a cabin here," Mr. Callahan said.

The sheriff nodded. "You summer here?"

"Not usually."

Cally continued to look at his dad, trying not to make eye contact with the sheriff.

"Where's your son's cabin?"

"What's the name of that lake?" Mr. Callahan asked Cally.

"There's not many inland lakes here," the sheriff said.

"I can't think of the name," Cally lied.

The sheriff uncrossed his arms and leaned forward in his chair, placing his elbows on the armrests. "What part of the island?"

"South side," Cally said.

"Lake Geneserath."

"That's it," Mr. Callahan said.

The sheriff cracked a slight smile and extended his hand across the desk. "I don't think I introduced myself. Sheriff Conlan Cooper."

Cally shook the sheriff's hand and smiled uneasily back at him. Mr. Callahan shook his hand.

"You didn't tell me your names."

Cally looked at his dad.

"Robert Callahan Senior."

"I'm junior. You can call me Cally."

"Named after your dad, eh," the sheriff said. He eased back into his chair and sat silent for a moment looking at them. The fan on the computer on the sheriff's desk buzzed.

Cally gripped the armrests on his chair. His palms began to sweat.

"Wait a minute," the sheriff said. "I think I saw you two by the marina when I ran to my boat," the sheriff said.

Cally nodded.

"Callahan," the sheriff said. "Alicia told me she knows you two."

"What else did she say?" Cally replied.

"Not much. She was pretty dazed. How do you two know Alicia?"

"We met her on the island."

"How long have you been on the island?"

"Just a few days."

"Did you take the ferry?"

"Uh . . ." Cally hesitated.

"By plane," Mr. Callahan said.

"Fresh Air?" the sheriff continued.

"Well," Cally started to say, then paused, unsure if he wanted to bring Daniel into the conversation. He continued to look at his dad.

Mr. Callahan smiled. "Actually, it was Island Airways."

Cally nodded and looked at the sheriff.

"And you met Alicia here?"

"Yeah."

The sheriff rubbed his chin thoughtfully.

Cally swallowed hard when the sheriff gave him a curious look.

"I'm trying to piece together what happened out there on Lake Michigan with the *Emerald Isle*," the sheriff said. "Before I caught up with Alicia and Fallon, I heard gunshots, then saw their boat blow up. It looked like something came at them out of the sky."

"You know more than I do," Cally said.

"Do you know Fallon McElliot?"

"We met him with Alicia," Mr. Callahan said.

The sheriff nodded.

Cally gripped the chair armrests tighter. "Fallon told me he works for the state police."

"That's right," the sheriff said. "And he told me there was going to be a terrorist attack. Did you know about that?"

"We were with Alicia when he called her to tell her there was going to be a terrorist attack."

"How did he know that it was targeting the *Emerald Isle*?"

"I don't know. I've already told you all I know."

"When he called me," the sheriff said, "he told me he was meeting Alicia at the marina—that he would try to stop it."

"And you believed him?"

"I've known Alicia for a long time."

Cally pointed to the picture on the wall. "That's her in the picture."

The sheriff glanced over his shoulder at the picture and chuckled. "Years ago, she was a dispatcher, then a deputy for Charlevoix County."

"You know her pretty well then," Cally said, welcoming the diversion.

"More than I like to admit," the sheriff said with a sigh as he turned to look at Cally and Mr. Callahan. "Did you know Alicia was investigating a potential terror plot against the ferry?"

"What?"

"Did you know she's with Homeland Security?"

"No."

Mr. Callahan looked at him with a surprised expression. "We thought she was Fallon's partner with the state police."

"Tell me, how exactly did you meet her?"

Cally scrambled for an explanation. "Well, my dad and I were visiting my brother here. She and Fallon showed up at my brother's cabin on the island."

"The one on Lake Geneserath?"

"Yes."

The sheriff waited several beats, staring at Cally, and then asked, "What's your brother's name?"

"Daniel," Mr. Callahan said.

Cally frowned at his dad.

"Where exactly is his cabin on the lake?" the sheriff asked.

"It's the one with a seaplane dock," his dad quickly replied.

Cally's heart sank.

"You took a seaplane here, then?" the sheriff continued.

"Yeah," Cally responded quietly. This was getting worse and worse.

The sheriff sat silent for a moment in his chair.

Cally shifted in his seat. The chair creaked.

"I know that place," the sheriff said as he swiveled in his seat to face the computer screen on his desk. "It's the only cabin on the lake with a seaplane." He clicked the computer mouse several times and typed at the keyboard for a few minutes. "According to Charlevoix County property records, that cabin has been owned for almost ten years by a Thomas Ferguson, not Daniel Callahan."

"What?" Cally exclaimed. "That can't be."

"Property records don't lie."

"But—"

"You want to tell me what's going on here?"

"Daniel told us . . ." Cally paused to think through his story.

"Told you what?"

"That he owned the cabin—that he bought it ten years ago."

"Wait a minute," the sheriff said, cocking his head with a puzzled look. "I saw Tom Ferguson on the news a few days ago. He was talking about a prisoner who escaped from a funeral in Detroit. He's the warden of Jackson State Prison."

Cally looked down at his worn shoes. They still had mud on them from the path on North Fox Island. He sat silent, trying not to make eye contact with the sheriff.

"Look, you two. It's better if you tell me the truth."

Cally looked at his dad, then back at the sheriff.

The sheriff and Cally stared at each other for a moment.

"Go ahead, tell him, Cally. It'll be okay," his dad said.

"You're the guy who escaped," the sheriff continued.

Cally nodded.

"I thought you looked familiar. They sent out an all-points bulletin a few days ago with your picture."

Cally felt his body slump. Now he would go back to prison, with no proof of the real story.

"This is getting more complicated by the second," the sheriff said with a sigh as he looked at Cally. "Look, you've been helpful. You were willing to come in and talk, and you didn't run." The sheriff paused, apparently trying to think through the complications. "But whether any of us like it or not, you know I'm going to have to take you into custody."

"But, Sheriff, listen. You don't understand," Cally said. "Ferguson is dirty. He was trying to kill us to cover up what he was doing."

The sheriff chuckled. "You have to admit that's a pretty far-fetched story."

"But it's true. Ferguson chased us to North Fox Island. Alicia got me and my dad out of there by plane because she knew he was after us—*all* of us. Ask her! We barely escaped with our lives. Call the airport. They'll tell you we made an emergency landing at Welke Airport. Ask them if there are bullet holes in the plane. Ferguson is probably still stranded on North Fox. We took his plane to escape."

The sheriff sat silent.

"He's telling the truth," Mr. Callahan said.

"Okay. I'll call the airport," the sheriff said. He picked up his desk phone and punched in a number.

Cally listened carefully to the sheriff's side of the conversation, but he couldn't hear the other person.

When the sheriff hung up, he said, "They confirm your story. They also said Ferguson rented the plane—the same plane you say Alicia made an emergency landing with."

Cally nodded.

They sat a moment in silence as the sheriff leaned back in his chair. "Tell you what. Since you've been so cooperative, we'll check North Fox Island, but we'll have to detain you two until we verify your story."

"Be careful. They had automatic rifles," Cally warned.

The sheriff nodded. "I'm calling in the state police to back us up. We'll search North Fox and get to the bottom of this."

* * *

The hours dragged by as Cally and his dad sat in the sheriff's office with a deputy.

"Thanks for the sandwiches," Mr. Callahan said.

Sitting in the sheriff's chair, the deputy nodded.

"Can you call the sheriff and find out what's going on?" Cally asked nervously.

"Sorry," the deputy said.

Cally stood and walked to the window. Fallon had said that he and Daniel had retrieved the hard drive, but where was it? If Fallon had it on him when he went after the drone, it was probably now on the bottom of Lake Michigan. Without the drive, there was no hope of getting the truth out. Why wasn't Daniel here? Where was he?

Cally rubbed his wrists, imagining the feel of the cuffs on him again. He looked at the woods across the street and the darkening sky. Would he ever again be free to walk in the woods or outside on the shore of a lake?

Two police cars pulled up in front of the sheriff's building. Feeling equal parts eagerness and fear to see what would happen, Cally was shocked to see a deputy pull Ferguson out of one of the cars. Just the sight of Ferguson was enough to scare him. The other two from North Fox Island, the man and the woman, were pulled out of the other car. He was relieved to see them all in handcuffs. A van pulled up next to the cars. When the deputies loaded Ferguson and the other two into the van, Cally felt a cautious hope.

A moment later, the sheriff entered the room. "It was just like you told us," he said, rubbing his forehead. "We searched the island and found them, but they didn't give up without a fight. There was a shootout. They were well armed and kept it up until they realized they were outnumbered with no place to run." The sheriff shook his head. "The irony is, until they started shooting at us, I didn't have anything on Ferguson but your story, and the word of a convict against a warden wouldn't go very far. Now he'll face charges of assaulting a sheriff, deputies, and the state police."

"Was anyone hurt?" Cally asked urgently.

"A couple of my deputies were hit, but fortunately we all had bulletproof vests. They'll be fine. I don't get why they put up such a fight."

"Ferguson is part of a crime ring," Cally said. "I think that's what Fallon has been investigating."

His dad looked at him.

"We'll need some time to sort all of this out," the sheriff said. "Look, you've been cooperative and I appreciate that, but I'm still going to have to take you in."

Cally swallowed hard. His eyes teared up. He looked at his dad.

"It'll be okay," his dad said.

The sheriff cuffed Cally. "State police confirmed that you escaped from prison, and they have a plane waiting at Welke Airport to take you to our jail in Charlevoix. I'm afraid you'll have to join Ferguson and the other two on that flight."

"I have to ride with Ferguson! The man wants me dead!"

"It's a short flight to Charlevoix," the sheriff said. "They're all cuffed."

Cally's stomach tightened at the thought of seeing Ferguson again. He felt powerless. "What about my dad?"

"We'll get him back to Detroit."

"Just keep cooperating, Cally. It'll be okay," Mr. Callahan said.

They all stood up.

"Your dad's right," the sheriff said, cuffing Cally's hands behind his back.

Cally turned to look at his dad.

His dad cracked a smile. "The truth will set you free."

Cally nodded.

The sheriff took Cally outside. Cally looked over his shoulder and saw his dad looking at him from inside the sheriff's office. He waved at Cally right before they loaded Cally into the van. How their relationship had changed over the past few days!

A deputy sat Cally down in a seat facing Ferguson. The deputy sat next to Cally as the back door closed. Cally tried to not look scared.

"Well, look who's riding with us," Ferguson said. "You're going back to prison, Cally."

"So are you," Cally said. "And all the prisoners you abused are going to be really glad to see you."

CHAPTER 31

W hat did you do to my boat?"

The voice was faint, and Fallon had a hard time making out what it was saying. He slowly opened his eyes. A thick fog surrounded him. A bright light shone through the fog, outlining the shape of a person.

"What happened to my boat?" the shadowy figure asked as it moved closer to him.

Fallon tried to respond, but couldn't find the words. He knew he'd been driving the boat . . .

"Did you sink my boat?"

"Granddad?" Fallon asked. He blinked to clear his vision.

"My boat. What did you do?"

"I, uh . . . ," Fallon said. Nothing seemed clear, in either his vision or his thoughts. He blinked again, trying to keep his eyes open, trying to get a clear look at the shadowy figure. The fog slowly lifted. No one was there.

He moved his head. His neck hurt. "Granddad?"

Someone next to him said something. It sounded like a woman. Carefully, he turned his head. A woman was sitting next to him. He winced at the pain in his neck.

"Fallon? You're awake!"

He tried to move his legs, but they felt too heavy to move. He looked down at his legs and realized he was lying on a bed. He tried to sit up, but his whole body hurt. He turned his head to the other side of the bed. There were monitors, and a bag with clear liquid hanging on a pole next to his bed. He tried to speak. His throat felt scratchy. "Where am I?"

"Nurse!" the woman shouted.

"Who are you?" Fallon said as he carefully turned his head. "Where's Granddad?"

"I'm Alicia," she said.

She acted like he knew her. He didn't recall knowing anyone named Alicia.

A man and a woman dressed in scrubs entered the room and scurried around his bed. The woman checked a monitor, then an intravenous tube attached to his arm. The man moved in close to him and shined a bright light into his eyes.

"What's going on?" Fallon asked feebly.

"You've been out for a while," the man said.

"Who are you?"

"I'm your nurse."

"Where am I?"

"You're at U of M hospital in Ann Arbor."

"How long have I been here?"

"About a week."

Fallon felt confused. He looked at the woman sitting next to his bed. "Alicia?"

"You remember me?"

"No . . ." Fallon lifted his hand to his aching head. "That's . . . the name you told me."

Alicia's face drooped. "I'm so glad you're awake."

Fallon couldn't place her. He felt the soft touch of her hand on his forehead, her fingers gently rubbing his head. He saw a large bandage on her arm. "What . . . happened?"

"Hush."

Fallon felt a hand on his wrist. It was the male nurse, who studied him and then turned to speak to the other nurse now standing at the foot of his bed.

"My head hurts," Fallon said. He looked at Alicia. It felt like he had a hat on, a stocking hat, but why? He never wore hats. "Such a pounding headache."

"We'll get you something for the pain," the female nurse said.

Fallon looked at Alicia. He wondered if he should know her. Was she his wife? He stared at her, trying hard to piece together how he knew this woman. Something about her was familiar, but why?

"Thanks, Nurse," Alicia said.

"He needs rest," the male nurse said.

"He seems to have memory problems," Alicia said.

"His vitals are good, but he still has a long recovery ahead. He took quite a blow to the head. The neurosurgeon will be in tomorrow to check him out again." Both nurses left.

"What happened?" Fallon asked Alicia.

"You don't remember anything?"

Fallon shook his head. He couldn't hold a thought together.

"We stopped a terrorist attack."

His mind was blank.

"You don't remember . . . There was a drone attack on the Beaver Island ferry."

Fallon stared at her. The only boat he could think of was his granddad's Chris-Craft. "Did I sink my granddad's boat?"

"Yes! You remember that?"

"My granddad's pretty upset about it. He was just talking to me." Alicia stared at Fallon.

"Are you upset too . . . about me sinking the boat?"

"No."

"How did I sink it?"

"We were in your granddad's boat . . . we stopped a drone attack."

Fallon stared at Alicia. He had no idea what she was talking about. Alicia shook her head. "You don't remember?"

"No. I just know Granddad is upset with me."

They sat silently for a moment. Alicia looked frustrated. What had he done to upset her? His brain was fuzzy. He tried to recall even a fragment of what she'd just told him, but nothing came to mind—except that he felt something as he looked at her—a feeling of affection. "Are you my wife?"

She gasped. She started to say something, then stopped with her mouth agape.

Fallon gazed into her hazel eyes. They seemed familiar, so captivating, so calming. "What were you going to say?"

"Well . . . we can talk later. Right now, you need to rest."

"Rest." Fallon felt so tired, so sore. He tried to lift his right leg, but it wouldn't move. His arm was lying by his side in a cast. He wiggled his fingers sticking out from the end of the cast. "Where's my wedding ring?" His eyes felt heavy. As he felt himself drifting off to sleep, he heard Alicia's voice.

"It's okay, Fallon," she said. "Get some rest."

CHAPTER 32

In the waiting area of the detention facility, Cally sat next to a court official. "You're lucky the judge expedited your release," the official said. "You'll be home in time for Thanksgiving."

"Barely. Thanksgiving is tomorrow."

"You're still lucky."

"It's not as if the judge had a choice—given the overwhelming evidence that I was wrongly accused and taken against my will."

"I can't believe the jury bought your attorney's line that you didn't escape from prison but was taken hostage at the church by terrorists."

"It was in their best interests. They wanted to stop me from releasing that evidence." Daniel had been right. No one had known it was Daniel at the church because of his gas mask.

"I can see why they wanted to stop you. That evidence implicated a lot of people," the official said. "Including a lot of higher-ups. It was pretty audacious of the director of Corrections to use the state warehouse system to distribute drugs."

"Is Brogan going to prison?"

"Her, Ferguson, and dozens of others in the police and state government. They still have to stand trial, of course."

"I tried to tell people, but no one believed me."

"Well, you're a hero now."

Cally still wondered how all the evidence on the hard drive and the videos Daniel had on his laptop had appeared on the internet. Somehow Daniel had made sure all the corruption, from that of the police to that within the state government, was revealed.

Cally shook his head. "My brother, Daniel, is the real hero."

"I don't know if the feds see it that way."

"They have no evidence that implicates him in anything."

"If he's innocent, then why has he been missing for the last three months?"

"I wish I knew."

"The feds just want to talk to him; there's no warrant for his arrest."

"I wish I could talk to him."

The official studied Cally's face. "Do you know where he is?"

"No! I keep telling people that, but they don't believe me. Fallon was the last person to see him."

"Well, unfortunately, Fallon's memory is shot," the official said. "But yours isn't. I don't think you're telling us everything you know."

Cally looked into the man's eyes, making a conscious effort to hide his deception. "I've said everything I need to say."

"Cally!" someone shouted from across the room.

He looked up. His sister, Sheila, ran toward him. He stood and embraced her. They both wept and held each other for a long moment.

"He's free to go," the official said, holding out a folder. "Here's a copy of his paperwork."

Sheila released Cally and took the folder. "Thanks for printing it off for me. I assume this is also on the court's Archipelago database?"

"Of course," the official said. "Well, good luck, Cally."

Cally shook his hand. He could see the skepticism in the man's eyes about his innocence. "Thanks," Cally said.

"And thanks for your help," Sheila said as she shook his hand.

"That's my job," the official said, then walked away.

"He seems a bit ornery," Sheila said.

"I think he was born a skeptic," Cally said.

"Well, you don't have to worry about it anymore, Cally. Come on, let's get you home."

Cally smiled and followed her to the exit. The word *home* stuck in his mind. He wasn't even sure where his home was anymore. For now, his parents' home would have to do.

On the steps outside, Cally stopped to look up at the gray sky. It reflected his mood. So much uncertainty in his life right now. It cast a cloud over the excitement of finally being free. He followed Sheila to her car and they headed for his parents' house.

"Thanks for all you've done, Sheila."

"I'm grateful the judge agreed to suspend your sentence based on the new evidence surrounding Chuck's murder. It was clear that you were set up."

"But that prosecutor still tried to get me for having a gun while on probation. I thought for sure I would have to do more jail time."

"It's good the judge listened to my argument for extending your probation instead. I'm just sorry you had to spend the last three months in jail while they sorted everything out."

"I can't believe it's over and now I can get on with my life—whatever that looks like."

"Just give it time. You'll find your way."

They rode in silence for a few minutes. Up ahead, Cally could see the tall church spire rising above the rooftops of a neighborhood. "Has anyone heard from Daniel?"

"No," Sheila said. She glanced at Cally, then back at the road. "The feds haven't given up on questioning me or Mom and Dad."

"They kept grilling me in jail. They think I know where he is."

"The feds have no hard evidence that he helped you escape, although they suspect as much. I told them Mom and I went into hiding in Canada after the church incident because we feared the crime ring was coming for us."

"I wish I knew where he was," Cally said, looking out the car window at the houses they passed. "Has he tried to contact you or Mom or Dad?"

"No."

"It just doesn't add up, Sheila. It's not like Daniel to go rogue. He loved his job with the FBI. He loves us. Why would he disappear like this? I'm worried that something happened to him."

Sheila sighed. "Me too." She glanced at Cally. "I spoke with his partner at the FBI a few weeks ago, and he's concerned too."

"You found no clues in his house?"

"No. His house was almost empty. It was as if he knew he wouldn't be back."

"Fallon seems to be the only one with the answers we need."

"Unfortunately, I don't think he's going to be able to tell us anything. I talked with Alicia yesterday. He's recovering well, but he still has no memory of what happened. There are still no leads."

"Except Henry Massey. Daniel told me he was going to work for him after he got the hard drive. He said Massey helped with my escape."

"I've tried several times to contact Massey, but his staff keeps telling me he doesn't know me and to stop making false claims that he knows where Daniel is hiding."

"But Daniel told me—"

"I know, but Massey's staff claims Daniel is lying."

"Daniel wouldn't lie to me."

"It's your word against a tech billionaire."

Cally sighed. "I know."

"I believe you, Cally."

He looked at Sheila and smiled. "Thanks again for all you did."

Sheila nodded. "Let's just try to enjoy Thanksgiving tomorrow."

Cally recognized the intersection ahead. They were almost at his parents' house. He felt apprehensive. This would be the first time he'd returned to the house since fleeing from the police last year.

"It'll be okay, Cally," Sheila said.

"I don't know."

Sheila turned onto the street leading to their parents' house. "It'll be good having you back at the Thanksgiving dinner table tomorrow."

Cally breathed deeply as he thought about being back in the house with his parents. He felt anxious.

"You know you can stay with me until you get back on your feet. You don't have to stay at Mom and Dad's house."

"Thanks."

The car pulled up in front of their parent's house. They climbed out of the car and stood a moment on the sidewalk looking at their mom and dad, who were just stepping out of the house. They all stood a moment on the concrete path awkwardly, looking at each other in silence.

"Oh, Cally," his mom said at last, and hugged him. She began to weep on Cally's shoulder. "It's such a blessing to have you here in time for Thanksgiving."

Cally looked over her shoulder at his dad. He released his mom and stared at his dad for a moment. He wanted to hug him, but couldn't bring himself to do it.

"Why are we standing out here in the cold? Let's go inside. Dinner is waiting," his dad said.

They walked up the steps to the house. Their mom entered first, followed by Sheila, as their dad held the door open. Cally stopped in the doorway to look back at their dad.

"It's good to have you here, Cally," his dad said.

"It's good to be here."

Cally's dad put his hand on Cally's shoulder and smiled. "We had quite the adventure together last summer."

Cally chuckled. "I guess you could call it that." He thought about the last time he'd seen Daniel, leaving the cabin with Fallon. "Any word from Daniel?"

His dad shook his head. "None. Any update on Fallon?"

"Alicia visited me last week. He's recovering well except his memory."

"Still no clues about where Daniel is?"

"He doesn't remember anything."

"Not even us?"

"Nothing."

"Are you two coming?" their mom called from inside. "You're letting all the cold in."

Cally followed his dad inside and stood in the entryway for a moment looking up the stairs. He savored the smell of a home-cooked meal.

"Can I get you some hot tea?" his dad asked from the kitchen.

"No thanks, Dad. I'm going upstairs to my room for a minute."

"Don't be long, Cally," his mom said. "Dinner's almost ready."

Sheila came back and stood next to him. "Are you okay?"

"I just need a minute alone in my room."

Cally climbed the stairs and went into his bedroom. It was quiet and cold, the air musty. He walked to his dresser and picked up the picture of him and Chuck sitting on the hood of the Shelby Mustang GT. He sat on the edge of his bed and stared at the picture as tears streamed down his cheeks. "Who's the boss?" he whispered.

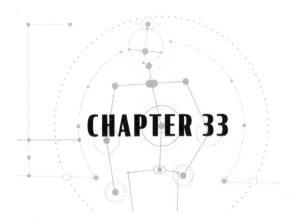

CHAPTER 33

I've never seen anyone quite as tough as you," the doctor said.

"I'm not feeling tough right now," Fallon said as he maneuvered back to his hospital bed with his crutches. "I hope this was the last surgery." He eased himself onto the bed and leaned the crutches against the wall.

"It should be—as long as you follow my orders."

Fallon picked up a plastic container next to his bed and examined the metal and wood fragments inside. "I guess there wasn't much left of my granddad's boat."

"We saved the pieces we took out of you."

As Fallon lay back onto his bed, pain shot up his leg. He winced and let his head drop onto his pillow.

"Your leg will be sensitive for a few days."

Fallon nodded. "No kidding."

"I heard the museum on Beaver Island wasn't too happy about your grandfather's boat being blown up, but they made allowances given that the owner's grandson used it to stop a terrorist attack. Do you remember any more about it?"

"I saw the videos taken by people on the ferry," Fallon said. "But I feel like I'm watching an actor playing me in a movie when I see myself driving the boat. I don't remember any of it."

"You're a hero."

"So I hear."

"But you remember your grandfather?"

"I remember taking rides in his boat when I was a kid." Fallon glanced at the doctor. "Do you think I'll get my short-term memory back?"

"The brain is very complex. It's hard to predict. No one knows for sure. The neurologist will follow up with you after Thanksgiving."

"I feel like I'm living in a fog. I'm so disoriented."

The doctor reconnected monitors to him. "It will take time, Fallon."

Fallon repositioned himself in the bed and winced again at the discomfort in his legs. "Time. I've lost track of time."

"You did well with your physical therapy today."

"That therapist knows how to torture me."

"I can up your pain medication." The doctor checked Fallon's vital signs on the monitor next to his bed.

Another jolt of pain shot up Fallon's leg. "I may need it."

"Try not to get discouraged. You're making good progress." The doctor walked to the door. "I'll see you tomorrow when I make my rounds. If everything still looks good, I might be able to release you so you can go home in time for Thanksgiving dinner."

"Is Thanksgiving tomorrow?"

"Yes. See you tomorrow."

"Thanks, Doc." As he pulled the sheet over himself, Fallon wasn't sure where he would go for Thanksgiving if he was released from the hospital. Maybe the two men who visited yesterday—the two men who claimed to be his sons—would want him to visit. Would Alicia invite him over for dinner?

Fallon smiled as he thought about Alicia. She was nice enough, visiting him almost every day. He looked forward to her visits. She said he had known her for a long time, but she insisted they were not married. He had a faint memory of dating her, but no memory of a wedding. Maybe she was right. Thoughts swirled in his head.

There were so many people and so many events he could not place. People who looked familiar, but he could not identify them no matter how many times they gave him their name. So many people asked him about a man named Daniel. He had a vague memory of working with him—sitting in a car with him at night talking. Some people from the FBI showed him a video of him and Daniel at an airport, but he had no recollection of it.

He tried to understand why the governor had visited him the other day—why she had an interest in him. Apparently, they were longtime friends. The governor told him someone named Chip was taking care of things for him. She looked so disappointed when he could not remember. So many disappointed looks from so many people who stopped by to talk to him. He sighed and let his head sink gently into his pillow, still feeling the tenderness from his injuries.

He reached for the television remote to find something to distract him. A newscaster appeared on the screen and droned on about the latest numbers on the state's economy. Suddenly a picture of someone named Tom Ferguson appeared behind the newscaster.

"The former warden of Jackson Correctional Facility is expected to go on trial soon," the newscaster said.

Fallon's body tensed as he looked at Ferguson. He remembered seeing this man wearing a helmet in a dark room—holding a rifle. The man had shouted at him as shots rang out. He grabbed the remote to turn off the screen, but his finger stopped when the newscaster mentioned going live to the State Capitol building.

"Tech billionaire Henry Massey is expected to announce his candidacy for governor," the newscaster said.

The picture changed. A man behind a podium with several microphones began to speak. The sound of his voice annoyed Fallon, but he listened anyway.

"With the revelation of corruption in our governor's administration, as well as her inability to protect the citizens of Michigan from terrorism right here in our Great Lakes State," Massey said, "I feel I have an obligation to provide an alternative for Michigan."

Massey seemed to be staring directly at Fallon. It made him feel uneasy. Something about Massey disturbed him. He felt anger toward this man, but he was unsure why.

"Someone independent and equipped to make our state a leader in this country and the world," Massey continued. "That's why today I am announcing my candidacy for governor of the great state of Michigan. Today, I am offering a clear alternative for the people of our state, an honest alternative. I guarantee you a Massey administration will not be politics as usual."

The view on the screen switched to a large crowd of people cheering and chanting, "Massey, Massey, Massey!"

"Mr. McElliot?" a nurse asked as he entered the room carrying a plant. He stopped to look at the television screen. "Looks like Massey finally announced he's running for governor?"

"I guess."

"That will make the campaign interesting."

"I don't like him."

The nurse ignored the comment as he held up a plant with an attached card. "This just came in for you."

"Set it on the windowsill with the others," Fallon said, pointing to the dozen or so plants and vases with flowers already there, with cards propped up in front of them. "Could you bring me the card?"

The nurse did as he asked.

"Thanks," Fallon said. He waited until the nurse had left the room, then opened the envelope. On the front of the card was a picture of a small, red tractor in a field. The tractor had the name "Massey" on its hood. It seemed like a strange picture for a get-well card. He opened the card and read the note scrawled inside in blue ink:

Get well soon, Fallon. When you're up to it, call me. We can talk some more about that tractor franchise. I hear you have a name that's known for great legal advice. I'd love to have you

*"connect" with our team! We need more heroes in this world. I
hope you'll join me. —Henry Massey.*

Fallon closed the card and examined the tractor picture on the
front. He glanced up at the television screen with Massey continuing
to speak to a large crowd, then looked again at the card. Why was
Massey sending him a note, and what exactly did he mean by, *"connect
with our team"*?

"We want to create a new future, a future of possibilities," Massey
said from the television. "A future full of new opportunities for you,
the people of our great state. I will make Michigan a leader in the
nation and the world."

The crowd cheered. Massey smiled. The grin on the man's face
disturbed Fallon. His speech sounded familiar, but why?

"I want you to join me," Massey said.

Fallon looked again at the card in his hand. The words "join me"
jumped off the card. What did it mean?

A voice broke Fallon's concentration. Alicia entered the room,
followed by a man in a nicely tailored suit. They sat next to Fallon's bed.

"Hi, Alicia. Who's this?"

"This is my boss at Homeland Security, Regional Director Trevor
Jackson," Alicia responded.

Fallon eyed the man, then Alicia. "You work for Homeland
Security?"

Alicia sighed. "I explained the whole thing to you—how Homeland
Security sent me to follow up on some chatter we heard about a
potential terror plot."

"Did I know that?"

"We talked about it before."

"Sorry," Fallon said. He set the card in his hand on the small table
next to his bed.

"I brought you a special gift to enjoy after you're off your
painkillers." Alicia set a bottle on the table.

"What's that?"

"Someone on Beaver Island wanted me to bring it to you. They so appreciated what you did to save all those people on the ferry that they found an old bottle of your grandpa's whiskey."

Fallon studied the bottle.

"You don't remember?"

Fallon shook his head.

"Mr. McElliot, I'd like to ask you a few questions if you're up to it," Trevor said.

"Sure," Fallon replied. He grabbed the remote.

Alicia looked at the screen, then at Fallon. "Can you believe the nerve of that guy?"

"What about him?" Fallon asked. He pushed the off button.

"Such an opportunist. What kind of guy runs against a sitting governor in his own party? He's already the richest person on the planet. It's like he's running for governor to have something to do."

"I think he might actually be good for the state," Trevor said.

Alicia sighed and looked at the card sitting on the table next to Fallon's bed. "Who's the card from?"

"Take a look," Fallon grabbed the card and handed it to Alicia. "It came with that plant over there."

"That's an odd picture for a get-well card."

"That's what I thought."

Alicia opened it and gasped. "Henry Massey!"

Fallon shrugged.

"What's this line supposed to mean, 'I hope you'll join me'?"

"I wondered the same thing."

"What connection do you have to Massey?" Trevor asked.

"I don't recall any connection."

"I think Massey wants to take advantage of Fallon because he's a hero," Alicia closed the card and handed it back to Fallon. "Like I said, he's an opportunist."

Trevor leaned closer. "I have just a few questions for you, Fallon."

Fallon set the card back on the table.

"We have some conflicting information," Trevor said. "Somehow you knew the *Emerald Isle* was going to be attacked by a drone."

"If that's true, I don't know why."

"Chip, your assistant—"

"Chip?"

"He worked with you. Chip told us that you called him and had him look up the address of a cabin. He said it was listed as being owned by Daniel Callahan, but the address Chip gave us shows it has been owned by Tom Ferguson for more than ten years. Do you have any memory of that?"

Fallon shook his head.

"We also have video of you talking with Ferguson in his office, but there's never any mention of terrorists or even the location of Ferguson's cabin."

"Ferguson? My army buddy?"

"Yes. In the video he tells you he thinks Daniel went rogue from the FBI, but we think maybe that was a setup to get you to help him out. Do you remember that?"

"No."

"You talk about going after Cally to capture him . . ." Trevor began.

Fallon held his head. "You can ask me all the questions you want, but I don't remember a thing."

"Look, Trevor. He has a brain injury," Alicia said. "Can't you see he doesn't remember?"

Trevor's intense, laser-like focus on him was making Fallon anxious.

"I told you Fallon told me Daniel Callahan owned the cabin," Alicia said. "Fallon gave me the address after we arrived on the island. I told you how Daniel helped Cally escape, how he planted the smoke bombs at the church, how he was at the cabin. Ferguson didn't show up on Beaver and North Fox islands until later."

Trevor leaned back in his chair. "Everything points to Ferguson as the mastermind behind the terror plot. We think his cabin on Beaver Island served as the headquarters for the terror cell. Pieces of the explosive device found by divers trace back to Ferguson. We even have video of Ferguson loading the stolen drone into a van at the Caspian warehouse. Why else would he pursue you all the way to North Fox Island? They were desperate to stop you."

Fallon shook his head. "Wait. That doesn't make sense. If it was Daniel's cabin and he was working with Ferguson, why would he let Ferguson hunt down his brother and dad?"

Trevor sighed. "Ferguson owned the cabin. That we know. The records are clear."

Alicia smiled. "At least you haven't lost your detective instincts, Fallon."

Fallon turned to her. "You said that I told you Daniel Callahan owned the cabin? How did I know that?"

"You told me you and Daniel worked some cases together—that he told you on a stakeout," Alicia said gently.

"I wish I could remember."

"Daniel could've lied to you," Trevor said. "There's a registered deed from ten years ago on file with Ferguson's name on it."

Fallon felt confused. He looked at Alicia, then Trevor. "Something doesn't sound right about that."

"And you say you have no memory of ever talking to Massey?" Trevor asked. He pointed to the card on the table by Fallon's bed with a skeptical look.

"None."

"It's okay, Fallon." Alicia reached out and took Fallon's hand. "Just give it time. I'm sure it will come back to you."

"I guess I'll leave now," Trevor said. "Stay on it, Alicia. Let me know if any new information turns up."

"Will do," Alicia replied.

Fallon watched Trevor close the door behind him. "I'm still not putting the pieces together," he said to Alicia, "but I'm glad I remember us."

Alicia smiled.

"Doc said they might release me tomorrow," Fallon said.

"Tomorrow is Thanksgiving. Where would you go?"

"I guess to my condo in Lansing."

"And spend Thanksgiving alone?"

"Apparently I have two sons. They told me I'm divorced and that they'll spend Thanksgiving with their mom. If I'm released tomorrow, they offered to stop by if I need help." Fallon looked into Alicia's hazel eyes. "You could stop by my place if I'm released tomorrow."

"I have plans."

"Well, maybe you could fit me into your plans."

Alicia smiled. "I'll think about it."

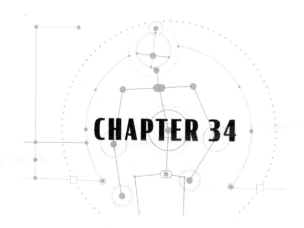

CHAPTER 34

Daniel adjusted his sunglasses and pulled his stocking cap below his ears as he watched Massey climb into the passenger side of the black SUV parked behind the Michigan Capitol building.

"Are you absolutely sure he still has no memory of anything that happened?" Massey asked.

"I talked with Trevor," Daniel said. "He just left Fallon's hospital bed. He says Fallon doesn't remember a thing. I don't think Fallon is bluffing. It's been three months."

"This turned out better than I planned."

Daniel saw a smile creep onto Massey's face.

"Take us back to Coleman Young Airport and my jet."

"Do you really think Fallon might join you?"

"I *know* he will," Massey said with a smug look on his face. "Do you doubt me?"

"I know better than to doubt you now. I wondered if we could really pull off Cally's escape and get the hard drive."

"I delivered on that one. You can trust me, Daniel. Our plan is unfolding on schedule. Even the drone performed better than we expected."

"What's next?"

"We'll go to my estate in Colorado."

"You're not having Thanksgiving at your mansion in Detroit?"

"No, that's only for my required residency so I can run for governor." Massey looked out the window as the traffic slowed. "I'm sorry you can't be with your family, Daniel."

They stopped at a red light. Daniel glanced at Massey. "It's okay. My family usually ends up fighting about religion and football on Thanksgiving."

"I promise you Thanksgiving at my place in Colorado will be much quieter. My daughters will be there from college. We usually talk about the latest books and movies."

"That'll be a welcome change for me," Daniel said. The light turned green and he drove toward the freeway.

"You sound like you're satisfied with the way things went."

"Cally is free. The truth came out about Ferguson. We shut down a major crime ring and exposed corrupt people in the police and state government. I'd say that's a good day's work."

"But I sense that something is bugging you, Daniel."

"I just wonder if we're missing something—if we're overconfident."

"That's what I like about you, Daniel. You're always thinking, always watching for things we might miss."

"I was trained well," Daniel said.

"I don't want you to think of yourself as just my employee. You're my trusted adviser. I want you to think of yourself as part of my family now. You'll be working from my compound in the Colorado Rockies. We'll have a nice Thanksgiving dinner there. My family will be delighted to have you join us."

Daniel nodded and glanced at Massey, then back at the road.

"I have to return a few calls from the media," Massey said. "I'll be on the phone for a while."

"I'll let you know when we're almost at the airport."

Massey tapped a number into his phone and put it to his ear.

Daniel tuned out Massey and thought about Cally and the rest of his family at their table on Thanksgiving. He recalled all the holidays when Cally's seat was empty. Now, for the first time in a long time, Cally would be at the family table for the holiday, but *his own* chair would be empty. He was now Massey's trusted adviser, his confidant.

Cally was free, but it was hard not being with him. He missed his brother. Briefly, as he drove, he relived their short time together during and after Cally's escape. And he was determined that they would once again be reunited on Beaver Island.

EPILOGUE

Daniel leaned back in his chair and dabbed his mouth with his napkin. "That was a great meal."

"So glad you're here with us, Daniel," Massey said from the head of the table as he took a sip of wine.

"And it's nice to meet *you*, Leigha and Carolyn," Daniel said, grinning at Massey's two college-age daughters. They looked back at him shyly from across the table, poking at the food on their plates. Daniel looked down the long table at Massey's wife, seated opposite Massey. "And thanks for being such a wonderful host, Helen."

Her large diamond ring twinkled as she lifted her wineglass. "I'm so glad I finally had a chance to meet you," Helen said as she sipped her wine. "Henry has talked so much about you. I hope you're enjoying your stay with us."

Daniel lifted his own glass. "I am." The fine crystal felt comfortable in his hand—the wine tasted smooth and expensive.

"I'm glad, too, that you're managing security for our estate," Helen said. "We've never had someone with so much experience. I wouldn't trust anyone else with our family's security."

"Thank you," Daniel said. They trusted him. Mission accomplished.

"I don't think I told you that Helen is now chair of Arpa," Massey said. "She used to be vice president of an investment firm in New York." Massey chuckled. "Her security is as much at risk as mine."

"Mr. Callahan?" Leigha said. "You said you worked with the FBI before Dad hired you. What was it like chasing hard-core criminals?"

"Well . . ." Daniel tried to keep his focus on Leigha, not Massey. He wanted to ask, *Like your dad?* "It's hard to sum it up. It's long hours of drudgery chasing leads that come up empty. Then short periods of high tension when you start closing in on the suspects."

"Did you ever kill someone?"

Daniel took a deep breath. An image from years ago slipped into his mind—a man aiming an automatic weapon, ready to fire. "A couple times. Only when I had no choice."

Awkward silence fell over the room for a moment.

"Well, that's a cheery topic for Thanksgiving dinner," Massey said.

"I'm sorry," Leigha said. "I'm thinking about switching my major to criminal justice. I just wondered—"

"That's okay," Daniel said. "If you're going into law enforcement, you need to know that's part of the job. But after all those long hours, there's nothing like finally bringing someone to justice who has eluded the law for years."

"That's what appeals to me," Leigha said with a smile.

"Then there's the security business," Daniel said as he turned his attention to Massey. "I'm sure we'll have to put in long hours with your gubernatorial campaign next year."

Massey cracked a big smile. "It will be intense. Unfortunately, there are a lot of people out there who dislike me just because I'm wealthy."

"Well, they don't know you like I do," Helen said. "He's really a teddy bear when you get to know him."

"Is that true?" Daniel asked Leigha and Carolyn with a smile.

"He's okay." They smirked in unison.

Daniel let his gaze drift to the wall of windows across the dining room and looked out at Fort Collins below. "I think I'd like to take a short walk to get some fresh air. It's such a beautiful setting."

"Sure," Massey said. "We have more than a thousand acres here. There's a nice trail behind the house that goes up into the foothills. You have about an hour before sunset." Massey stood up. "I'll show you."

Daniel followed him out of the dining room to a large entryway.

Massey grabbed Daniel's coat from the closet and handed it to him.

"I won't take more than just a few minutes," Daniel said.

"We'll have pumpkin pie when Daniel gets back," Helen called from the dining room, her voice echoing off the high ceiling.

Daniel followed Massey up a long stone stairway that wound around the back of the mansion to a large stone patio. Massey sat on one of the benches that circled a large firepit and looked up. "Isn't the view spectacular?" he said.

Daniel nodded as he shifted his gaze from the snow-capped Rocky Mountains rising in front of them to Massey.

"You'll need to keep your head down for a while," Massey said. "Until the time is right to bring you out of hiding to help with my campaign security."

"Even if I surfaced tomorrow, there's nothing the FBI can pin on me."

"True. Your name never came up as being involved in any of it. In fact, they think the crime ring was responsible for Cally's escape from the church. Give it some time. We'll get this worked out."

"I appreciate all you've done for me."

"There's no turning back now," Massey said, his face growing serious as he looked pointedly at Daniel. "This will be your home for the foreseeable future. You'll run security for me from my compound here."

"I'm okay with that," Daniel said. "Right now, I just need a little time to walk and clear my head."

"Good," Massey said. "The trail starts right there. Be sure to turn around before thirty minutes so you can get back before dark."

Daniel starting walking toward the trailhead.

"Oh, one more thing," Massey said.

Daniel stopped.

"There's no cell coverage out here," Massey said. "I know you miss your family, but it's better if you don't contact them."

"I know," Daniel said.

They stood a moment looking at each other.

"Enjoy your walk," Massey said as he headed back to the mansion.

Daniel made his way along the trail, keeping his eyes focused on the underbrush along the trail. He glanced at his watch, recalling the instructions he'd received from the FBI before he went deep undercover. The drop would be fifteen minutes into his hike.

He timed his walk, stopped, and scanned the underbrush. There, barely visible, was the GPS hiking device for remote communication. He quickly turned it on and keyed in a short message:

Fully embedded. All systems go.

A moment later, a reply message appeared on the tiny screen: *Engage.*

He took a deep breath. It was the agreed code word from the FBI to start the second phase of his deep-undercover assignment. Outsmarting Massey would not be easy. He had to build a bulletproof case against him. He had to stop Massey's effort to take over Michigan's government, and he had to do it before the election.

He smashed the GPS unit with a rock and buried the pieces under several more. He crouched and stared at the rocks, then at the snow-capped mountains above. He thought about his empty seat at his family's Thanksgiving meal. By now they would've finished having pumpkin pie. He smiled as he retraced his steps to the mansion. He doubted Helen's pie would be as good as his mom's, but he would still tell her it was the best he'd ever had.

* * *

"Thanks, Chip," Fallon said as he unlocked the door to his condo. He leaned on his cane as he opened the door.

"Any progress on your leg?" Chip asked.

"Physical therapy is helping, but I'm not sure I'll regain full function."

Chip set Fallon's bag down in the entryway. "Alicia's not going to be happy I gave you a ride from the hospital. Why didn't you want her to pick you up?"

"She's with her mom for Thanksgiving. Besides, I wasn't sure they were going to release me until late this afternoon."

"Do you want me to stay?"

"No, that's okay."

Chip pulled a plastic container out of the bag and held it up. "I can't believe they pulled all these pieces of the boat out of you."

"Me either," Fallon said. Chip handed him the container. "Didn't you tell me the cabin on Beaver Island was owned by Daniel?" Fallon asked.

"You remember?"

"I was driving somewhere and I called you."

Chip smiled.

"But some guy in the hospital told me it was owned by . . ."

"Ferguson."

Fallon nodded. "I've been working with a therapist on my memory issues. Maybe after New Year's I'll be able to get back to the office."

"Maybe, but right now, you need to take care of yourself," Chip said.

"That's all I've been doing for three months."

"You sure you don't want me to stay?"

"I'll be fine. I just need some time alone."

Chip nodded. "I'll talk to you after Thanksgiving."

Fallon made his way to the living room as the door closed behind Chip. He set the plastic container on an end table and leaned over to turn on a lamp. His leg felt weak. He used the cane to steady himself. The room was eerily quiet, void of the sound of medical equipment, hospital staff, and visitors peppering him with questions.

From his bag by the door, he retrieved the whiskey bottle Alicia had given him. "McElliot Whiskey Works," the label read. No drinking alcohol while on painkillers, the doctor had advised him. But no one was here now to stop him. A little drink might help. No more doctors or nurses to tell him what he should or shouldn't do.

He parked himself on the couch and took a sip from the snifter. The whiskey was smooth and flavorful. The thought of his granddad brought a smile to his face for a moment.

The plastic container on the end table caught his eye. Splinters of wood and twisted pieces of metal shuffled inside as he rolled the container in his hand, just like all the jumbled memories and thoughts in his head. Pushing the throttle on the Chris-Craft boat. Granddad sitting in the boat with him, or was it Alicia? The triangular Chris-Craft flag on the bow of the boat flapping in the wind as it raced across the glassy water of Lake Michigan.

Fallon set the plastic container back on the end table. *They don't make boats like that anymore. Fast, powerful, and beautiful.* He picked up the snifter and watched the golden liquid swirl in it. Somewhere, sometime he had done this before with someone—shared a drink of whiskey. Was it Chip? Or maybe Massey? *You know what you have to do.* Why would Massey say that?

A buzzing noise came from the kitchen. The refrigerator turning on. Or was it something else? *Drones are great for instant delivery of most anything like shoes, food, or . . .* Or what? Or maybe something more damaging. He felt angry. Massey was so smug, so confident. The feeling that he had to stop him was overwhelming, but why? Another sip of whiskey.

A knock at the door startled him. Cautiously, he stepped close to it. Through the peephole he saw a familiar face. He opened the door.

"I called the hospital to check on you," Alicia said quietly, her face downcast as if her feelings were hurt. "They said you were released." She stepped inside.

"You were with your mom. I didn't want to bother you."

Fallon closed the door behind them. Alicia set a large bag on the kitchen table.

"What's that?" Fallon said.

"My mom fixed you a turkey sandwich and sent along some of the Thanksgiving fixings for you. I *was* going to bring it to you in the hospital."

"I appreciate that," Fallon smiled.

Alicia emptied the bag, and they each took a chair at the table.

"You have a little bit of everything here," Fallon said. "That was nice of your mom."

"She was concerned you'd spend Thanksgiving with only hospital food." Alicia smiled at him.

"Maybe in a couple weeks after I'm more settled in my home I can personally thank her." He unwrapped the sandwich and took a bite. "Alicia—did Henry Massey's name come up in any of the investigations about the drone attack?"

Alicia gave Fallon a puzzled look. "Why do you ask?"

"For some reason Massey keeps coming to mind."

"Massey did fund the restoration of your granddad's boat."

"He did?"

"I told you," Alicia sighed.

"Like so many things you've told me that I can't seem to remember." Fallon took another bite of his sandwich.

"You need to stop thinking about all of that and give your brain time to heal."

"There's something about Massey that bothers me. I can't seem to pinpoint it."

"Hey—it's Thanksgiving," Alicia said "Let's take this food to the living room and watch some football while you eat."

Fallon nodded. He followed Alicia to the couch with his plate. As she sat down on the couch he glanced at the plastic container on the end table. So many fragments of memories rolling around in his head. He could not shake the uneasy feeling about Massey. Somehow he would put the pieces together and find the truth.

ACKNOWLEDGMENTS

Writing and publishing this book has been a journey. I am grateful to the many people who have helped me along the way. First, a big thank you to my wife, Joanne, who first introduced me to Beaver Island where the idea for this book was born. Thank you, Joanne, for encouraging me throughout the years and for the hours you spent editing many of my initial drafts. You helped make me a better writer and my novel more readable. I also want to thank my daughters, who listened to many of my stories when they were kids and for continuing to encourage me to keep writing. Thanks, too, to my granddaughter, who helps spur my creativity when we play make-believe.

So many people have helped me along the way as I pursued a writing career: my high school English teacher who first piqued my interest in writing; my journalism professors in college who endured many of my very rough article drafts and helped me hone my writing skills; and the editors and writers I worked with in my advertising and communications jobs who taught me a lot about putting words together in an effective way.

I also want to thank my book launch team for agreeing to participate in promoting the book. I am grateful that they joined me early on to provide feedback on the manuscript, book cover design, and promotional items. Because of their feedback, you have an epilogue that extends the book a few more pages. I also want to give a shout out to my aviation friends who provided technical expertise on the airplane scenes in the book. Thanks, Neil, for teaching me that seaplanes have floats, not pontoons.

I am grateful for the many people who helped on the self-publishing journey. A big thank-you to my editor Dave, who helped me polish the manuscript and gave me advice on self-publishing. I also want to recognize Jeanette and her expertise in helping direct the marketing effort. Thank you, too, to the folks at Brookstone Publishing Group and Iron Stream Media for their guidance in bringing this book to print.

I especially want to thank Brian Preuss for his creative expertise in designing the cover and back cover and for help with the photo expedition on Beaver Island. Thanks, Brian!

There are likely others I've overlooked who have helped me along the way. I am grateful to them and so many others I have encountered in my life—people who have helped to shape me over the years. I am blessed beyond measure.

If you enjoyed this book, will you consider sharing the message with others?

Let us know your thoughts. You can let the author know by visiting or sharing a photo of the cover on our social media pages or leaving a review at a retailer's site. All of it helps us get the message out!

Email: info@ironstreammedia.com

 @ironstreammedia

Iron Stream, Iron Stream Fiction, Iron Stream Kids, Brookstone Publishing Group, and Life Bible Study are imprints of Iron Stream Media, which derives its name from Proverbs 27:17, "As iron sharpens iron, so one person sharpens another." This sharpening describes the process of discipleship, one to another. With this in mind, Iron Stream Media provides a variety of solutions for churches, ministry leaders, and nonprofits ranging from in-depth Bible study curriculum and Christian book publishing to custom publishing and consultative services.

For more information on ISM and its imprints, please visit IronStreamMedia.com

Made in the USA
Middletown, DE
09 April 2023